To Larry

From
Dad and Mom
1952

BOB

SON OF BATTLE

BOB

SON OF BATTLE

By ALFRED OLLIVANT

GROSSET & DUNLAP

Publishers, NEW YORK

CONTENTS

PART I

THE COMING OF THE TAILLESS TYKE

PART II

THE LITTLE MAN

PART III

THE SHEPHERDS' TROPHY

CONTENTS

PART IV

THE BLACK KILLER

PART V

OWD BOB O' KENMUIR

PART VI

THE BLACK KILLER

PART I

THE COMING OF THE TAILLESS TYKE

CHAPTER I

THE GRAY DOG

THE sun stared brazenly down on a gray farmhouse lying long and low in the shadow of the Muir Pike; on the ruins of peel-tower and barmkyn, relics of the time of raids, it looked; on ranges of whitewashed outbuildings; on a goodly array of dark-thatched ricks.

In the stack-yard, behind the lengthy range of stables, two men were thatching. One lay sprawling on the crest of the rick, the other stood perched on a ladder at a lower level.

The latter, small, old, with shrewd nutbrown countenance, was Tammas Thornton, who had served the Moores of Kenmuir for more than half a century. The other, on top of the stack, wrapped apparently in gloomy meditation, was Sam'l Todd. A solid Dalesman, he, with huge hands and hairy arms; about his face an uncomely aureole of stiff, red hair; and on his features, deep-seated, an expression of resolute melancholy.

"Ay, the Gray Dogs, bless 'em!" the old man was saying. "Yo' canna beat 'em not nohow. Known 'em ony time this sixty year, I have, and niver knew a bad un yet. Not as I say, mind ye, as any of 'em cooms up to Rex son o' Rally. Ah, he was a one, was Rex! We's never won Cup since his day."

"Nor niver shall agin, you' may depend," said the other gloomily.

Tammas clucked irritably.

"G'long, Sam'l Todd!" he cried. "Yo' niver happy onless yo' making' yo'self miser'ble. I niver see sich a chap. Niver win agin? Why, oor young Bob he'll mak' a right un, I tell yo', and I should know. Not as what he'll touch Rex son o' Rally, mark ye! I'm niver saying' so, Sam'l Todd. Ah, he was a one, was Rex! I could tell yo' a tale or two o' Rex. I mind me hoo——"

The big man interposed hurriedly.

"I've heard it afore, Tammas, I welly 'ave," he said.

Tammas paused and looked angrily up.

"Yo've heard it afore, have yo', Sam'l Todd?" he asked sharply. "And what have yo' heard afore?"

"Yo' stories, owd lad—yo' stories o' Rex son o' Rally."

"Which on' em?"

"All on 'em, Tammas, all on 'em—mony a time. I'm fair sick on 'em, Tammas, I welly am," he pleaded.

The old man gasped. He brought down his mallet with a vicious smack.

"I'll niver tell yo' a tale again, Sam'l Todd, not if yo' was to go on yo' bended knees for't. Nay; it bain't no manner o' use talkin'. Niver agin, says I."

"I niver askt yo'," declared honest Sam'l.

"Nor it wouldna ha' bin no manner o' use if yo' had "

said the other viciously. "I'll niver tell yo' a tale agin if I was to live to be a hundred."

"Yo'll not live to be a hundred, Tammas Thornton, nor near it," said Sam'l brutally.

"I'll live as long as some, I warrant," the old man replied with spirit. "I'll live to see Cup back i' Kenmuir, as I said afore."

"If yo' do," the other declared with emphasis, "Sam'l Todd niver spake a true word. Nay, nay, lad; yo're owd, yo're wambly, your time's near run or I'm the more mistook."

"For mussy's sake hold yo' tongue, Sam'l Todd! It's clack-clack all day——" The old man broke off suddenly, and buckled to his work with suspicious vigour. "Mak' a show yo' bin workin', lad," he whispered. "Here's Master and oor Bob."

As he spoke, a tall gaitered man with weather-beaten face, strong, lean, austere, and the blue-gray eyes of the hill-country, came striding into the yard. And trotting soberly at his heels, with the gravest, saddest eyes you ever saw, a sheep-dog puppy.

A rare dark gray he was, his long coat, dashed here and there with lighter touches, like a stormy sea moonlit. Upon his chest an escutcheon of purest white, and the dome of his head showered, as it were, with a sprinkling of snow. Perfectly compact, utterly lithe, inimitably graceful with his airy-fairy action; a gentleman every inch, you could not help but stare at him—Owd Bob o' Kenmuir.

At the foot of the ladder the two stopped. And the young dog, placing his forepaws on a lower rung, looked up, slowly waving his silvery brush.

"A proper Gray Dog!" mused Tammas, gazing down

into the dark face beneath him. "Small, yet big; light to get about on backs o' his sheep, yet not too light. Wi' a coat hard a-top to keep oot Daleland weather, soft as sealskin beneath. And wi' them sorrerful eyes on him as niver goes but wi' a good un. Amaist he minds me o' Rex son o' Rally."

"Oh, dear! Oh, dear!" groaned Sam'l. But the old man heard him not.

"Did 'Enry Farewether tell yo' hoo he acted this mornin', Master?" he inquired, addressing the man at the foot of the ladder.

"Nay," said the other, his stern eyes lighting.

"Why, 'twas this way, it seems," Tammas continued. "Young bull gets 'isself loose somegate and marches oot into yard, o'erturns milkpail, and prods owd pigs i' ribs. And as he stands lookin' about un, thinking' what he shall be up to next, oor Bob sees un. 'An' what yo' doin' here, Mr. Bull?' he seems to say, cockin' his ears and trottin' up gaylike. Wi' that bull bloats fit to bust 'isself, lashes wi's tail, waggles his head, and gets agate o' chargin' 'im. But Bob leaps oot o' way, quick as lightnin' yet cool as butter, and when he's done his foolin drives un back agin."

"Who seed all this?" interposed Sam'l, sceptically.

"'Enry Farewether from the loft. So there, Fat'ead!" Tammas replied, and continued his tale. "So they goes on; bull chargin' and Bob drivin' un back and back, hoppin' in and oot agin, quiet as a cowcumber, yet determined. At last Mr. Bull sees it's no manner o' use that gate, so he turns, rares up, and tries to jump wall. Nary a bit. Young dog jumps in on un and nips him by tail. Wi' that, bull tumbles down in a hurry, turns wi' a

kind o' groan, and marches back into stall, Bob after un.
And then, dang me!"—the old man beat the ladder as he
loosed off this last titbit,—"if he doesna sit' isself i' door
like a sentrynel till 'Enry Farewether coom up. Hoo's
that for a tyke not yet a year?"

Even Sam'l Todd was moved by the tale.

"Well done, oor Bob!" he cried.

"Good, lad!" said the Master, laying a hand on the
dark head at his knee.

"Yo' may well say that," cried Tammas in a kind of
ecstasy. "A proper Gray Dog, I tell yo'. Wi' the brains
of a man and the way of a woman. Ah, yo' canna beat 'em
nohow, the Gray Dogs o' Kenmuir!"

The patter of cheery feet rang out on the plank-bridge
over the stream below them. Tammas glanced round.

"Here's David," he said. "Late this mornin' he be."

A fair-haired boy came spurring up the slope, his face
all aglow with the speed of his running. Straightway the
young dog dashed off to meet him with a fiery speed his
sober gait belied. The two raced back together into the
yard.

"Poor lad!" said Sam'l gloomily, regarding the new-
comer.

"Poor heart!" muttered Tammas. While the Master's
face softened visibly. Yet there looked little to pity in
this jolly, rocking lad with the tousle of light hair and
fresh, rosy countenance.

"G'mornin', Mister Moore! Morn'n, Tammas!
Morn'n, Sam'l!" he panted as he passed; and ran on
through the hay-carpeted yard, round the corner of the
stable, and into the house.

In the kitchen, a long room with red-tiled floor and

latticed windows, a woman, white-aproned and frail-faced, was bustling about her morning business. To her skirts clung a sturdy, bare-legged boy; while at the oak table in the centre of the room a girl with brown eyes and straggling hair was seated before a basin of bread and milk.

"So yo've coom at last, David!" the woman cried, as the boy entered; and, bending, greeted him with a tender, motherly salutation, which he returned as affectionately. "I welly thowt yo'd forgot us this mornin'. Noo sit you' doon beside oor Maggie." And soon he, too, was engaged in a task twin to the girl's.

The two children munched away in silence, the little bare-legged boy watching them the while, critically. Irritated by this prolonged stare, David at length turned on him.

"Weel, little Andrew," he said, speaking in that paternal fashion in which one small boy loves to address another. "Weel, ma little lad, yo'm cooming' along gradely." He leant back in his chair the better to criticise his subject. But Andrew, like all the Moores, slow of speech, preserved a stolid silence, sucking a chubby thumb, and regarding his patron a thought cynically.

David resented the expression on the boy's countenance, and half rose to his feet.

"Yo' put another face on yo', Andrew Moore," he cried threateningly, "or I'll put it for yo'."

Maggie, however, interposed opportunely.

"Did yo' fether beat yo' last night?" she inquired in a low voice; and there was a shade of anxiety in the soft brown eyes.

"Nay," the boy answered; "he was a-goin' to, but he never did. Drunk," he added in explanation.

"What was he goin' to beat yo' for, David?" asked Mrs. Moore.

"What for? Why, for the fun o't—to see me squiggle," the boy replied, and laughed bitterly.

"Yo' shouldna speak so o' your dad, David," reproved the other as severely as was in her nature.

"Dad! a fine dad! I'd dad him an I'd the chance," the boy muttered beneath his breath. Then, to turn the conversation:

"Us should be startin', Maggie," he said, and going to the door. "Bob! Owd Bob, lad! Ar't coomin' along?" he called.

The gray dog came springing up like an antelope, and the three started off for school together.

Mrs. Moore stood in the doorway, holding Andrew by the hand, and watched the departing trio.

" 'Tis a pretty pair, Master, surely," she said softly to ner husband, who came up at the moment.

"Ay, he'll be a fine lad if his fether'll let him," the tall man answered.

" 'Tis a shame Mr. M'Adam should lead him such a life," the woman continued indignantly. She laid a hand on her husband's arm, and looked up at him coaxingly. "Could yo' not say summat to un, Master, think 'ee? Happen he'd 'tend to you," she pleaded. For Mrs. Moore imagined that there could be no one but would gladly heed what James Moore, Master of Kenmuir, might say to him. "He's not a bad un at bottom, I do believe," she continued. "He never took on so till his missus died. Eh, but he was main fond o' her."

Her husband shook his head.

"Nay, mother," he said. " 'Twould nob' but mak' it

worse for t' lad. M'Adam'd listen to no one, let alone me." And, indeed, he was right; for the tenant of the Grange made no secret of his animosity for his straight-going, straight-speaking neighbour.

.   .   .   .   .

Owd Bob, in the meantime, had escorted the children to the larch-copse bordering on the lane which leads to the village. Now he crept stealthily back to the yard, and established himself behind the water-butt.

How he played and how he laughed; how he teased old Whitecap till that gray gander all but expired of apoplexy and impotence; how he ran the roan bull-calf, and aroused the bitter wrath of a portly sow, mother of many, is of no account.

At last, in the midst of his merry mischief-making, a stern voice arrested him.

"Bob, lad, I see 'tis time we larned you yo' letters."

So the business of life began for that dog of whom the simple farmer-folk of the Daleland still love to talk—Bob, son of Battle, last of the Gray Dogs of Kenmuir.

CHAPTER II

A SON OF HAGAR

IT IS a lonely country, that about the Wastrel-dale.
Parson Leggy Hornbut will tell you that his is the
smallest church in the biggest parish north of the Derwent,
and that his cure numbers more square miles than parishioners. Of fells and ghylls it consists, of becks and
lakes; with here a scattered hamlet and there a solitary
hill sheep-farm. It is a country in which sheep are
paramount; and every other Dalesman is engaged in that
profession which is as old as Abel. And the talk of the
men of the land is of wethers and gimmers, of tup-hoggs,
ewe tegs in wool, and other things which are but fearsome
names to you and me; and always of the doings or mis-
doings, the intelligence or stupidity, of their adjutants, the
sheep-dogs.

Of all the Daleland, the country from the Black Water
to Grammoch Pike is the wildest. Above the tiny stone-
built village of Wastrel-dale the Muir Pike nods its massive

head. Westward, the desolate Mere Marches, from which the Sylvesters' great estate derives its name, reach away in mile on mile of sheep-infested, windswept moor-land. On the far side of the Marches is that twin dale where flows the gentle Silver Lea. And it is there in the paddocks at the back of the Dalesman's Daughter, that, in the late summer months, the famous sheep-dog Trials of the North are held. There that the battle for the Dale Cup, the world-known Shepherds' Trophy, is fought out.

Past the little inn leads the turnpike road to the market-centre of the district—Grammoch-town. At the bottom of the paddocks at the back of the inn winds the Silver Lea. Just there a plank bridge crosses the stream, and, beyond, the Murk Muir Pass crawls up the sheer side of the Scaur on to the Mere Marches.

At the head of the Pass, before it debouches on to those lonely sheep-walks which divide the two dales, is that hollow, shuddering with gloomy possibilities, aptly called the Devil's Bowl. In its centre the Lone Tarn, weirdly suggestive pool, lifts its still face to the sky. It was beside that black, frozen water, across whose cold surface the storm was swirling in white snow-wraiths, that, many, many years ago (not in this century) old Andrew Moore came upon the mother of the Gray Dogs of Kenmuir.

In the North, every one who has heard of the Muir Pike —and who has not?—has heard of the Gray Dogs of Kenmuir, every one who has heard of the Shepherd's Trophy— and who has not?—knows their fame. In that country of good dogs and jealous masters the pride of place has long been held unchallenged. Whatever line may claim to follow the Gray Dogs always lead the van. And there is a saying in the land: "Faithfu' as the Moores and their tykes."

. . . . .

On the top dresser to the right of the fireplace in the kitchen of Kenmuir lies the family Bible. At the end you will find a loose sheet—the pedigree of the Gray Dogs; at the beginning, pasted on the inside, an almost similar sheet, long since yellow with age—the family register of the Moores of Kenmuir.

Running your eye down the loose leaf, once, twice, and again it will be caught by a small red cross beneath a name, and under the cross the one word "Cup." Lastly, opposite the name of Rex son of Rally, are two of those proud, tell-tale marks. The cup referred to is the renowned Dale Cup—Champion Challenge Dale Cup, open to the world. Had Rex won it but once again the Shepherds' Trophy, which many men have lived to win, and died still striving after, would have come to rest forever in the little gray house below the Pike.

It was not to be, however. Comparing the two sheets, you read beneath the dog's name a date and a pathetic legend; and on the other sheet, written in his son's boyish hand, beneath the name of Andrew Moore the same date and the same legend.

From that day James Moore, then but a boy, was master of Kenmuir.

So past Grip and Rex and Rally, and a hundred others until at the foot of the page you come to that last name—Bob, son of Battle.

. . . . .

From the very first the young dog took to his work in a manner to amaze even James Moore. For a while he watched his mother, Meg, at her business, and with that seemed to have mastered the essentials of sheep tactics.

Rarely had such fiery élan been seen on the sides of the Pike; and with it the young dog combined a strange sobriety, an admirable patience, that justified, indeed, the epithet "Owd." Silent he worked, and resolute; and even in those days had that famous trick of coaxing the sheep to do his wishes;—blending, in short, as Tammas put it, the brains of a man with the way of a woman.

Parson Leggy, who was reckoned the best judge of a sheep or sheep-dog 'twixt Tyne and Tweed, summed him up in the one word "Genius." And James Moore himself, cautious man, was more than pleased.

In the village, the Dalesmen, who took a personal pride in the Gray Dogs of Kenmuir, began to nod sage heads when "oor" Bob was mentioned. Jim Mason, the post-man, whose word went as far with the villagers as Parson Leggy's with the gentry, reckoned he'd never seen a young un as so took his fancy.

That winter it grew quite the recognized thing, when they had gathered of a night round the fire in the Sylvester Arms, with Tammas in the centre, old Jonas Maddox on his right, Rob Saunderson of the Holt on the left, and the others radiating away toward the sides, for some one to begin with:

"Well, and what o' oor Bob, Mr. Thornton?"

To which Tammas would always make reply:

"Oh, yo' ask Sam'l there. He'll tell yo' better'n me,"— and would forthwith plunge, himself, into a yarn.

And the way in which, as the story proceeded, Tupper of Swinsthwaite winked at Ned Hoppin of Fellsgarth, and Long Kirby, the smith, poked Jem Burton, the publican,

in the ribs, and Sexton Ross said, "Ma w
more eloquently than many words.

One man only never joined in the chorus
Sitting always alone in the background,
would listen with an incredulous grin on

"Oh, ma certes! The devil's in the ⌊og! It's no
cannie ava!" he would continually exclaim, as Tammas
told his tale.

.   .   .   .   .

In the Daleland you rarely see a stranger's face. Wan-
dering in the wild country about the twin dales at the time
of this story, you might have met Parson Leggy, striding
along with a couple of varmint terriers at his heels, and
young Cyril Gilbraith, whom he was teaching to tie flies
and fear God, beside him; or Jim Mason, postman by
profession, poacher by predilection, honest man and
sportsman by nature, hurrying along with the mail-bags
on his shoulder, a rabbit in his pocket, and the faithful
Betsy a yard behind. Besides these you might have hit
upon a quiet shepherd and a wise-faced dog; Squire
Sylvester, going his rounds upon a sturdy cob; or, had you
been lucky, sweet Lady Eleanor bent upon some errand
of mercy to one of the many tenants.

It was while the Squire's lady was driving through the
village on a visit* to Tammas's slobbering grandson—it
was shortly after Billy Thornton's advent into the world
—that little M'Adam, standing in the door of the Sylvester

*NOTE—It was this visit which figured in the Grammoch-town *Argus* (local and
radical) under the heading of "Alleged Wholesale Corruption by Tory Agents."
And that is why, on the following market day, Herbert Trotter, journalist,
erstwhile gentleman, and Secretary of the Dale Trials, found himself trying to
swim in the public horse-trough.

Arms, with a twig in his mouth and a sneer fading from his lips, made his ever-memorable remark:

"Sall!" he said, speaking in low, earnest voice; "'tis a muckle wumman."

"What? What be sayin', mon?" cried old Jonas, startled out of his usual apathy.

M'Adam turned sharply on the old man.

"I said the wumman wears a muckle hat!" he snapped.

Blotted out as it was, the observation still remains—a tribute of honest admiration. Doubtless the Recording Angel did not pass it by. That one statement anent the gentle lady of the manor is the only personal remark ever credited to little M'Adam not born of malice and all uncharitableness. And that is why it is ever memorable.

The little Scotsman with the sardonic face had been the tenant of the Grange these many years; yet he had never grown acclimatized to the land of the Southron. With his shrivelled body and weakly legs he looked among the sturdy, straight-limbed sons of the hill-country like some brown, wrinkled leaf holding its place midst a galaxy of green. And as he differed from them physically, so he did morally.

He neither understood them nor attempted to. The North-country character was an unsolved mystery to him, and that after ten years' study. "One-half o' what ye say they doot, and they let ye see it; t'ither half they disbelieve, and they tell ye so," he once said. And that explained his attitude toward them, and consequently theirs toward him.

He stood entirely alone; a son of Hagar, mocking. His sharp, ill tongue was rarely still, and always bitter. There was hardly a man in the land, from Langholm How

to the market-cross in Grammoch-town, but had at
one time known its sting, endured it in silence—for
they are slow of speech, these men of the fells and meres—
and was nursing his resentment till a day should bring
that chance which always comes. And when at the Sylvester Arms, on one of those rare occasions when M'Adam
was not present, Tammas summed up the little man in
that historic phrase of his, "When he's drunk he's wi'lent,
and when he bain't he's wicious," there was an applause
to gratify the blasé heart of even Tammas Thornton.

Yet it had not been till his wife's death that the little
man had allowed loose rein to his ill-nature. With her
firmly gentle hand no longer on the tiller of his life, it
burst into fresh being. And alone in the world with
David, the whole venom of his vicious temperament was
ever directed against the boy's head. It was as though he
saw in his fair-haired son the unconscious cause of his
ever-living sorrow. All the more strange this, seeing
that, during her life, the boy had been to poor Flora
M'Adam as her heart's core. And the lad was growing
up the very antithesis of his father. Big and hearty, with
never an ache or ill in the whole of his sturdy young body;
of frank, open countenance; while even his speech was
slow and burring like any Dale-bred boy's. And the fact
of it all, and that the lad was palpably more Englishman
than Scot—ay, and gloried in it—exasperated the little
man, a patriot before everything, to blows. While, on
top of it, David evinced an amazing pertness fit to have
tried a better man than Adam M'Adam.

On the death of his wife, kindly Elizabeth Moore had,
more than once, offered such help to the lonely little man
as a woman only can give in a house that knows no

mistress. On the last of these occasions, after crossing the Stony Bottom, which divides the two farms, and toiling up the hill to the Grange, she had met M'Adam in the door.

"Yo' maun let me put yo' bit things straight for yo', mister," she had said shyly; for she feared the little man.

"Thank ye, Mrs. Moore," he had answered with the sour smile the Dalesmen knew so well, "but ye maun think I'm a waefu' cripple." And there he had stood, grinning sardonically, opposing his small bulk in the very centre of the door.

Mrs. Moore had turned down the hill, abashed and hurt at the reception of her offer; and her husband, proud to a fault, had forbidden her to repeat it. Nevertheless her motherly heart went out in a great tenderness for the little orphan David. She knew well the desolateness of his life; his father's aversion from him, and its inevitable consequences.

It became an institution for the boy to call every morning at Kenmuir, and trot off to the village school with Maggie Moore. And soon the lad came to look on Kenmuir as his true home, and James and Elizabeth Moore as his real parents. His greatest happiness was to be away from the Grange. And the ferret-eyed little man there noted the fact, bitterly resented it, and vented his illhumour accordingly.

It was this, as he deemed it, uncalled-for trespassing on his authority which was the chief cause of his animosity against James Moore. The Master of Kenmuir it was at whom he was aiming when he remarked one day at the Arms: "Masel', I aye prefaire the good man who does no go to church, to the bad man who does. But then, as ye say, Mr. Burton, I'm peculiar."

The little man's treatment of David, exaggerated as it was by eager credulity, became at length such a scandal to the Dale that Parson Leggy determined to bring him to task on the matter.

Now M'Adam was the parson's pet antipathy. The bluff old minister, with his brusque manner and big heart, would have no truck with the man who never went to church, was perpetually in liquor, and never spoke good of his neighbours. Yet he entered upon the interview fully resolved not to be betrayed into an unworthy expression of feeling; rather to appeal to the little man's better nature.

The conversation had not been in progress two minutes, however, before he knew that, where he had meant to be calmly persuasive, he was fast become hotly abusive.

"You, Mr. Hornbut, wi' James Moore to help ye, look after the lad's soul, I'll see to his body," the little man was saying.

The parson's thick gray eyebrows lowered threateningly over his eyes.

"You ought to be ashamed of yourself to talk like that. Which d'you think the more important, soul or body? Oughtn't you, his father, to be the very first to care for the boy's soul? If not, who should? Answer me, sir."

The little man stood smirking and sucking his eternal twig, entirely unmoved by the other's heat.

"Ye're right, Mr. Hornbut, as ye aye are. But my argiment is this: that I get at his soul best through his leetle carcase."

The honest parson brought down his stick with an angry thud.

"M'Adam, you're a brute—a brute!" he shouted.

At which outburst the little man was seized with a spasm of silent merriment.

"A fond dad first, a brute afterward, aiblins—he! he! Ah, Mr. Hornbut! ye 'ford me vast diversion, ye do indeed, 'my loved, my honoured, much-respected friend.'"

"If you paid as much heed to your boy's welfare as you do to the bad poetry of that profligate ploughman——"

An angry gleam shot into the other's eyes.

"D'ye ken what blasphemy is, Mr. Hornbut?" he asked, shouldering a pace forward.

For the first time in the dispute the parson thought he was about to score a point, and was calm accordingly.

"I should do; I fancy I've a specimen of the breed before me now. And d'you know what impertinence is?"

"I should do; I fancy I've—I awd say it's what gentlemen aften are unless their mammies whipped 'em as lads."

For a moment the parson looked as if about to seize his opponent and shake him.

"M'Adam," he roared, "I'll not stand your insolences!"

The little man turned, scuttled indoors, and came running back with a chair.

"Permit me!" he said blandly, holding it before him like a haircutter for a customer.

The parson turned away. At the gap in the hedge he paused.

"I'll only say one thing more," he called slowly. "When your wife, whom I think we all loved, lay dying in that room above you, she said to you in my presence——"

It was M'Adam's turn to be angry. He made a step forward with burning face.

"Aince and for a', Mr. Hornbut," he cried passionately, "onderstand I'll not ha' you and yer likes lay yer tongues on ma wife's memory whenever it suits ye. You can say what ye like aboot me—lies, sneers, snash—and I'll say naethin'. I dinna ask ye to respect me; I think ye might do sae muckle by her, puir lass. She never harmed ye. Gin ye canna let her bide in peace where she lies doon yonder"—he waved in the direction of the churchyard—"ye'll no come on ma land. Though she is dead she's mine."

Standing in front of his house, with flushed face and big eyes, the little man looked almost noble in his indignation. And the parson, striding away down the hill, was uneasily conscious that with him was not the victory.

CHAPTER III

RED WULL

THE winter came and went; the lambing season was over, and spring already shyly kissing the land. And the back of the year's work broken, and her master well started on a fresh season, M'Adam's old collie, Cuttie Sark, lay down one evening and passed quietly away.

The little black-and-tan lady, Parson Leggy used to say, had been the only thing on earth M'Adam cared for. Certainly the two had been wondrously devoted; and for many a market-day the Dalesmen missed the shrill, chuckling cry which heralded the pair's approach: "Weel done, Cuttie Sark!"

The little man felt his loss acutely, and, according to his wont, vented his ill-feeling on David and the Dalesmen. In return, Tammas, whose forte lay in invective and alliteration, called him behind his back, "A wenomous one!" and "A wiralent wiper!" to the applause of tinkling pewters.

A shepherd without his dog is like a ship without a rudder, and M'Adam felt his loss practically as well as otherwise. Especially did he experience this on a day when he had to take a batch of draft-ewes over to Grammoch-town. To help him Jem Burton had lent the services of his herring-gutted, herring-hearted, greyhound lurcher, Monkey. But before they had well topped Braithwaite Brow, which leads from the village on to the marches, M'Adam was standing in the track with a rock in his hand, a smile on his face, and the tenderest blandishments in his voice as he coaxed the dog to him. But Master Monkey knew too much for that. However, after gamboling a while longer in the middle of the flock, a boulder, better aimed than its predecessors, smote him on the hinder parts and sent him back to the Sylvester Arms, with a sore tail and a subdued heart.

For the rest, M'Adam would never have won over the sheep-infested marches alone with his convoy had it not been for the help of old Saunderson and Shep, who caught him on the way and aided him.

It was in a very wrathful mood that on his way home he turned into the Dalesman's Daughter in Silverdale.

The only occupants of the tap-room, as he entered, were Teddy Bolstock, the publican, Jim Mason, with the faithful Betsy beneath his chair and the post-bags flung into the corner, and one long-limbed, drover-like man—a stranger.

"And he coom up to Mr. Moore," Teddy was saying, "and says he: 'I'll gie ye twal' pun for yon gray dog o' yourn.' 'Ah,' says Moore, 'yo' may gie me twal' hunner'd and yet you'll not get ma Bob.'—Eh, Jim?"

"And he did thot," corroborated Jim. "'Twal' hun-ner'd,' says he."

"James Moore and his dog agin,'" snapped M'Adam. "There's ithers in the warld for bye them twa,"

"Ay, but none like 'em," quoth loyal Jim.

"Na, thanks be. Gin there were there'd be no room for Adam M'Adam in this 'melancholy vale.'"

There was silence a moment, and then—:

"You're wantin' a tyke, bain't you, Mr. M'Adam?" Jim asked.

The little man hopped round all in a hurry.

"What!" he cried in well-affected eagerness, scanning the yellow mongrel beneath the chair. "Betsy for sale! Guid life! Where's ma check-book!" Whereat Jim, most easily snubbed of men, collapsed.

M'Adam took off his dripping coat and crossed the room to hang it on a chair-back. The stranger drover followed the meagre, shirt-clad figure with shifty eyes; then he buried his face in his mug.

M'Adam reached out a hand for the chair; and as he did so, a bomb in yellow leapt out from beneath it, and, growling horribly, attacked his ankles.

"Curse ye!" cried M'Adam, starting back. "Ye devil, let me alone!" Then turning fiercely on the drover, "Yours, mister?" he asked. The man nodded. "Then call him aff, can't ye? D—n ye!" At which Teddy Bolstock withdrew, sniggering; and Jim Mason slung the post-bags on to his shoulder and plunged out into the rain, the faithful Betsy following, disconsolate.

The cause of the squall, having beaten off the attacking force, had withdrawn again beneath its chair. M'Adam stooped down, still cursing, his wet coat on his arm, and beheld a tiny yellow puppy, crouching defiant in the dark, and glaring out with fiery light eyes. Seeing itself remarked, it bared its little teeth, raised its little bristles, and growled a hideous menace.

A sense of humour is many a man's salvation, and was M'Adam's one redeeming feature. The laughableness of the thing—this ferocious atomy defying him—struck home to the little man. Delighted at such a display of vice in so tender a plant, he fell to chuckling.

"Ye leetle devil!" he laughed. "He! he! ye leetle devil!" and flipped together finger and thumb in vain endeavour to coax the puppy to him.

But it growled, and glared more terribly.

"Stop it, ye little snake, or I'll flatten you!" cried the big drover, and shuffled his feet threateningly. Whereat the puppy, gurgling like hot water in a kettle, made a feint as though to advance and wipe them out, these two bad men.

M'Adam laughed again, and smote his leg.

"Keep a ceevil tongue and yer distance," says he, "or I'll e'en ha' to mak' ye. Though he is but as big as a man's thumb, a dog's a dog for a' that— he! he! the leetle devil." And he fell to flipping finger and thumb afresh.

"Ye're maybe wantin' a dog?" inquired the stranger. "Yer friend said as much."

"Ma friend lied; it's his way," M'Adam replied.

"I'm willin' to part wi' him," the other pursued.

The little man yawned. "Weel, I'll tak' him to oblige ye," he said indifferently.

The drover rose to his feet.

"It's givin' 'im ye, fair givin' 'im ye, mind! But I'll do it!"—he smacked a great fist into a hollow palm. "Ye may have the dog for a pun'—I'll only ask *you* a pun'," and he walked away to the window.

M'Adam drew back, the better to scan his would-be benefactor; his lower jaw dropped, and he eyed the stranger with a drolly sarcastic air.

"A poun', man! A poun'—for yon noble dorg!" he pointed a crooked forefinger at the little creature, whose scowling mask peered from beneath the chair. "Man, I couldna do it. Na, na; ma conscience wadna permit me. 'Twad be fair robbin' ye. Ah, ye Englishmen!" he spoke half to himself, and sadly, as if deploring the unhappy accident of his nationality; "it's yer grand, open-hairted generosity that grips a puir Scotsman by the throat. A poun'! and for yon!" He wagged his head mournfully, cocking it sideways the better to scan his subject.

"Take him or leave him," ordered the drover truculently, still gazing out of the window.

"Wi' yer permission I'll leave him," M'Adam answered meekly.

"I'm short o' the ready," the big man pursued, "or I wouldna part with him. Could I bide me time there's many'd be glad to give me a tenner for one o' that bree——" he caught himself up hastily—"for a dog sic as that."

"And yet ye offer him me for a poun'! Noble indeed!" Nevertheless the little man had pricked his ears at the other's slip and quick correction. Again he approached the puppy, dangling his coat before him to protect his ankles; and again that wee wild beast sprang out, seized the coat in its small jaw, and worried it savagely.

M'Adam stooped quickly and picked up his tiny assailant; and the puppy, suspended by its neck, gurgled and slobbered; then, wriggling desperately round, made its teeth meet in its adversary's shirt. At which M'Adam shook it gently and laughed. Then he set to examining it.

Apparently some six weeks old; a tawny coat, fiery eyes, a square head with small, cropped ears, and a comparatively immense jaw; the whole giving promise of great strength, if little beauty. And this effect was enhanced by the manner of its docking. For the miserable relic of a tail, yet raw, looked little more than a red button adhering to its wearer's stern.

M'Adam's inspection was as minute as it was apparently absorbing; he omitted nothing from the square muzzle to the lozenge-like scut. And every now and then he threw a quick glance at the man at the window, who was watching the careful scrutiny a thought uneasily.

"Ye've cut him short," he said at length, swinging round on the drover.

"Ay; strengthens their backs," the big man answered with averted gaze.

M'Adam's chin went up in the air; his mouth partly opened and his eyelids partly closed as he eyed his informant.

"Oh, ay," he said.

"Gie him back to me," ordered the drover surlily. He took the puppy and set it on the floor; whereupon it immediately resumed its former fortified position. "Ye're no buyer; I knoo that all along by that face on ye," he said in insulting tones.

"Ye wad ha' bought him yerself', nae doot?" M'Adam inquired blandly.

"In course; if you says so."

"Or airblins ye bred him?"

"'Appen I did."

"Ye'll no be from these parts?"

"Will I no?" answered the other.

A smile of genuine pleasure stole over M'Adam's face. He laid his hand on the other's arm.

"Man," he said gently, "ye mind me o' hame." Then almost in the same breath: "Ye said ye found him?"

It was the stranger's turn to laugh.

"Ha! ha! Ye teeckle me, little mon. Found 'im? Nay; I was give 'im by a friend. But there's nowt amiss wi' his breedin', ye may believe me."

The great fellow advanced to the chair under which the puppy lay. It leapt out like a lion, and fastened on his huge boot.

"A rare bred un, look 'ee! a rare game un. Ma word, he's a big-hearted un! Look at the back on him; see the jaws to him; mark the pluck of him!" He shook his booted foot fiercely, tossing his leg to and fro like a tree in a wind. But the little creature, now raised ceilingward, now dashed to the ground, held on with incomparable doggedness, till its small jaw was all bloody and muzzle wrinkled with the effort.

"Ay, ay, that'll do," M'Adam interposed, irritably.

The drover ceased his efforts.

"Now, I'll mak' ye a last offer." He thrust his head down to a level with the other's, shooting out his neck. "It's throwin' him at ye, mind. 'Tain't buyin' him ye'll be—don't go for to deceive yourself. Ye may have him for fifteen shillin'. Why do I do it, ye ask? Why,' cos 1 think ye'll be kind to him," as the puppy retreated to its chair, leaving a spotted track of red along its route.

"Ay, ye wadna be happy gin ye thocht he'd no a comfortable hame, conseederate man?" M'Adam answered, eyeing the dark track on the floor. Then he put on his coat.

"Na, na, he's no for me. Weel, I'll no detain ye. Good-nicht to ye, mister!" and he made for the door.

"A gran' worker he'll be," called the drover after him.

"Ay; muckle wark he'll mak' amang the sheep wi' sic a jaw and sic a temper. Weel, I maun be steppin'. Good-nicht to ye."

"Ye'll niver have sich anither chanst."

"Nor niver wush to. Na, na; he'll never mak' a sheep-dog"; and the little man turned up the collar of his coat.

"Will he not?" cried the other scornfully. "There niver yet was one o' that line——" he stopped abruptly.

The little man spun round.

"Iss?" he said, as innocent as any child; "ye were sayin'?"

The other turned to the window and watched the rain falling monotonously.

"Ye'll be wantin' wet," he said adroitly.

"Ay, we could do wi' a drappin'. And he'll never mak' a sheep-dog." He shoved his cap down on his head. "Weel, good-nicht to ye!" and he stepped out into the rain.

.   .   .   .   .

It was long after dark when the bargain was finally struck.

Adam M'Adam's Red Wull became that little man's property for the following realizable assets: ninepence in cash—three coppers and a doubtful sixpence; a plug of suspicious tobacco in a well-worn pouch; and an old watch.

"It's clean givin' 'im ye," said the stranger bitterly, at the end of the deal.

"It's mair the charity than aught else mak's me sae leeberal," the other answered gently. "I wad not like to see ye pinched."

"Thank ye kindly," the big man replied with some acerbity, and plunged out into the darkness and rain. Nor was that long-limbed drover-man ever again seen in the countryside. And the puppy's previous history— whether he was honestly come by or no, whether he was, indeed, of the famous Red McCulloch* strain, ever remained a mystery in the Daleland.

*N.B.—You may know a Red McCulloch anywhere by the ring of white upon his tail some two inches from the root.

CHAPTER IV

FIRST BLOOD

AFTER that first encounter in the Dalesman's
Daughter, Red Wull, for so M'Adam called him,
resigned himself complacently to his lot; recognizing,
perhaps, his destiny.

Thenceforward the sour little man and the vicious puppy
grew, as it were, together. The two were never apart.
Where M'Adam was, there was sure to be his tiny attendant, bristling defiance as he kept ludicrous guard over his
master.

The little man and his dog were inseparable. M'Adam
never left him even at the Grange.

"I couldna trust ma Wullie at hame alone wi' the dear
lad," was his explanation. "I ken weel I'd come back to
find a wee corpse on the floor, and David singin':

'My heart is sair, I daur na tell,
My heart is sair for somebody.'

Ay, and he'd be sair elsewhere by the time I'd done wi'
him—he! he!"

The sneer at David's expense was as characteristic as it
was unjust. For though the puppy and the boy were
already sworn enemies, yet the lad would have scorned to
harm so small a foe. And many a tale did David tell at
Kenmuir of Red Wull's viciousness, of his hatred of him
(David), and his devotion to his master; how, whether
immersed in the pig-bucket or chasing the fleeting rabbit,
he would desist at once, and bundle, panting, up at his
master's call; how he routed the tomcat and drove him
from the kitchen; and how he clambered on to David's
bed and pinned him murderously by the nose.

Of late the relations between M'Adam and James
Moore had been unusually strained. Though they were
neighbours, communications between the two were of the
rarest; and it was for the first time for many a long day
that, on an afternoon shortly after Red Wull had come into
his possession, M'Adam entered the yard of Kenmuir,
bent on girding at the master for an alleged trespass at the
Stony Bottom.

"Wi' yer permission, Mr. Moore," said the little man,
"I'll wheestle ma dog," and, turning, he whistled a shrill,
peculiar note like the cry of a disturbed peewit.

Straightway there came scurrying desperately up, ears
back, head down, tongue out, as if the world depended on
his speed, a little tawny beetle of a thing, who placed his
forepaws against his master's ankles and looked up into
his face; then, catching sight of the strangers, hurriedly he
took up his position between them and M'Adam, assuming
his natural attitude of grisly defiance. Such a laughable
spectacle he made, that martial mite, standing at bay with

bristles up and teeth bared, that even James Moore smiled.

"Ma word! Ha' yo' brought his muzzle, man?" cried old Tammas, the humourist; and, turning, climbed all in a heat on to an upturned bucket that stood by. Whereat the puppy, emboldened by his foe's retreat, advanced savagely to the attack, buzzing round the slippery pail like a wasp on a windowpane, in a vain attempt to reach the old man.

Tammas stood on the top, hitching his trousers and looking down on his assailant, the picture of mortal fear.

"'Elp! Oh, 'elp!" he bawled. "Send for the sogers! Fetch the p'lice! For lawk-a-mussy's sake call him off, man!" Even Sam'l Todd, watching the scene from the cart-shed, was tickled and burst into a loud guffaw, heartily backed by 'Enry and oor Job. While M'Adam remarked: "Ye're fitter for a stage than a stable-bucket, Mr. Thornton."

"How didst come by him?" asked Tammas, nodding at the puppy.

"Found him," the little man replied, sucking his twig. 'Found him in ma stockin' on ma birthday. A present from ma leetle David for his auld dad, I doot."

"So do I," said Tammas, and was seized with sudden spasm of seemingly causeless merriment. For looking up, as M'Adam was speaking, he had caught a glimpse of a boy's fair head, peering cautiously round the cowshed, and, behind, the flutter of short petticoats. They disappeared as silently as they had come; and two small figures, just returned from school, glided away and sought shelter in the friendly darkness of a coal-hole.

"Coom awa', Maggie, coom awa'! 'Tis th' owd un, isself," whispered a disrespectful voice.

M'Adam looked round suspiciously.

"What's that?" he asked sharply.

At that moment, however, Mrs. Moore put her head out of the kitchen window.

"Coom thy ways in, Mister M'Adam, and tak' a soop o' tea," she called hospitably.

"Thank ye kindly, Mrs. Moore, I will," he answered, politely for him. And this one good thing must be allowed of Adam M'Adam: that, if there was only one woman of whom he was ever known to speak well, there was also only one, in the whole course of his life, against whom he ever insinuated evil—and that was years afterward, when men said his brain was sapped. Flouts and jeers he had for every man, but a woman, good or bad, was sacred to him. For the sex that had given him his mother and his wife he had that sentiment of tender reverence which, if a man still preserve, he cannot be altogether bad. As he turned into the house he looked back at Red Wull.

"Ay, we may leave him," he said. "That is, gin ye're no afraid, Mr. Thornton?"

.   .   .   .   .   .

Of what happened while the men were within doors, it is enough to tell two things. First, that Owd Bob was no bully. Second, this: In the code of sheep-dog honour there is written a word in stark black letters; and opposite it another word, writ large in the colour of blood. The first is "Sheep-murder"; the second, "Death." It is the one crime only to be wiped away in blood; and to accuse of the crime is to offer the one unpardonable insult. Every sheep-dog knows it, and every shepherd.

That afternoon, as the men still talked, the quiet echoes of the farm rung with a furious animal cry, twice *ι*epeated: "Shot for sheep-murder"—"Shot for sheep-murder"; followed by a hollow stillness.

  .   .   .   .   .

The two men finished their colloquy. The matter was concluded peacefully, mainly owing to the pacifying influence of Mrs. Moore. Together the three went out into the yard; Mrs. Moore seizing the opportunity to shyly speak on David's behalf.

"He's such a good little lad, I do think," she was saying.

"Ye should ken, Mrs. Moore," the little man answered, a thought bitterly; "ye see enough of him."

"Yo' mun be main proud of un, mester," the woman continued, heedless of the sneer: "an' 'im growin' such a gradely lad."

M'Adam shrugged his shoulders.

"I barely ken the lad," he said. "By sight I know him, of course, but barely to speak to. He's but seldom at hame."

"An' hoo proud his mother'd be if she could see him," the woman continued, well aware of his one tender place. "Eh, but she was fond o' him, so she was."

An angry flush stole over the little man's face. Well he understood the implied rebuke; and it hurt him like a knife.

"Ay, ay, Mrs. Moore," he began. Then breaking off, and looking about him—"Where's ma Wullie?" he cried excitedly. "James Moore!" whipping round on the Master, "ma Wullie's gone—gone, I say!"

Elizabeth Moore turned away indignantly.

"I do declar' he tak's more fash after yon little yaller beastie than iver he does after his own flesh," she muttered.

"Wullie, ma wee doggie! Wullie, where are ye? James Moore, he's gone—ma Wullie's gone!" cried the little man, running about the yard, searching everywhere.

"Cannot 'a' gotten far," said the Master, reassuringly, looking about him.

"Niver no tellin'," said Sam'l, appearing on the scene, pig-bucket in hand. "I misdoot yo'll iver see your dog agin, mister." He turned sorrowfully to M'Adam.

That little man, all dishevelled, and with the perspiration standing on his face, came hurrying out of the cow-shed and danced up to the Master.

"It's robbed I am—robbed, I tell ye!" he cried recklessly. "Ma wee Wull's bin stolen while I was ben your hoose, James Moore!"

"Yo' munna say that, ma mon. No robbin' at Kenmuir," the Master answered sternly.

"Then where is he? It's for you to say."

"I've ma own idee, I 'ave," Sam'l announced opportunely, pig-bucket uplifted.

M'Adam turned on him.

"What, man? What is it?"

"I misdoot yo'll iver see your dog agin, mister," Sam'l repeated, as if he was supplying the key to the mystery.

"Noo, Sam'l, if yo' know owt tell it," ordered his master.

Sam'l grunted sulkily.

"Wheer's oor Bob, then?" he asked.

At that M'Adam turned on the Master.

"'Tis that, nae doot. It's yer gray dog, James Moore, yer —— dog. I might ha' kent it,"—and he loosed off a volley of foul words.

"Sweerin' will no find him," said the Master coldly. "Noo, Sam'l."

The big man shifted his feet, and looked mournfully at M'Adam.

"'Twas 'appen 'alf an hour agone, when I sees oor Bob goin' oot o' yard wi' little yaller tyke in his mouth. In a minnit I looks agin—and theer! little yaller 'un was gone, and oor Bob a-sittin' a-lickin' his chops. Gone foriver, I do reck'n. Ah, yo' may well take on, Tammas Thornton!" For the old man was rolling about the yard, bent double with merriment.

M'Adam turned on the Master with the resignation of despair.

"Man, Moore," he cried piteously, "it's yer gray dog has murdered ma wee Wull! Ye have it from yer ain man."

"Nonsense," said the Master encouragingly. "'Tis but yon girt oof."

Sam'l tossed his head and snorted.

"Coom, then, and I'll show yo'," he said, and led the way out of the yard. And there below them on the slope to the stream, sitting like Justice at the Courts of Law, was Owd Bob.

Straightway Sam'l whose humour was something of the calibre of old Ross's, the sexton, burst into horse-merriment. "Why's he sittin' so still, think 'ee? Ho! ho! See un lickin' his chops—ha! ha!"—and he roared afresh. While from afar you could hear the distant rumbling of 'Enry and oor Job.

At the sight, M'Adam burst into a storm of passionate invective, and would have rushed on the dog had no James Moore forcibly restrained him.

"Bob, lad," called the Master, "coom here!"

But even as he spoke, the gray dog cocked his ears, listened a moment, and then shot down the slope. At the same moment Tammas hallooed: "Theer he be! yon's yaller un coomin' oot o' drain! La, Sam'l!" And there, indeed, on the slope below them, a little angry, smutty-faced figure was crawling out of a rabbit-burrow.

"Ye murderin' devil, wad ye duar touch ma Wullie?" yelled M'Adam, and, breaking away, pursued hotly down the hill; for the gray dog had picked up the puppy, like a lancer a tent-peg, and was sweeping on, his captive in his mouth, toward the stream.

Behind, hurried James Moore and Sam'l, wondering what the issue of the comedy would be. After them toddled old Tammas, chuckling. While over the yard-wall was now a little cluster of heads: 'Enry, oor Job, Maggie and David, and Vi'let Thornton, the dairymaid.

Straight on to the plank-bridge galloped Owd Bob. In the middle he halted, leant over, and dropped his prisoner; who fell with a cool plop into the running water beneath.

Another moment and M'Adam had reached the bank of the stream. In he plunged, splashing and cursing, and seized the struggling puppy; then waded back, the waters surging about his waist, and Red Wull, limp as a wet rag, in his hand. The little man's hair was dripping, for his cap was gone; his clothes clung to him, exposing the miserableness of his figure; and his eyes blazed like hot ashes in' his wet face.

He sprang on to the bank, and, beside himself with passion, rushed at Owd Bob.

"Curse ye for a——"

"Stan' back, or yo'll have him at your throat!" shouted

the Master, thundering up. "Stan' back, I say, yo' fule!" And, as the little man still came madly on, he reached forth his hand and hurled him back; at the same moment, bending, he buried the other hand deep in Owd Bob's shaggy neck. It was but just in time; for if ever the fierce desire of battle gleamed in gray eyes, it did in the young dog's as M'Adam came down on him.

The little man staggered, tottered, and fell heavily. At the shock, the blood gushed from his nose, and, mixing with the water on his face, ran down in vague red streams, dripping off his chin; while Red Wull, jerked from his grasp, was thrown afar, and lay motionless.

"Curse ye!" M'Adam screamed, his face dead-white save for the running red about his jaw. "Curse ye for a cowardly Englishman!" and, struggling to his feet, he made at the Master.

But Sam'l interposed his great hulk between the two.

"Easy, little mon," he said leisurely, regarding the small fury before him with mournful interest. "Eh, but thee do be a little spit-cat, surely!"

James Moore stood, breathing deep, his hand still buried in Owd Bob's coat.

"If yo'd touched him," he explained, "I couldna ha' stopped him. He'd ha' mauled yo' afore iver I could ha' had him off. They're bad to hold, the Gray Dogs, when they're roosed."

"Ay, ma word, that they are!" corroborated Tammas, speaking from the experience of sixty years. "Once on, yo' canna get 'em off."

The little man turned away.

"Ye're all agin me," he said, and his voice shook. A pitiful figure he made, standing there with the water dripping from him. A red stream was running slowly from his chin; his head was bare, and face working.

James Moore stood eyeing him with some pity and some contempt. Behind was Tammas, enjoying the scene. While Sam'l regarded them all with an impassive melancholy.

M'Adam turned and bent over Red Wull, who still lay like a dead thing. As his master handled him, the button-tail quivered feebly; he opened his eyes, looked about him, snarled faintly, and glared with devilish hate at the gray dog and the group with him.

The little man picked him up, stroking him tenderly. Then he turned away and on to the bridge. Half-way across he stopped. It rattled feverishly beneath him, for he still trembled like a palsied man.

"Man, Moore!" he called, striving to quell the agitation in his voice—"I wad shoot yon dog."

Across the bridge he turned again.

"Man, Moore!" he called and paused. "Ye'll not forget this day." And with that the blood flared up a dull crimson into his white face.

PART II

THE LITTLE MAN

CHAPTER V

A MAN'S SON

THE storm, long threatened, having once burst,
M'Adam allowed loose rein to his bitter animosity
against James Moore.

The two often met. For the little man frequently
returned home from thé village by the footpath across
Kenmuir. It was out of his way, but he preferred it in
order to annoy his enemy and keep a watch upon his
doings.

He haunted Kenmuir like its evil genius. His sallow
face was perpetually turning up at inopportune moments.
When Kenmuir Queen, the prize short-horn heifer, calved
unexpectedly and unattended in the dip by the lane, Tammas and the Master, summoned hurriedly by Owd Bob,
came running up to find the little man leaning against the
stile, and shaking with silent merriment. Again, poor old
Staggy, daring still in his dotage, took a fall while scrambling on the steep banks of the Stony Bottom. There he

lay for hours, unnoticed and kicking, until James Moore and Owd Bob came upon him at length, nearly exhausted. But M'Adam was before them.

Standing on the far bank with Red Wull by his side, he called across the gulf with apparent concern: "He's bin so sin' yesternight." Often James Moore, with all his great strength of character, could barely control himself.

There were two attempts to patch up the feud. Jim Mason, who went about the world seeking to do good, tried in his shy way to set things right. But M'Adam and his Red Wull between them soon shut him and Betsy up.

"You mind yer letters and yer wires, Mr. Poacher-Postman. Ay, I saw 'em baith: th' ain doon by the Haughs, t'ither in the Bottom. And there's Wullie, the humorsome chiel, havin' a rare game wi' Betsy." There, indeed, lay the faithful Betsy, suppliant on her back, paws up, throat exposed, while Red Wull, now a great-grown puppy, stood over her, his habitually evil expression intensified into a fiendish grin, as with wrinkled muzzle and savage wheeze he waited for a movement as a pretext to pin: "Wullie, let the leddy be—ye've had yer dinner."

Parson Leggy was the other would-be mediator; for he hated to see the two principal parishioners of his tiny cure at enmity. First he tackled James Moore on the subject; but that laconic person cut him short with, "I've nowt agin the little mon," and would say no more. And, indeed, the quarrel was none of his making.

Of the parson's interview with M'Adam, it is enough to say here that, in the end, the angry old minister would of a surety have assaulted his mocking adversary had not Cyril Gilbraith forcibly withheld him.

And after that the vendetta must take its course unchecked.

David was now the only link between the two farms.
Despite his father's angry commands, the boy clung to his
intimacy with the Moores with a doggedness that no
thrashing could overcome.   Not a minute of the day when
out of school, holidays and Sundays included, but was
passed at Kenmuir.   It was not till late at night that he
would sneak back to the Grange, and creep quietly up to
his tiny bare room in the roof—not supperless, indeed,
motherly Mrs. Moore had seen to that.   And there he
would lie awake and listen with a fierce contempt as his
father, hours later, lurched into the kitchen below, lilting
liquorishly:

> "We are na fou, we're nae that fou,
>   But just a drappie in our e'e;
> The cock may craw, the day may daw',
>   And ay we'll taste the bareley bree!"

And in the morning the boy would slip quietly out of the
house while his father still slept; only Red Wull would
thrust out his savage head as the lad passed, and snarl
hungrily.

Sometimes father and son would go thus for weeks without sight of one another.   And that was David's aim—to
escape attention.   It was only his cunning at this game of
evasion that saved him a thrashing.

The little man seemed devoid of all natural affection for
his son.   He lavished the whole fondness of which his
small nature appeared capable on the Tailless Tyke, for
so the Dalesmen called Red Wull.   And the dog he
treated with a careful tenderness that made David smile
bitterly.

The little man and his dog were as alike morally as physically they were contrasted. Each owed a grudge against the world and was determined to pay it. Each was an Ishmael among his kind.

You saw them thus, standing apart, leper-like, in the turmoil of life; and it came quite as a revelation to happen upon them in some quiet spot of nights, playing together, each wrapped in the game, innocent, tender, forgetful of the hostile world.

The two were never separated except only when M'Adam came home by the path across Kenmuir. After that first misadventure he never allowed his friend to accompany him on the journey through the enemy's country; for well he knew that sheep-dogs have long memories.

To the stile in the lane, then, Red Wull would follow him. There he would stand, his great head poked through the bars, watching his master out of sight; and then would turn and trot, self-reliant and defiant, sturdy and surly, down the very centre of the road through the village— no playing, no enticing away, and woe to that man or dog who tried to stay him in his course! And so on, past Mother Ross's shop, past the Sylvester Arms, to the right by Kirby's smithy, over the Wastrel by the Haughs, to await his master at the edge of the Stony Bottom.

The little man, when thus crossing Kenmuir, often met Owd Bob, who had the free run of the farm. On these occasions he passed discreetly by; for, though he was no coward, yet it is bad, single-handed, to attack a Gray Dog of Kenmuir; while the dog trotted soberly on his way, only a steely glint in the big gray eyes betraying his knowledge of the presence of his foe. As surely, however, as the little man, in his desire to spy out the nakedness of the land, strayed off the public path, so surely a gray figure, seeming to spring from out the blue, would come fiercely, silently driving down on him; and he would turn and run for his life, amid the uproarious jeers of any of the farm-hands who were witness to the encounter.

On these occasions David vied with Tammas in face-tiousness at his father's expense.

"Good on yo', little un!" he roared from behind a wall, on one such occurrence.

"Bain't he a runner, neither?" yelled Tammas, not to be outdone. "See un skip it—ho! ho!"

"Look to his knees a-wamblin';" from the undutiful son in ecstasy. "An' I'd knees like yon, I'd wear petti-coats." As he spoke, a swinging box on the ear nearly knocked the young reprobate down.

"D' yo' think God gave you a dad for you to jeer at? Y' ought to be ashamed o' yo'self. Serve yo' right if he does thrash yo' when yo' get home." And David, turn-ing round, found James Moore close behind him, his heavy eyebrows lowering over his eyes.

Luckily, M'Adam had not distinguished his son's voice among the others. But David feared he had; for on the following morning the little man said to him:

"David, ye'll come hame immediately after school to-day."

"Will I?" said David pertly.

"Ye will."

"Why?"

"Because I tell ye to, ma lad"; and that was all the reason he would give. Had he told the simple fact that he wanted help to drench a "husking" ewe, things might have gone differently. As it was, David turned away defiantly down the hill.

The afternoon wore on. Schooltime was long over; still there was no David.

The little man waited at the door of the Grange, fuming, hopping from one leg to the other, talking to Red Wull, who lay at his feet, his head on his paws, like a tiger waiting for his prey.

At length he could restrain himself no longer; and started running down the hill, his heart burning with indignation.

"Wait till we lay hands on ye, ma lad," he muttered as he ran. "We'll warm ye, we'll teach ye."

At the edge of the Stony Bottom, he, as always, left Red Wull. Crossing it himself, and rounding Langholm How, he espied James Moore, David, and Owd Bob walking away from him and in the direction of Kenmuir. The gray dog and David were playing together, wrestling, racing, and rolling. The boy had never a thought for his father.

The little man ran up behind them, unseen and unheard, his feet softly pattering on the grass. His hand had fallen on David's shoulder before the boy had guessed his approach.

"Did I bid ye come hame after school, David?" he asked, concealing his heat beneath a suspicious suavity.

"Maybe. Did I say I would come?"

The pertness of tone and words, alike, fanned his father's resentment into a blaze. In a burst of passion he lunged forward at the boy with his stick. But as he smote, a gray whirlwind struck him fair on the chest, and he fell like a snapped stake, and lay, half stunned, with a dark muzzle an inch from his throat.

"Git back, Bob!" shouted James Moore, hurrying up. "Git back, I tell yo'!" He bent over the prostrate figure, propping it up anxiously. "Are yo' hurt, M'Adam? Eh, but I am sorry. He thought yo' were goin' for to strike the lad."

David had now run up, and he, too, bent over his father with a very scared face.

"Are yo' hurt, feyther?" he asked, his voice trembling.

The little man rose unsteadily to his feet and shook off his supporters. His face was twitching, and he stood, all dust-begrimed, looking at his son.

"Ye're content, aiblins, noo ye've seen yer father's gray head bowed in the dust," he said.

"'Twas an accident," pleaded James Moore. "But I *am* sorry. He thought yo' were goin' to beat the lad."

"So I was—so I will."

"If ony's beat it should be ma Bob here tho' he nob'but thought he was doin' right. An' yo' were aff the path."

The little man looked at his enemy, a sneer on his face.

"Ye canna thrash him for doin' what ye bid him. Set yer dog on me, if ye will, but dinna beat him when he does yer biddin'!"

"I did not set him on yo', as you know," the Master replied warmly.

M'Adam shrugged his shoulders.

"I'll no argie wi' ye, James Moore," he said. "I'll leave you and what ye call yer conscience to settle that. My business is not wi' you.—David!" turning to his son.

A stranger might well have mistaken the identity of the boy's father. For he stood now, holding the Master's

arm; while a few paces above them was the little man
pale but determined, the expression on his face betraying
his consciousness of the irony of the situation.

"Will ye come hame wi' me and have it noo, or stop wi'
him and wait till ye get it?" he asked the boy.

"M'Adam, I'd like yo' to——"

"None o' that, James Moore,—David, what d'ye say?"
David looked up into his protector's face.

"Yo'd best go wi' your feyther, lad," said the Master
at last, thickly. The boy hesitated, and clung tighter to
the shielding arm; then he walked slowly over to his
father.

A bitter smile spread over the little man's face as he
marked this new test of the boy's obedience to the other.

"To obey his frien' he foregoes the pleasure o' disobeyin'
his father," he muttered. "Noble!" Then he turned
homeward, and the boy followed in his footsteps.

James Moore and the gray dog stood looking after them.

"I know yo'll not pay off yer spite agin me on the lad's
head, M'Adam," he called, almost appealingly.

"I'll do ma duty, thank ye, James Moore, wi'oot
respect o' persons," the little man cried back, never
turning.

Father and son walked away, one behind the other,
like a man and his dog, and there was no word said
between them. Across the Stony Bottom, Red Wull,
scowling with bared teeth at David, joined them. Together the three went up the hill to the Grange.

In the kitchen M'Adam turned.

"Noo, I'm gaein' to gie ye the gran'est thrashin' ye iver
dreamed of. Tak' aff yer coat!"

The boy obeved, and stood up in his thin shirt, his face

white and set as a statue's.   Red Wull seated himself on
his haunches close by, his ears pricked, licking his lips, all
attention.

The little man suppled the great ash-plant in his hands
and raised it.   But the expression on the boy's face
arrested his arm.

"Say ye're sorry and I'll let yer aff easy."

"I'll not."

"One mair chance—yer last! Say yer 'shamed o
yerself'!''

"I'm not."

The little man brandished his cruel white weapon, and
Red Wull shifted a little to obtain a better view.

"Git on wi' it," ordered David angrily.

The little man raised the stick again and—threw it intc
the farthest corner of the room.

It fell with a rattle on the floor, and M'Adam turned
away.

"Ye're the pitifulest son iver a man had," he cried
brokenly.   "Gin a man's son dinna haud to him, wha can
he expect to?—no one.   Ye're ondootiful, ye're disrespect-
fu', ye're maist ilka thing ye shouldna be; there's but ae
thing I thocht ye were not—a coward.   And as to that,
ye've no the pluck to say ye're sorry when, God knows,
ye might be.   I canna thrash ye this day.   But ye shall
gae nae mair to school.   I send ye there to learn.   Ye'll
not learn—ye've learnt naethin' except disobedience to
me—ye shall stop at hame and work."

His father's rare emotion, his broken voice and working
face, moved David as all the stripes and jeers had failed to
do.   His conscience smote him.   For the first time in his
life it dimly dawned on him that, perhaps, his father, too,

had some ground for complaint; that, perhaps, he was not a good son.

He half turned.

"Feyther——"

"Git oot o' ma sight!" M'Adam cried.

And the boy turned and went.

CHAPTER VI

A LICKING OR A LIE

THENCEFORWARD David buckled down to work at home, and in one point only father and son resembled—industry. A drunkard M'Adam was, but a drone, no.

The boy worked at the Grange with tireless, indomitable energy; yet he could never satisfy his father.

The little man would stand, a sneer on his face and his thin lips contemptuously curled, and flout the lad's brave labours.

"Is he no a gran' worker, Wullie? 'Tis a pleasure to watch him, his hands in his pockets, his eyes turned heavenward!" as the boy snatched a hard-earned mo-! ment's rest. "You and I, Wullie, we'll brak' oorsel's slavin' for him while he looks on and laffs."

And so on, the whole day through, week in, week out, till he sickened with weariness of it all.

In his darkest hours David thought sometimes to run away. He was miserably alone on the cold bosom of the world. The very fact that he was the son of his father

isolated him in the Daleland. Naturally of a reserved
disposition, he had no single friend outside Kenmuir.
And it was only the thought of his friends there that
withheld him. He could not bring himself to part from
them; they were all he had in the world.

So he worked on at the Grange, miserably, doggedly,
taking blows and abuse alike in burning silence. But
every evening, when work was ended, he stepped off to his
other home beyond the Stony Bottom. And on Sundays
and holidays—for of these latter he took, unasking, what
he knew to be his due—all day long, from cock-crowing to
the going down of the sun, he would pass at Kenmuir. In
this one matter the boy was invincibly stubborn. Nothing his father could say or do sufficed to break him of the
habit. He endured everything with white-lipped, silent
doggedness, and still held on his way.

Once past the Stony Bottom, he threw his troubles
behind him with a courage that did him honour. Of all the
people at Kenmuir two only ever dreamed the whole depth
of his unhappiness, and that not through David. James
Moore suspected something of it all, for he knew more of
M'Adam than did the others. While Owd Bob knew it as
did no one else. He could tell it from the touch of the
boy's hand on his head; and the story was writ large upon
his face for a dog to read. And he would follow the lad
about with a compassion in his sad gray eyes greater than
words.

David might well compare his gray friend at Kenmuir
with that other at the Grange.

The Tailless Tyke had now grown into an immense dog
heavy of muscle and huge of bone. A great bull head;
undershot jaw, square and lengthy and terrible; vicious,

yellow-gleaming eyes; cropped ears; and an expression incomparably savage. His coat was a tawny, lion-like yellow, short, harsh, dense; and his back, running up from shoulder to loins, ended abruptly in the knob-like tail. He looked like the devil of a dogs' hell. And his repu-cation was as bad as his looks. He never attacked un-provoked; but a challenge was never ignored, and he was greedy of insults. Already he had nigh killed Rob Saunderson's collie, Shep; Jem Burton's Monkey fled incontinently at the sound of his approach; while he had even fought a round with that redoubtable trio, the Vexer, Venus, and Van Tromp.

Nor, in the matter of war, did he confine himself to his own kind. His huge strength and indomitable courage made him the match of almost anything that moved. Long Kirby once threatened him with a broomstick; the smith never did it again. While in the Border Ram he attacked Big Bell, the Squire's underkeeper, with such murderous fury that it took all the men in the room to pull him off.

More than once had he and Owd Bob essayed to wipe out mutual memories, Red Wull, in this case only, the aggressor. As yet, however, while they fenced a moment for that deadly throat-grip, the value of which each knew so well, James Moore had always seized the chance to intervene.

"That's right, hide him ahint yer petticoats," sneered M'Adam on one of these occasions.

"Hide? It'll not be him I'll hide, I warn you, M'Adam," the Master answered grimly, as he stood, twirling his good oak stick between the would-be duellists. Whereat there was a loud laugh at the little man's expense.

It seemed as if there were to be other points of rivalry between the two than memories. For, in the matter of his own business—the handling of sheep—Red Wull bid fair to be second only throughout the Daleland to the Gray Dog of Kenmuir. And M'Adam was patient and painstaking in the training of his Wullie in a manner to astonish David. It would have been touching, had it not been so unnatural in view of his treatment of his own blood, to watch the tender carefulness with which the little man moulded the dog beneath his hands. After a promising display he would stand, rubbing his palms together, as near content as ever he was.

"Weel done, Wullie! Weel done. Bide a wee and we'll show 'em a thing or two, you and I, Wullie.

> "'The warld's wrack we share o't,
> The warstle and the care o't.'

For it's you and I alane, lad." And the dog would trot up to him, place his great forepaws on his shoulders, and stand thus with his great head overtopping his master's, his ears back, and stump tail vibrating.

You saw them at their best when thus together, displaying each his one soft side to the other.

From the very first David and Red Wull were open enemies: under the circumstances, indeed, nothing else was possible. Sometimes the great dog would follow on the lad's heels with surly, greedy eyes, never leaving him from sunrise to sundown, till David could hardly hold his hands.

So matters went on for a never-ending year. Then there came a climax.

One evening, on a day throughout which Red Wull had dogged him thus hungrily, David, his work finished, went to pick up his coat, which he had left hard by. On it lay Red Wull.

"Git off ma coat!" the boy ordered angrily, marching up. But the great dog never stirred: he lifted a lip to show a fence of white, even teeth, and seemed to sink lower in the ground; his head on his paws, his eyes in his forehead.

"Come and take it!" he seemed to say.

Now what, between master and dog, David had endured almost more than he could bear that day.

"Yo' won't, won't yo', girt brute!" he shouted, and bending, snatched a corner of the coat and attempted to jerk it away. At that, Red Wull rose, shivering, to his feet, and with a low gurgle sprang at the boy.

David, quick as a flash, dodged, bent, and picked up an ugly stake, lying at his feet. Swinging round, all in a moment, he dealt his antagonist a mighty buffet on the side of the head. Dazed with the blow, the great dog fell; then, recovering himself, with a terrible, deep roar he sprang again. Then it must have gone hard with the boy, fine-grown, muscular young giant though he was. For Red Wull was now in the first bloom of that great strength which earned him afterward an undying notoriety in the land.

As it chanced, however, M'Adam had watched the scene from the kitchen. And now he came hurrying out of the house, shrieking commands and curses at the combatants. As Red Wull sprang, he interposed between the two, head back and eyes flashing. His small person received the full shock of the charge. He staggered, but recovered, and in an imperative voice ordered the dog to heel.

Then he turned on David, seized the stake from his hand, and began furiously belabouring the boy.

"I'll teach ye to strike—a puir—dumb—harmless—creetur, ye—cruel—cruel—lad!" he cried. "Hoo dau ye strike—ma—Wullie? yer—father's—Wullie? Adam—M'Adam's—Red Wull?" He was panting from his exertions, and his eyes were blazing. "I pit up as best I can wi' all manner o' disrespect to masel'; but when it comes to takin' ma puir Wullie, I canna thole it. Ha' ye no heart?" he asked, unconscious of the irony of the question.

"As much as some, I reck'n," David muttered.

"Eh, what's that? What d'ye say?"

"Ye may thrash me till ye're blind; and it's nob'but yer duty; but if only one daurs so much as to look at yer Wullie ye're mad," the boy answered bitterly. And with that he turned away defiantly and openly in the direction of Kenmuir.

M'Adam made a step forward, and then stopped.

"I'll see ye agin, ma lad, this evenin'," he cried with cruel significance.

"I doot but yo'll be too drunk to see owt—except, 'appen, your bottle," the boy shouted back; and swaggered down the hill.

.   .   .   .   .   .

At Kenmuir that night the marked and particular kindness of Elizabeth Moore was too much for the overstrung lad. Overcome by the contrast of her sweet motherliness, he burst into a storm of invective against his father, his home, his life—everything.

"Don't 'ee, Davie, don't 'ee, dearie!" cried Mrs. Moore, much distressed. And taking him to her she talked to the 'great, sobbing boy as though he were a child. At length he lifted his face and looked up; and, seeing the white, wan countenance of his dear comforter, was struck with tender remorse that he had given way and pained her, who looked so frail and thin herself.

He mastered himself with an effort; and, for the rest of the evening, was his usual cheery self. He teased Maggie into tears; chaffed stolid little Andrew; and bantered Sam'l Todd until that generally impassive man threatened to bash his snout for him.

Yet it was with a great swallowing at his throat that, later, he turned down the slope for home.

James Moore and Parson Leggy accompanied him to the bridge over the Wastrel, and stood a while watching as he disappeared into the summer night.

"Yon's a good lad," said the Master half to himself.

"Yes," the parson replied; "I always thought there was good in the boy, if only his father'd give him a chance. And look at the way Owd Bob there follows him. There's not another soul outside Kenmuir he'd do that for."

"Ay, sir," said the Master. "Bob knows a mon when he sees one."

"He does," acquiesced the other. "And by the by, James, the talk in the village is that you've settled not to run him for the Cup. Is that so?"

The Master nodded.

"It is, sir. They're all mad I should, but I mun cross 'em. They say he's reached his prime—and so he has o' his body, but not o' his brain. And a sheep-dog—unlike other dogs—is not at his best till his brain is at its best—and that takes a while developin', same as in a mon, I reck'n."

"Well, well," said the parson, pulling out a favourite phrase, "waiting's winning—waiting's winning."

David slipped up into his room and into bed unseen, he hoped. Alone with the darkness, he allowed himself the rare relief of tears; and at length fell asleep. He awoke to find his father standing at his bedside. The little man held a feeble dip-candle in his hand, which lit his sallow face in crude black and white. In the doorway, dimly outlined, was the great figure of Red Wull.

"Whaur ha' ye been the day?" the little man asked. Then, looking down on the white stained face beneath him, he added hurriedly: "If ye like to lie, I'll believe ye."

David was out of bed and standing up in his night-shirt. He looked at his father contemptuously.

"I ha' bin at Kenmuir. I'll not lie for yo' or your likes," he said proudly.

The little man shrugged his shoulders.

"'Tell a lee and stick to it,' is my rule, and a good one too, in honest England. I for one 'll no think ony the worse o' ye if yer memory plays yer false."

"D'yo' think I care a kick what yo' think o' me?" the boy asked brutally. "Nay; there's 'nough liars in this fam'ly wi'oot me."

The candle trembled and was still again.

"A lickin' or a lie—tak' yer choice!"

The boy looked scornfully down on his father. Standing on his naked feet, he already towered half a head above the other and was twice the man.

"D'yo' think I'm fear'd o' a thrashin' fra yo'? Goo' gracious me!" he sneered. "Why, I'd as lief let owd Grammer Maddox lick me, for all I care."

A reference to his physical insufficiencies fired the little man as surely as a lighted match powder.

"Ye maun be cauld, standin' there so. Rin ye doon and fetch oor little frien'"—a reference to a certain strap hanging in the kitchen. "I'll see if I can warm ye."

David turned and stumbled down the unlit, narrow stairs. The hard, cold boards struck like death against his naked feet. At his heels followed Red Wull, his hot breath fanning the boy's bare legs.

So into the kitchen and back up the stairs, and Red Wull always following.

"I'll no despair yet o' teachin' ye the fifth commandment, though I kill masel' in doin' it!" cried the little man, seizing the strap from the boy's numb grasp.

.   .   .   .   .

When it was over, M'Adam turned, breathless, away. At the threshold of the room he stopped and looked round; a little, dim-lit, devilish figure, framed in the door; while from the blackness behind, Red Wull's eyes gleamed yellow.

Glancing back, the little man caught such an expression on David's face that for once he was fairly afraid. He banged the door and hobbled actively down the stairs.

CHAPTER VII

THE WHITE WINTER

M'ADAM—in his sober moments at least—never touched David again; instead, he devoted himself to the more congenial exercise of the whiplash of his tongue. And he was wise; for David, who was already nigh a head the taller of the two, and comely and strong in proportion, could, if he would, have taken his father in the hollow of his hand and crumpled him like a dry leaf. Moreover, with his tongue, at least, the little man enjoyed the noble pleasure of making the boy wince. And so the war was carried on none the less vindictively.

Meanwhile another summer was passing away, and every day brought fresh proofs of the prowess of Owd Bob. Tammas, whose stock of yarns anent Rex son of Rally had after forty years' hard wear begun to pall on the loyal ears of even old Jonas, found no lack of new material now. In the Dalesman's Daughter in Silverdale and in the Border Ram at Grammoch-town, each succeeding market day brought some fresh tale. Men told how the gray dog had outdone Gypsy Jack, the sheep-sneak; how he had cut out a Kenmuir shearling from the very centre of Londesley's pack; and a thousand like stories.

The Gray Dogs of Kenmuir have always been equally heroes and favourites in the Daleland. And the confidence of the Dalesmen in Owd Bob was now invincible. Sometimes on market days he would execute some unaccountable maneuver, and a strange shepherd would ask: "What's the gray dog at?" To which the nearest Dalesman would reply: "Nay, I canno tell ye! But he's reet enough. Yon's Owd Bob o' Kenmuir."

Whereon the stranger would prick his ears and watch with close attention.

"Yon's Owd Bob o' Kenmuir, is he?" he would say; for already among the faculty the name was becoming known. And never in such a case did the young dog fail to justify the faith of his supporters.

It came, therefore, as a keen disappointment to every Dalesman, from Herbert Trotter, Secretary of the Trials, to little Billy Thornton, when the Master persisted in his decision not to run the dog for the Cup in the approaching Dale Trials; and that though parson, squire, and even Lady Eleanour essayed to shake his purpose. It was nigh fifty years since Rex son O' Rally had won back the Trophy for the land that gave it birth; it was time, they thought, for a Daleland dog, a Gray Dog of Kenmuir— the terms are practically synonymous—to bring it home again. And Tammas, that polished phrase-maker, was only expressing the feelings of every Dalesman in the room when, one night at the Arms, he declared of Owd Bob that "to ha' run was to ha' won." At which M'Adam snig-

gered audibly and winked at Red Wull. "To ha' run was
to ha' one—lickin'; to rin next year'll be to——"

"Win next year," Tammas interposed dogmatically.
"Onless"—with shivering sarcasm—"you and yer Wullie
are thinkin' o' winnin'."

The little man rose from his solitary seat at the back of
the room and pattered across.

"Wullie and I are thinkin' o' t," he whispered loudly
in the old man's ear. "And mair: what Adam M'Adam
and his Red Wull think o' doin', that, ye may remairk,
Mr. Thornton, they do. Next year we rin, and next
year—we win. Come, Wullie, we'll leave 'em to chew
that"; and he marched out of the room amid the jeers of
the assembled topers. When quiet was restored, it was
Jim Mason who declared: "One thing certain, win or no,
they'll not be far off."

.   .   .   .   .

Meanwhile the summer ended abruptly. Hard on the
heels of a sweltering autumn the winter came down. In
that year the Daleland assumed very early its white cloak.
The Silver Mere was soon ice-veiled; the Wastrel rolled
sullenly down below Kenmuir, its creeks and quiet places
tented with jagged sheets of ice; while the Scaur and
Muir Pike raised hoary heads against the frosty blue. It
was the season still remembered in the North as the
White Winter—the worst, they say, since the famous 1808.

For days together Jim Mason was stuck with his bags
in the Dalesman's Daughter, and there was no communi-
cation between the two Dales. On the Mere Marches the
snow massed deep and impassable in thick, billowy drifts.
In the Devil's Bowl men said it lay piled some score feet

deep. And sheep, seeking shelter in the ghylls and pro-
tected spots, were buried and lost in their hundreds.

That is the time to test the hearts of shepherds and
sheep-dogs, when the wind runs ice-cold across the waste
of white, and the low woods on the upland walks shiver
black through a veil of snow, and sheep must be found and
folded or lost: a trial of head as well as heart, of resource
as well as resolution.

In that winter more than one man and many a dog lost
his life in the quiet performance of his duty, gliding to
death over the slippery snow-shelves, or overwhelmed
beneath an avalanche of the warm, suffocating white:
"smoored," as they call it. Many a deed was done, many
a death died, recorded only in that Book which holds the
names of those—men or animals, souls or no souls—who
Tried.

They found old Wrottesley, the squire's head shepherd,
lying one morning at Gill's foot, like a statue in its white
bed, the snow gently blowing about the venerable face,
calm and beautiful in death. And stretched upon his
bosom, her master's hands blue, and stiff, still clasped
about her neck, his old dog Jess. She had huddled there,
as a last hope, to keep the dear, dead master warm, her
great heart riven, hoping where there was no hope.

That night she followed him to herd sheep in a better
land. Death from exposure, Dingley, the vet., gave it;
but as little M'Adam, his eyes dimmer than their wont,
declared huskily; "We ken better, Wullie."

Cyril Gilbraith, a young man not overburdened with
emotions, told with a sob in his voice how, at the terrible
Rowan Rock, Jim Mason had stood, impotent, dumb,
big-eyed, watching Betsy—Betsy, the friend and partner

of the last ten years—slipping over the ice-cold surface, silently appealing to the hand that had never failed her before—sliding to Eternity.

In the Daleland that winter the endurance of many a shepherd and his dog was strained past breaking-point. From the frozen Black Water to the white-peaked Grammoch Pike two men only, each always with his shaggy adjutant, never owned defeat; never turned back; never failed in a thing attempted.

In the following spring, Mr. Tinkerton, the squire's agent, declared that James Moore and Adam M'Adam— Owd Bob, rather, and Red Wull—had lost between them fewer sheep than any single farmer on the whole March Mere Estate—a proud record.

Of the two, many a tale was told that winter. They were invincible, incomparable; worthy antagonists.

It was Owd Bob who, when he could not *drive* the band of Black Faces over the narrow Razorback which led to safety, induced them to *follow* him across that ten-inch death-track, one by one, like children behind their mistress. It was Red Wull who was seen coming down the precipitous Saddler's How, shouldering up that grand old gentleman, King o' the Dale, whose leg was broken.

The gray dog it was who found Cyril Gilbraith by the White Stones, with a cigarette and a sprained ankle, on the night the whole village was out with lanterns searching for the well-loved young scapegrace. It was the Tailless Tyke and his master who one bitter evening came upon little Mrs. Burton, lying in a huddle beneath the lea of the fast-whitening Druid's Pillar with her latest baby on her breast. It was little M'Adam who took off his coat and wrapped the child in it; little M'Adam who unwound his plaid, threw it like a breastband across the dog's great chest, and tied the ends round the weary woman's waist. Red Wull it was who dragged her back to the Sylvester Arms and life, straining like a giant through the snow, while his master staggered behind with the babe in his arms. When they reached the inn it was M'Adam who, with a smile on his face, told the landlord what he thought of him for sending his wife across the Marches on such a day and on *his* errand. To which: "I'd a cauld," pleaded honest Jem.

For days together David could not cross the Stony Bottom to Kenmuir. His enforced confinement to the Grange led, however, to no more frequent collisions than usual with his father. For M'Adam and Red Wull were out at all hours, in all weathers, night and day, toiling at their work of salvation.

At last, one afternoon, David managed to cross the Bottom at a point where a fallen thorn-tree gave him a bridge over the soft snow. He stayed but a little while at Kenmuir, yet when he started for home it was snowing again.

By the time he had crossed the ice-draped bridge over the Wastrel, a blizzard was raging. The wind roared past him, smiting him so that he could barely stand; and the snow leaped at him so that he could not see. But he held on doggedly; slipping, sliding, tripping, down and up again, with one arm shielding his face. On, on, into the white darkness, blindly on sobbing, stumbling, dazed.

At length, nigh dead, he reached the brink of the Stony Bottom. He looked up and he looked down, but nowhere in that blinding mist could he see the fallen thorn-tree. He took a step forward into the white morass, and sank up to his thigh. He struggled feebly to free himself, and sank deeper. The snow wreathed, twisting, round him like a white flame, and he collapsed, softly crying on that soft bed.

"I canna—I canna!" he moaned.

. . . . . .

Little Mrs. Moore, her face whiter and frailer than ever, stood at the window, looking out into the storm.

"I canna rest for thinkin' o' th' lad," she said. Then, turning, she saw her husband, his fur cap down over his ears, buttoning his pilot-coat about his throat, while Owd Bob stood at his feet, waiting.

"Ye're no goin', James?" she asked, anxiously.

"But I am, lass," he answered; and she knew him too well to say more.

So those two went quietly out to save life or lose it, nor counted the cost.

Down a wind-shattered slope—over a spar of ice—up an eternal hill—a forlorn hope.

In a whirlwind chaos of snow, the tempest storming at them, the white earth lashing them, they fought a good fight. In front, Owd Bob, the snow clogging his shaggy coat, his hair cutting like lashes of steel across eyes, his head lowered as he followed the finger of God; and close behind, James Moore, his back stern against the storm, stalwart still, yet swaying like a tree before the wind.

So they battled through to the brink of the Stony Bottom—only to arrive too late.

For, just as the Master peering about him, had caught sight of a shapeless lump lying motionless in front, there loomed across the snow-choked gulf through the white riot of the storm a gigantic figure forging, doggedly forward,

his great head down to meet the hurricane. And close
behind, buffeted and bruised, stiff and staggering, a little
dauntless figure holding stubbornly on, clutching with one
hand at the gale; and a shrill voice, whirled away on the
trumpet tones of the wind, crying:

"Noo, Wullie, wi' me!

> "'Scots wha' hae wi' Wallace bled!
> Scots wham Bruce has often led!
> Welcome to——!'

Here he is, Wullie!

> "'——or to victorie!'"

The brave little voice died away. The quest was over;
the lost sheep found. And the last James Moore saw of
them was the same small, gallant form, half carrying, half
dragging the rescued boy out of the Valley of the Shadow
and away.

David was none the worse for his adventure, for on
reaching home M'Adam produced a familiar bottle.

"Here's something to warm yer inside, and"—making a
feint at the strap on the wall—"here's something to do the
same by yer—— But, Wullie, oot again!"

And out they went—unreckoned heroes.

.   .   .   .   .

It was but a week later, in the very heart of the bitter
time, that there came a day when, from gray dawn to
grayer eve, neither James Moore nor Owd Bob stirred out
into the wintry white. And the Master's face was hard
and set as it always was in time of trouble.

Outside, the wind screamed down the Dale; while the
snow fell relentlessly; softly fingering the windows,
blocking the doors, and piling deep against the walls.

Inside the house there was a strange quiet; no sound save
for hushed voices, and upstairs the shuffling of muffled feet.

Below, all day long, Owd Bob patrolled the passage like
some silent, gray spectre.

Once there came a low knocking at the door; and David,
his face and hair and cap smothered in the all-pervading
white, came in with an eddy of snow. He patted Owd
Bob, and moved on tiptoe into the kitchen. To him came
Maggie softly, shoes in hand, with white, frightened face.
The two whispered anxiously awhile like brother and
sister as they were; then the boy crept quietly away;
only a little pool of water on the floor and wet, treacherous
foot-dabs toward the door testifying to the visitor.

Toward evening the wind died down, but the mourning
flakes still fell.

With the darkening of night Owd Bob retreated to the
porch and lay down on his blanket. The light from the
lamp at the head of the stairs shone through the crack of
open door on his dark head and the eyes that never slept.

The hours passed, and the gray knight still kept his
vigil. Alone in the darkness—alone, it almost seemed,
in the house—he watched. His head lay motionless
along his paws, but the steady gray eyes never flinched
or drooped.

Time tramped on on leaden foot, and still he waited;
and ever the pain of hovering anxiety was stamped deeper
in the gray eyes.

At length it grew past bearing; the hollow stillness of
the house overcame him. He rose, pushed open the door,
and softly pattered across the passage.

At the foot of the stairs he halted, his forepaws on the
first step, his grave face and pleading eyes uplifted, as

though he were praying. The dim light fell on the raised head; and the white escutcheon on his breast shone out like the snow on Salmon.

At length, with a sound like a sob, he dropped to the ground, and stood listening, his tail dropping and head raised. Then he turned and began softly pacing up and down, like some velvet-footed sentinel at the gate of death.

Up and down, up and down, softly as the falling snow, for a weary, weary while.

Again he stopped and stood, listening intently, at the foot of the stairs; and his gray coat quivered as though there were a draught.

Of a sudden, the deathly stillness of the house was broken. Upstairs, feet were running hurriedly. There was a cry, and again silence.

A life was coming in; a life was going out.

The minutes passed; hours passed; and, at the sunless dawn, a life passed.

And all through that night of age-long agony the gray figure stood, still as a statue, at the foot of the stairs. Only, when, with the first chill breath of the morning, a dry, quick-quenched sob of a strong man sorrowing for the helpmeet of a score of years, and a tiny cry of a new-born child wailing because its mother was not, came down to his ears, the Gray Watchman dropped his head upon his bosom, and, with a little whimpering note, crept back to his blanket.

A little later the door above opened, and James Moore tramped down the stairs. He looked taller and gaunter than his wont, but there was no trace of emotion on his face.

At the foot of the stairs Owd Bob stole out to meet him.

He came crouching up, head and tail down, in a manner no man ever saw before or since. At his master's feet he stopped and whined pitifully.

Then, for one short moment, James Moore's whole face quivered.

"Well, lad," he said, quite low, and his voice broke; 'she's awa'!"

That was all; for they were an undemonstrative couple.

Then they turned and went out together into the bleak morning.

CHAPTER VIII

M'ADAM AND HIS COAT

TO David M'Adam the loss of gentle Elizabeth Moore was as real a grief as to her children. Yet he manfully smothered his own aching heart and devoted himself to comforting the mourners at Kenmuir.

In the days succeeding Mrs. Moore's death the boy recklessly neglected his duties at the Grange. But little M'Adam forbore to rebuke him. At times, indeed, he essayed to be passively kind. David, however, was too deeply sunk in his great sorrow to note the change.

The day of the funeral came. The earth was throwing off its ice-fetters; and the Dale was lost in a mourning mist.

In the afternoon M'Adam was standing at the window of the kitchen, contemplating the infinite weariness of the scene, when the door of the house opened and shut noiselessly. Red Wull raised himself on to the sill and growled, and David hurried past the window making for Kenmuir. M'Adam watched the passing figure indifferently; then with an angry oath sprang to the window. "Bring me back that coat, ye thief!" he cried, tapping fiercely on the pane. "Tak' it off at onst, ye muckle gowk, or I'll come and tear it aff ye. D'ye see him, Wullie? the great coof has ma coat—me black coat, new last Michaelmas, and it rainin' 'nough to melt it."

He threw the window up with a bang and leaned out.

"Bring it back, I tell ye, ondootiful, or I'll summons ye. Though ye've no respect for me, ye might have for ma claithes. Ye're too big for yer ain boots, let alane ma coat. D'ye think I had it cut for a elephant? It's burstin', I tell ye. Tak' it aff! Fetch it here, or I'll e'en send Wullie to bring it!"

David paid no heed except to begin running heavily down the hill. The coat was stretched in wrinkled agony across his back; his big, red wrists protruded like shank-bones from the sleeves; and the little tails flapped wearily in vain attempts to reach the wearer's legs.

M'Adam, bubbling over with indignation, scrambled half through the open window. Then, tickled at the amazing impudence of the thing, he paused, smiled, dropped to the ground again, and watched the uncouth, retreating figure with chuckling amusement.

"Did ye ever see the like o' that, Wullie?" he muttered. "Ma puir coat—puir wee coatie! it gars me greet to see her in her pain. A man's coat, Wullie, is aften unco sma' for his son's back; and David there is strainin' and stretchin' her nigh to brakin', for a' the world as he does ma forbearance. And what's he care aboot the one or t'ither?—not a finger-flip."

As he stood watching the disappearing figure there began the slow tolling of the minute-bell in the little Dale church.

Now near, now far, now loud, now low, its dull chant rang out through the mist like the slow-dropping tears of a mourning world.

M'Adam listened, almost reverently, as the bell tolled on, the only sound in the quiet Dale. Outside, a drizzling rain was falling; the snow dribbled down the hill in muddy tricklets and trees and roofs and windows dripped.

And still the bell tolled on, calling up relentlessly sad memories of the long ago.

It was on just such another dreary day, in just such another December, and not so many years gone by, that the light had gone forever out of his life.

The whole picture rose as instant to his eyes as if it had been but yesterday. That insistent bell brought the scene surging back to him: the dismal day; the drizzle; the few mourners; little David decked out in black, his fair hair contrasting with his gloomy clothes, his face swollen with weeping; the Dale hushed, it seemed in death, save for the tolling of the bell; and his love had left him and gone to the happy land the hymn-books talk of.

Red Wull, who had been watching him uneasily, now came up and shoved his muzzle into his master's hand. The cold touch brought the little man back to earth. He shook himself, turned wearily away from the window, and went to the door of the house.

He stood there looking out; and all round him was the eternal drip, drip of the thaw. The wind lulled, and again the minute-bell tolled out clear and inexorable, resolute to recall what was and what had been.

With a choking gasp the little man turned into the house, and ran up the stairs and into his room. He dropped on his knees beside the great chest in the corner, and unlocked the bottom drawer, the key turning noisily in its socket.

In the drawer he searched with feverish fingers, and produced at length a little paper packet wrapped about with a stained yellow ribbon. It was the ribbon she had used to weave on Sundays into her soft hair.

Inside the packet was a cheap, heart-shaped frame, and in it a photograph.

Up there it was too dark to see. The little man ran down the stairs, Red Wull jostling him as he went, and hurried to the window in the kitchen.

It was a sweet, laughing face that looked up at him from frame, demure yet arch, shy yet roguish—a face to look at and a face to love.

As he looked a wintry smile, wholly tender, half tearful, stole over the little man's face.

"Lassie," he whispered, and his voice was infinitely soft, "it's lang sin' I've daured look at ye. But it's no that ye're forgotten, dearie."

Then he covered his eyes with his hand as though he were blinded.

"Dinna look at me sae, lass!" he cried, and fell on his knees, kissing the picture, hugging it to him and sobbing passionately.

Red Wull came up and pushed his face compassionately into his master's; but the little man shoved him roughly away, and the dog retreated into a corner, abashed and reproachful.

Memories swarmed back on the little man.

It was more than a decade ago now, and yet he dared barely think of that last evening when she had lain so white and still in the little room above.

"Pit the bairn on the bed, Adam man," she had said in low tones. "I'll be gaein' in a wee while noo. It's the lang good-by to you—and him."

He had done her bidding and lifted David up. The tiny boy lay still a moment, looking at this white-faced mother whom he hardly recognized.

"Minnie!" he called piteously. Then, thrusting a small, dirty hand into his pocket, he pulled out a grubby sweet.

"Minnie, ha' a sweetie—ain o' Davie's sweeties!" and he held it out anxiously in his warm plump palm, thinking it a certain cure for any ill.

"Eat it for mither," she said, smiling tenderly; and then: "Davie, ma heart, I'm leavin' ye."

The boy ceased sucking the sweet, and looked at her, the corners of his mouth drooping pitifully.

"Ye're no gaein' awa', mither?" he asked, his face all working. "Ye'll no leave yer wee laddie?"

"Ay, laddie, awa'—reet awa'. He's callin' me." She tried to smile; but her mother's heart was near to bursting.

"Ye'll tak' yer wee Davie wi' ye mither!" the child pleaded, crawling up toward her face.

The great tears rolled, unrestrained, down her wan cheeks, and M'Adam, at the head of the bed, was sobbing openly.

"Eh, ma bairn, ma bairn, I'm sair to leave ye!" she cried brokenly. "Lift him for me, Adam."

He placed the child in her arms; but she was too weak to hold him. So he laid him upon his mother's pillows; and the boy wreathed his soft arms about her neck and sobbed tempestuously.

And the two lay thus together.

Just before she died, Flora turned her head and whis▾pered:

"Adam, ma man, ye'll ha' to be mither and father baith to the lad noo": and she looked at him with tender confidence in her dying eyes.

"I wull! afore God as I stan' here I wull!" he declared passionately. Then she died, and there was a look of ineffable peace upon her face.

.   .   .   .   .

"Mither and father baith!"

The little man rose to his feet and flung the photograph from him. Red Wull pounced upon it; but M'Adam leapt at him as he mouthed it.

"Git awa', ye devil!" he screamed; and, picking it up, stroked it lovingly with trembling fingers.

"Maither and father baith!"

How had he fulfilled his love's last wish? How!

"Oh God!"—and he fell upon his knees at the table-side, hugging the picture, sobbing and praying.

Red Wull cowered in the far corner of the room, and then crept whining up to where his master knelt. But M'Adam heeded him not, and the great dog slunk away again.

There the little man knelt in the gloom of the winter's afternoon, a miserable penitent. His gray-flecked head was bowed upon his arms; his hands clutched the picture; and he prayed aloud in gasping, halting tones.

"Gie me grace, O God! 'Father and mither baith,' ye said, Flora—and I ha'na done it. But 'tis no too late— say it's no, lass. Tell me there's time yet, and say ye forgie me. I've tried to bear wi' him mony and mony a time. But he's vexed me, and set himself agin me, and

stiffened my back, and ye ken hoo I was aye quick to tak'
offence. But I'll mak' it up to him—mak' it up to him,
and mair. I'll humble masel' afore him, and that'll be
bitter enough. And I'll be father and mither baith to
him. But there's bin none to help me; and it's bin sair
wi'oot ye. And—but, eh lassie, I'm wearyin' for ye!"

   .   .   .   .   .   .

It was a dreary little procession that wound in the
drizzle from Kenmuir to the little Dale Church. At the
head stalked James Moore, and close behind David in
his meagre coat. While last of all, as if to guide the
stragglers in the weary road, came Owd Bob.

There was a full congregation in the tiny church now.
In the squire's pew were Cyril Gilbraith, Muriel Sylvester,
and, most conspicuous, Lady Eleanour. Her slender
figure was simply draped in gray, with gray fur about the
neck and gray fur edging sleeves and jacket; her veil was
lifted, and you could see the soft hair about her temples,
like waves breaking on white cliffs, and her eyes big with
tender sympathy as she glanced toward the pew upon her
right.

For there were the mourners from Kenmuir: the Master,
tall, grim, and gaunt; and beside him Maggie, striving to
be calm, and little Andrew, the miniature of his father.

Alone, in the pew behind, David M'Adam in his father's
coat.

The back of the church was packed with farmers from
the whole March Mere Estate; friends from Silverdale and
Grammoch-town; and nearly every soul in Wastrel-dale,
come to show their sympathy for the living and reverence
for the dead.

At last the end came in the wet dreariness of the little churchyard, and slowly the mourners departed, until at length were left only the parson, the Master, and Owd Bob.

The parson was speaking in rough, short accents, digging nervously at the wet ground. The other, tall and gaunt, his face drawn and half-averted, stood listening. By his side was Owd Bob, scanning his master's countenance, a wistful compassion deep in the sad gray eyes; while close by, one of the parson's terriers was nosing inquisitively in the wet grass.

Of a sudden, James Moore, his face still turned away, stretched out a hand. The parson broke off abruptly and grasped it. Then the two men strode away in opposite directions, the terrier hopping on three legs and shaking the rain off his hard coat.

.   .   .   .   .

David's steps sounded outside. M'Adam rose from his knees. The door of the house opened, and the boy's feet shuffled in the passage.

"David!" the little man called in a tremulous voice.

He stood in the half-light, one hand on the table, the other clasping the picture. His eyes were bleared, his thin hair all tossed, and he was shaking.

"David," he called again; "I've somethin' I wush to say to ye!"

The boy burst into the room. His face was stained with tears and rain; and the new black coat was wet and slimy all down the front, and on the elbows were green-brown, muddy blots. For, on his way home, he had flung himself down in the Stony Bottom just as he was, heedless of the wet earth and his father's coat, and, lying on his face

thinking of that second mother lost to him, had wept his
heart out in a storm of passionate grief.

Now he stood defiantly, his hand upon the door.

"What d'yo' want?"

The little man looked from him to the picture in his hand.

"Help me, Flora—he'll no," he prayed.   Then raising
his eyes, he began: "I'd like to say—I've bin thinkin'—
I think I should tell ye—it's no an easy thing for a man to
say——"

He broke off short.   The self-imposed task was almost
more than he could accomplish.

He looked appealingly at David.   But there was no
glimmer of understanding in that white, set countenance.

"O God, it's maist mair than I can do!" the little man
muttered; and the perspiration stood upon his forehead.
Again he began: "David, after I saw ye this afternoon
steppin' doon the hill——"

Again he paused.   His glance rested unconsciously upon
the coat.   David mistook the look; mistook the dimness
in his father's eyes; mistook the tremor in his voice.

"Here 'tis! tak' yo' coat!" he cried passionately; and
tearing it off, flung it down at his father's feet.   "Tak' it—
and—and—curse yo'."

He banged out of the room and ran upstairs; and,
locking himself in, threw himself on to his bed and sobbed.

Red Wull made a movement to fly at the retreating
figure; then turned to his master, his stump-tail vibrating
with pleasure.

But little M'Adam was looking at the wet coat now
lying in a wet bundle at his feet.

"Curse ye," he repeated softly.   "Curse ye—ye heard
him, Wullie?"

A bitter smile crept across his face.   He looked again at
the picture now lying crushed in his hand.

"Ye canna say I didna try; ye canna ask me to agin,"
he muttered, and slipped it into his pocket.   "Niver agin,
Wullie; not if the Queen were to ask it."

Then he went out into the gloom and drizzle, still
smiling the same bitter smile.

.   .   .   .   .

That night, when it came to closing-time at the Sylvester
Arms, Jem Burton found a little gray-haired figure lying
on the floor in the tap-room.   At the little man's head
lay a great dog.

"Yo' beast!" said the righteous publican, regarding the
figure of his best customer with fine scorn.   Then catching
sight of a photograph in the little man's hand:

"Oh, yo're that sort, are yo', foxy?" he leered.   "Gie us
a look at 'er," and he tried to disengage the picture from
the other's grasp.   But at the attempt the great dog rose,
bared his teeth, and assumed such a diabolical expression
that the big landlord retreated hurriedly behind the bar.

"Two on ye!" he shouted viciously, rattling his heels;
"beasts baith!"

PART III

THE SHEPHERDS' TROPHY

CHAPTER IX

RIVALS

M'ADAM never forgave his son. After the scene on the evening of the funeral there could be no alternative but war for all time. The little man had attempted to humble himself, and been rejected; and the bitterness of defeat, when he had deserved victory, rankled like a poisoned barb in his bosom.

Yet the heat of his indignation was directed not against David, but against the Master of Kenmuir. To the influence and agency of James Moore he attributed his discomfiture, and bore himself accordingly. In public or in private, in tap-room or market, he never wearied of abusing his enemy.

"Feel the loss o' his wife, d'ye say?" he would cry. "Ay, as muckle as I feel the loss o' my hair. James Moore can feel naethin', I tell ye, except, aiblins, a mischance to his meeserable dog."

When the two met, as they often must, it was always

M'Adam's endeavour to betray his enemy into an unworthy expression of feeling. But James Moore, sorely tried as he often was, never gave way. He met the little man's sneers with a quelling silence, looking down on his asp-tongued antagonist with such a contempt flashing from his blue-gray eyes as hurt his adversary more than words.

Only once was he spurred into reply. It was in the tap-room of the Dalesman's Daughter on the occasion of the big spring fair in Grammoch-town, when there was a goodly gathering of farmers and their dogs in the room.

M'Adam was standing at the fireplace with Red Wull at his side.

"It's a noble pairt ye play, James Moore," he cried loudly across the room, "settin' son against father, and dividin' hoose against hoose. It's worthy o' ye we' yer churchgoin', and yer psalm-singin', and yer godliness."

The Master looked up from the far end of the room.

"Happen yo're not aware, M'Adam," he said sternly, "that, an' it had not bin for me, David'd ha' left you years agone—and 'twould nob'but ha' served yo' right, I'm thinkin'."

The little man was beaten on his own ground, so he changed front.

"Dinna shout so, man—I have ears to hear. Forbye ye irritate Wullie."

The Tailless Tyke, indeed, had advanced from the fireplace, and now stood, huge and hideous, in the very centre of the room. There was distant thunder in his throat, a threat upon his face, a challenge in every wrinkle. And the Gray Dog stole gladly out from behind his master to take up the gage of battle.

Straightway there was silence; tongues ceased to wag,

tankards to clink. Every man and every dog was quietly gathering about those two central figures. Not one of them all but had his score to wipe off against the Tailless Tyke; not one of them but was burning to join in, the battle once begun. And the two gladiators stood looking past one another, muzzle to muzzle, each with a tiny flash of teeth glinting between his lips.

But the fight was not to be; for the twentieth time the Master intervened.

"Bob, lad, coom in!" he called, and, bending, grasped his favourite by the neck.

M'Adam laughed softly.

"Wullie, Wullie, to me!" he cried. "The look o' you's enough for that gentleman."

"If they get fightin' it'll no be Bob here I'll hit, I warn yo', M'Adam," said the Master grimly.

"Gin ye sae muckle as touched Wullie d'ye ken what I'd do, James Moore?" asked the little man very smoothly.

"Yes—sweer," the other replied, and strode out of the room amid a roar of derisive laughter at M'Adam's expense.

Owd Bob had now attained wellnigh the perfection of his art. Parson Leggy declared roundly that his like had not been seen since the days of Rex son of Rally. Among the Dalesmen he was a heroic favourite, his prowess and gentle ways winning him friends on every hand. But the point that told most heavily for him was that in all things he was the very antithesis of Red Wull.

Barely a man in the country-side but owed that ferocious savage a grudge; not a man of them all who dared pay it. Once Long Kirby. full of beer and valor, tried to settle his account. Coming on M'Adam and Red Wull as he was driving into Grammoch-town, he leant over and with his thong dealt the dog a terrible sword-like flash that raised an angry ridge of red from hip to shoulder; and was twenty yards down the road before the little man's shrill curse reached his ear, drowned in a hideous bellow.

He stood up and lashed the colt, who, quick on his legs for a young un, soon settled to his gallop. But, glancing over his shoulder, he saw a hounding form behind, catching him as though he were walking. His face turned sickly white; he screamed; he flogged; he looked back. Right beneath the tail-board was the red devil in the dust; while racing a furlong behind on the turnpike road was the mad figure of M'Adam.

The smith struck back and flogged forward. It was of no avail. With a tiger-like bound the murderous brute leapt on the flying trap. At the shock of the great body the colt was thrown violently on his side; Kirby was tossed over the hedge; and Red Wull pinned beneath the débris.

M'Adam had time to rush up and save a tragedy. "I've a mind to knife ye, Kirby," he panted, as he bandaged the smith's broken head.

After that you may be sure the Dalesmen preferred to swallow insults rather than to risk their lives; and their impotence only served to fan their hatred to white heat.

The working methods of the antagonists were as contrasted as their appearances. In a word, the one compelled where the other coaxed.

His enemies said the Tailless Tyke was rough; not even Tammas denied he was ready. His brain was as big as his body, and he used them both to some purpose. "As quick as a cat, with the heart of a lion and the temper of Nick's self," was Parson Leggy's description.

What determination could effect, that could Red Wull; but achievement by inaction—supremest of all strategies— was not for him. In matters of the subtlest handling, where to act anything except indifference was to lose, with sheep restless, fearful forebodings hymned to them by the wind, panic hovering unseen above them, when an ill-considered movement spelt catastrophe—then was Owd Bob o' Kenmuir incomparable.

Men still tell how, when the squire's new thrashing-machine ran amuck in Grammoch-town, and for some minutes the market square was a turbulent sea of blaspheming men, yelping dogs, and stampeding sheep, only one flock stood calm as a mill-pond by the bull-ring, watching the riot with almost indifference. And in front, sitting between them and the storm, was a quiet gray dog, his mouth stretched in a capacious yawn: to yawn was to win, and he won.

When the worst of the uproar was over, many a glance of triumph was shot first at that one still pack, and then at M'Adam, as he waded through the disorder of huddling sheep.

"And wheer's your Wullie noo?" asked Tupper scornfully.

"Weel," the little man answered with a quiet smile, "at this minute he's killin' your Rasper doon by the pump." Which was indeed the case; for big blue Rasper had interfered with the great dog in the performance of his duty, and suffered accordingly.

.   .   .   .   .

Spring passed into summer; and the excitement as to the event of the approaching Trials, when at length the rivals would be pitted against one another, reached such a height as old Jonas Maddox, the octogenarian, could hardly recall.

Down in the Sylvester Arms there was almost nightly a conflict between M'Adam and Tammas Thornton, spokesmen of the Dalesmen. Many a long-drawn bout of words had the two anent the respective merits and Cup chances of red and gray. In these duels Tammas was usually worsted. His temper would get the better of his discretion; and the cynical debator would be lost in the hot-tongued partisan.

During these encounters the others would, as a rule, maintain a rigid silence. Only when their champion was being beaten, and it was time for strength of voice to vanquish strength of argument, they joined in right lustily and roared the little man down, for all the world like the gentlemen who rule the Empire at Westminster.

Tammas was an easy subject for M'Adam to draw, but David was an easier. Insults directed at himself the boy bore with a stolidity born of long use. But a poisonous dart shot against his friends at Kenmuir never failed to achieve its object. And the little man evinced an amazing talent for the concoction of deft lies respecting James Moore.

"I'm hearin'," said he, one evening, sitting in the kitchen, sucking his twig; "I'm hearin' James Moore is gaein' to git married agin."

"Yo're hearin' lies—or mair-like tellin' 'em," David answered shortly. For he treated his father now with contemptuous indifference.

"Seven months sin' his wife died," the little man continued meditatively. "Weel, I'm on'y 'stonished he's

waited sae lang. Ain buried, anither come on—that's
James Moore."

David burst angrily out of the room.

"Gaein' to ask him if it's true?" called his father after
him. "Gude luck to ye—and him."

David had now a new interest at Kenmuir. In Maggie
he found an endless source of study. On the death of her
mother the girl had taken up the reins of government at
Kenmuir; and gallantly she played her part, whether in
tenderly mothering the baby, wee Anne, or in the sterner
matters of household work. She did her duty, young
though she was, with a surprising, old-fashioned womanli-
ness that won many a smile of approval from her father,
and caused David's eyes to open with astonishment.

And he soon discovered that Maggie, mistress of
Kenmuir, was another person from his erstwhile play-
fellow and servant.

The happy days when might ruled right were gone,
never to be recalled. David often regretted them,
especially when in a conflict of tongues, Maggie, with
her quick answers and teasing eyes, was driving him sulky
and vanquished from the field. The two were perpetually
squabbling now. In the good old days, he remembered
bitterly, squabbles between them were unknown. He had
never permitted them; any attempt at independent
thought or action was as sternly quelled as in the Middle
Ages. She must follow where he led on—"Ma word!"

Now she was mistress where he had been master; hers
was to command, his to obey. In consequence they were
perpetually at war. And yet he would sit for hours in the
kitchen and watch her, as she went about her business,
with solemn, interested eyes, half of admiration, half of

amusement. In the end Maggie always turned on him with a little laugh touched with irritation.

"Han't yo' got nothin' better'n that to do, nor lookin' at me?" she asked one Saturday about a month before Cup Day.

"No, I han't," the pert fellow rejoined.

"Then I wish yo' had. It mak's me fair jumpety yo' watchin' me so like ony cat a mouse."

"Niver yo' fash yo'sel' account o' me, ma wench," he answered calmly.

"Yo' wench, indeed!" she cried, tossing her head.

"Ay, or will be," he muttered.

"What's that?" she cried, springing round, a flush of color on her face.

"Nowt, my dear. Yo'll know so soon as I want yo' to, yo' may be sure, and no sooner."

The girl resumed her baking, half angry, half suspicious.

"I dunno' what yo' mean, Mr. M'Adam," she said.

"Don't yo', Mrs. M'A——"

The rest was lost in the crash of a falling plate; whereat David laughed quietly, and asked if he should help pick up the bits.

.   .   .

On the same evening at the Sylvester Arms an announcement was made that knocked the breath out of its hearers.

In the debate that night on the fast-approaching Dale Trials and the relative abilities of red and gray, M'Adam on the one side, and Tammas, backed by Long Kirby and the rest, on the other, had cudgelled each other with more than usual vigour. The controversy rose to fever-heat; abuse succeeded argument; and the little man again and again was hooted into silence.

"It's easy laffin'," he cried at last, "but ye'll laff t'ither side o' yer ugly faces on Cup Day."

"Will us, indeed? Us'll see," came the derisive chorus.

"We'll whip ye till ye're deaf, dumb, and blind, Wullie and I."

"Yo'll not!"

"We will!"

The voices were rising like the east wind in March.

"Yo'll not, and for a very good reason too," asseverated Tammas loudly.

"Gie us yer reason, ye muckle liar," cried the little man, turning on him.

"Becos——" began Jim Mason and stopped to rub his nose.

"Yo' 'old yo' noise, Jim," recommended Rob Saunderson.

"Becos——" it was Tammas this time who paused.

"Git on wi' it, ye stammerin' stirk!" cried M'Adam. "Why?"

"Becos—Owd Bob'll not rin."

Tammas sat back in his chair.

"What!" screamed the little man, thrusting forward.

"What's that!" yelled Long Kirby, leaping to his feet.

"Mon, say it agin!" shouted Rob.

"What's owd addled eggs tellin'?" cried Liz Burton.

"Dang his 'ead for him!" shouts Tupper.

"Fill his eye!" says Ned Hoppin.

They jostled round the old man's chair: M'Adam in front; Jem Burton and Long Kirby leaning over his shoulder; Liz behind her father; Saunderson and Tupper tackling him on either side; while the rest peered and elbowed in the rear.

The announcement had fallen like a thunderbolt among them.

Tammas looked slowly up at the little mob of eager faces above him. Pride at the sensation caused by his news struggled in his countenance with genuine sorrow for the matter of it.

"Ay, yo' may well 'earken all on yo'. 'Tis enough to mak' the deadies listen. I says agin: We's'll no rin oor Bob fot' Cup. And yo' may guess why. Bain't every mon, Mr. M'Adam, as'd pit aside his chanst o' thc Cup, and that 'masit a gift for him"—M'Adam's tongue was in his cheek—"and it a certainty," the old man continued warmly, "oot o' respect for his wife's memory."

The news was received in utter silence. The shock of the surprise, coupled with the bitterness of the disappointment, froze the slow tongues of his listeners.

Only one small voice broke the stillness.

"Oh, the feelin' man! He should git a reduction o' rent for sic a display o' proper speerit. I'll mind Mr. Hornbut to let auld Sylvester ken o't."

Which he did, and would have got a thrashing for his pains had not Cyril Gilbraith thrown him out of the parsonage before the angry cleric could lay hands upon him.

CHAPTER X

RED WULL WINS

TAMMAS had but told the melancholy truth. Owd Bob was not to run for the cup. And this self-denying ordinance speaks more for James Moore's love of his lost wife than many a lordly cenotaph.

To the people of the Daleland, from the Black Water to the market-cross in Grammoch-town, the news came with the shock of a sudden blow. They had set their hearts on the Gray Dog's success; and had felt serenely confident of his victory. But the sting of the matter lay in this: that now the Tailless Tyke might well win.

M'Adam, on the other hand, was plunged into a fervour of delight at the news. For to win the Shepherd's Trophy was the goal of his ambition. David was now less than nothing to the lonely little man, Red Wull everything to him. And to have that name handed down to posterity, gallantly holding its place among those of the most famous sheep-dogs of all time, was his heart's desire.

As Cup Day drew near, the little man, his fine-drawn temperament strung to the highest pitch of nervousness, was tossed on a sea of apprehension. His hopes and fears ebbed and flowed on the tide of the moment. His moods were as uncertain as the winds in March; and there was no dependence on his humor for a unit of time. At one minute he paced up and down the kitchen, his face already flushed with the glow of victory, chanting:

"Scots wha hae wi' Wallace bled!"

At the next he was down at the table, his head buried in his hands, his whole figure shaking, as he cried in choking voice: "Eh, Wullie, Wullie, they're all agin us."

David found that life with his father now was life with an unamiable hornet. Careless as he affected to be of his father's vagaries, he was tried almost to madness, and fled away at every moment to Kenmuir; for, as he told Maggie, "I'd sooner put up wi' your h'airs and h'imperences, miss, than wi' him, the wemon that he be!"

.   .   .   .   .

At length the great day came. Fears, hopes, doubts, dismays, all dispersed in the presence of the reality.

Cup Day is always a general holiday in the Daleland, and every soul crowds over to Silverdale. Shops were shut; special trains ran in to Grammoch-town; and the road from the little town was dazed with char-a-bancs, brakes, wagonettes, carriages, carts, foot-passengers, wending toward the Dalesman's Daughter. And soon the paddock below that little inn was humming with the crowd of sportsmen and spectators come to see the battle for the Shepherd's Trophy.

There, very noticeable with its red body and yellow

wheels, was the great Kenmuir wagon. Many an eye was directed on the handsome young pair who stood in it, conspicuous and unconscious, above the crowd: Maggie, looking in her simple print frock as sweet and fresh as any mountain flower; while David's fair face was all gloomy and his brows knit.

In front of the wagon was a black cluster of Dalesmen, discussing M'Adam's chances. In the centre was Tammas holding forth. Had you passed close to the group you might have heard: "A man, d'yo say, Mr. Maddox? A h'ape, I call him"; or: "A dog? more like an 'og, I tell yo'." Round the old orator were Jonas, 'Enry, and oor Job, Jem Burton, Rob Saunderson, Tupper, Jim Mason, Hoppun, and others; while on the outskirts stood Sam'l Todd prophesying rain and M'Adam's victory. Close at hand Bessie Bolstock, who was reputed to have designs on David, was giggling spitefully at the pair in the Kenmuir wagon, and singing:

> "Let a lad aloan, lass,
> Let a lad a-be."

While her father, Teddy, dodged in and out among the crowd with tray and glasses: for Cup Day was the great day of the year for him.

Past the group of Dalesmen and on all sides was a mass of bobbing heads—Scots, Northerners, Yorkshiremen, Taffies. To right and left a long array of carriages and carts, ranging from the squire's quiet landau and Viscount Birdsaye's gorgeous barouche to Liz Burton's three-legged moke-cart with little Mrs. Burton, the twins, young Jake (who should have walked), and Monkey (ditto) packed away inside. Beyond the Silver Lea the gaunt Scaur raised its craggy peak, and the Pass, trending along its side, shone white in the sunshine.

At the back of the carriages were booths, cocoanut-shies, Aunt Sallies, shows, bookmakers' stools, and all the panoply of such a meeting. Here Master Launcelot Bilks and Jacky Sylvester were fighting; Cyril Gilbraith was offering to take on the boxing man; Long Kirby was snapping up the odds against Red Wull; and Liz Burton and young Ned Hoppin were being photographed together, while Melia Ross in the background was pretending she didn't care.

On the far bank of the stream was a little bevy of men and dogs, observed of all.

The Juvenile Stakes had been run and won; Londesley's Lassie had carried off the Locals; and the fight for the Shepherds' Trophy was about to begin.

"Yo're not lookin' at me noo," whispered Maggie to the silent boy by her side.

"Nay: nor niver don't wush to agin." David answered roughly. His gaze was directed over the array of heads in front to where, beyond the Silver Lea, a group of shepherds and their dogs was clustered. While standing apart from the rest, in characteristic isolation, was the bent figure of his father, and beside him the Tailless Tyke.

"Doest'o not want yo' feyther to win?" asked Maggie softly, following his gaze.

"I'm prayin' he'll be beat," the boy answered moodily.

"Eh, Davie, hoo can ye?" cried the girl, shocked.

"It's easy to say, 'Eh, David,'" he snapped. "But if yo' lived along o' them two"—he nodded toward the stream—"'appen yo'd understand a bit. . . . 'Eh, David.' indeed! I never did!"

"I know it, lad," she said tenderly; and he was appeased.

"He'd give his right hand for his bless'd Wullie to win; I'd give me right arm to see him beat. . . . And oor Bob there all the while,—he nodded to the far left of the line, where stood James Moore and Owd Bob, with Parson Leggy and the Squire.

When at length Red Wull came out to run his course, he worked with the savage dash that always characterized him. His method was his own; but the work was admirably done.

"Keeps right on the back of his sheep," said the parson, watching intently. "Strange thing they don't break!" But they didn't. There was no waiting, no coaxing; it was drive and devilry all through. He brought his sheep along at a terrific rate, never missing a turn, never faltering, never running out. And the crowd applauded, for the crowd loves a dashing display. While little M'Adam, hopping agilely about, his face ablaze with excitement, handled dog and sheep with a masterly precision that compelled the admiration even of his enemies.

"M'Adam wins!" roared a bookmaker. "Twelve to one agin the field!"

"He wins, dang him!" said David, low.

"Wull wins!" said the parson, shutting his lips.

"And deserves too!" said James Moore.

"Wull wins!" softly cried the crowd.

"We don't!" said Sam'l gloomily.

And in the end Red Wull did win; and there were none save Tammas, the bigot, and Long Kirby, who had lost a good deal of his wife's money and a little of his own, to challenge the justice of the verdict.

The win had but a chilling reception. At first there was faint cheering; but it sounded like the echo of an echo, and soon died of inanition. To get up an ovation, there must be money at the back, or a few roaring fanatics to lead the dance. Here there was neither; ugly stories, disparaging remarks, on every hand. And the hundreds who did not know took their tone, as always, from those who said they did.

M'Adam could but remark the absence of enthusiasm as he pushed up through the throng toward the committee tent. No single voice hailed him victor; no friendly hand smote its congratulations. Broad backs were turned; contemptuous glances levelled; spiteful remarks shot. Only the foreign element looked curiously at the little bent figure with the glowing face, and shrank back at the size and savage aspect of the great dog at his heels.

But what cared he? His Wullie was acknowledged champion, the best sheep-dog of the year; and the little man was happy. They could turn their backs on him; but they could not alter that; and he could afford to be indifferent. "They dinna like it, lad—he! he! But they'll e'en ha' to thole it. Ye've won it, Wullie—won it fair."

He elbowed through the press, making for the rope-guarded inclosure in front of the committee tent, round which the people were now packing. In the door of the tent stood the secretary, various stewards, and members of the committee. In front, alone in the roped-off space, was Lady Eleanour, fragile, dainty, graceful, waiting with a smile upon her face to receive the winner. And on a table beside her, naked and dignified, the Shepherds' Trophy.

There it stood, kingly and impressive; its fair white sides inscribed with many names; cradled in three shepherds' crooks; and on the top, as if to guard the Cup's contents, an exquisitely carved collie's head. The Shepherds' Trophy, the goal of his life's race, and many another man's.

He climbed over the rope, followed by Red Wull, and took off his hat with almost courtly deference to the fair lady before him.

As he walked up to the table on which the Cup stood, a shrill voice, easily recognizable, broke the silence.

"You'd like it better if 'twas full and yo' could swim in it, you and yer Wullie," it called. Whereat the crowd giggled, and Lady Eleanour looked indignant.

The little man turned.

"I'll mind drink yer health, Mr. Thornton, never fear, though I ken ye'd prefaire to drink yer ain," he said. At which the crowd giggled afresh; and a gray head at the back, which had hoped itself unrecognized, disappeared suddenly.

The little man stood there in the stillness, sourly smiling, his face still wet from his exertions; while the Tailless Tyke at his side fronted defiantly the serried ring of onlookers, a white fence of teeth faintly visible between his lips.

Lady Eleanour looked uneasy. Usually the lucky winner was unable to hear her little speech, as she gave the Cup away, so deafening was the applause. Now there was utter silence. She glanced up at the crowd, but there was no response to her unspoken appeal in that forest of hostile faces. And her gentle heart bled for the forlorn little man before her. To make it up she smiled on him so sweetly as to more than compensate him.

"I'm sure you deserve your success, Mr. M'Adam," she said. "You and Red Wull there worked splendidly— everybody says so."

"I've heard naethin' o't," the little man answered dryly. At which some one in the crowd sniggered.

"And we all know what a grand dog he is; though"— with a reproving smile as she glanced at Red Wull's square, truncated stern—"he's not very polite."

"His heart is good, your Leddyship, if his manners are not," M'Adam answered, smiling.

"Liar!" came a loud voice in the silence. Lady Eleanour looked up, hot with indignation, and half rose from her seat. But M'Adam merely smiled.

"Wullie, turn and mak' yer bow to the leddy," he said. "They'll no hurt us noo we're up; it's when we're doon they'll flock like corbies to the carrion."

At that Red Wull walked up to Lady Eleanour, faintly wagging his tail; and she put her hand on his huge bull head and said, "Dear old Ugly!" at which the crowd cheered in earnest.

After that, for some moments, the only sound was the gentle ripple of the good lady's voice and the little man's caustic replies.

"Why, last winter the country was full of Red Wull's doings and yours. It was always M'Adam and his Red Wull have done this and that and the other. I declare I got quite tired of you both, I heard such a lot about you."

The little man, cap in hand, smiled, blushed, and looked genuinely pleased.

"And when it wasn't you it was Mr. Moore and Owd Bob."

"Owd Bob, bless him!" called a stentorian voice. "Three cheers for oor Bob!"

"'Ip! 'ip! 'ooray!" It was taken up gallantly, and cast from mouth to mouth; and strangers, though they did not understand, caught the contagion and cheered, too; and the uproar continued for some minutes.

When it was ended Lady Eleanour was standing up, a faint flush on her cheeks and her eyes flashing dangerously, like a queen at bay.

"Yes," she cried, and her clear voice thrilled through the air like a trumpet. "Yes; and now three cheers for Mr. M'Adam and his Red Wull! Hip! hip——"

"Hooray!" A little knowt of stalwarts at the back— James Moore, Parson Leggy, Jim Mason, and you may be sure in heart, at least, Owd Bob—responded to the call right lustily. The crowd joined in; and, once off, cheered and cheered again.

"Three cheers more for Mr. M'Adam!"

But the little man waved to them.

"Dinna be bigger heepocrites than ye can help," he said. "Ye've done enough for one day, and thank ye for it."

Then Lady Eleanour handed him the Cup.

"Mr. M'Adam, I present you with the Champion Challenge Dale Cup, open to all comers. Keep it, guard it, love it as your own, and win it again if you can. Twice more and it's yours, you know, and it will stop forever beneath the shadow of the Pike. And the right place for it, say I—the Dale Cup for Dalesmen."

The little man took the Cup tenderly.

"It shall no leave the Estate or ma hoose, yer Leddyship, gin Wullie and I can help it," he said emphatically.

Lady Eleanour retreated into the tent, and the crowd swarmed over the ropes and round the little man, who held the Cup beneath his arm.

Long Kirby laid irreverent hands upon it.

"Dinna finger it!" ordered M'Adam.

"Shall!"

"Shan't! Wullie, keep him aff." Which the great dog proceeded to do amid the laughter of the onlookers.

Among the last, James Moore was borne past the little man. At sight of him, M'Adam's face assumed an expression of intense concern.

"Man, Moore!" he cried, peering forward as though in alarm; "man, Moore, ye're green—positeevely verdant. Are ye in pain?" Then, catching sight of Owd Bob, he started back in affected horror.

"And, ma certes! so's yer dog! Yer dog as was gray is green. Oh, guid life!"—and he made as though about to fall fainting to the ground.

Then, in bantering tones; "Ah, but ye shouldna covet——"

"He'll ha' no need to covet it long, I can tell yo'," interposed Tammas's shrill accents.

"And why for no?"

"Becos next year he'll win it fra yo'. Oor Bob'll win it. little mon. Why? thot's why."

The retort was greeted with a yell of applause from the sprinkling of Dalesmen in the crowd.

But M'Adam swaggered away into the tent, his head up, the Cup beneath his arm, and Red Wull guarding his rear.

"First of a' ye'll ha' to beat Adam M'Adam and his Red Wull!" he cried back proudly.

CHAPTER XI

OOR BOB

M'ADAM'S pride in the great Cup that now graced his kitchen was supreme. It stood alone in the very centre of the mantelpiece, just below the old bell-mouthed blunderbuss that hung upon the wall. The only ornament in the bare room, it shone out in its silvery chastity like the moon in a gloomy sky.

For once the little man was content. Since his mother's death David had never known such peace. It was not that his father became actively kind; rather that he forgot to be actively unkind.

"Not as I care a brazen button one way or t'ither," the boy informed Maggie.

"Then yo' should," that proper little person replied.

M'Adam was, indeed, a changed being. He forgot to curse James Moore; he forgot to sneer at Owd Bob; he rarely visited the Sylvester Arms, to the detriment of Jem Burton's pocket and temper; and he was never drunk.

"Soaks 'isself at home, instead," suggested Tammas, the prejudiced. But the accusation was untrue.

"Too drunk to git so far," said Long Kirby, kindly man.

"I reck'n the Cup is kind o' company to him," said Jim Mason. "Happen it's lonesomeness as drives him here so much." And happen you were right, charitable Jim.

"Best mak' maist on it, while he has it, 'cos he'll not have it for long," Tammas remarked amid applause.

Even Parson Leggy allowed—rather reluctantly, indeed, for he was but human—that the little man was changed wonderfully for the better.

"But I am afraid it may not last," he said. "We shall see what happens when Owd Bob beats him for the Cup, as he certainly will. That'll be the critical moment."

As things were, the little man spent all his spare moments with the Cup between his knees, burnishing it and crooning to Wullie:

"I never saw a fairer,
I never lo'ed a dearer,
And neist my heart I'll wear her,
For fear my jewel tine."

There, Wullie! look at her! is she no bonnie? She shines like a twinkle—twinkle in the sky." And he would hold it out at arm's length, his head cocked sideways the better to scan its bright beauties.

The little man was very jealous for his treasure. David might not touch it; might not smoke in the kitchen lest the fumes should tarnish its glory; while if he approached too closely he was ordered abruptly away.

"As if I wanted to touch his nasty Cup!" he complained to Maggie. "I'd sooner ony day——"

"Hands aff, Mr. David, immediate!" she cried indignantly. "'Pertinence, indeed!" as she tossed her
head clear of the big fingers that were fondling her pretty
hair.

So it was that M'Adam, on coming quietly into the
kitchen one day, was consumed with angry resentment to
find David actually handling the object of his reverence;
and the manner of his doing it added a thousandfold to the
offence.

The boy was lolling indolently against the mantelpiece,
his fair head shoved right into the Cup, his breath dimming
its lustre, and his two hands, big and dirty, slowly re-
volving it before his eyes.

Bursting with indignation, the little man crept up
behind the boy. David was reading through the long list
of winners.

"Theer's the first on 'em," he muttered, shooting out
his tongue to indicate the locality: "'Andrew Moore's
Rough, 178–' And theer agin—'James Moore's Pinch,
179.–' And agin—'Beck, 182–.' Ah, and theer's 'im
Tammas tells on! 'Rex 183–,' and 'Rex, 183–.' Ay,
but he was a rare un by all tellin's! If he'd nob'but won
but onst agin! Ah, and theer's none like the Gray Dogs—
they all says that, and I say so masel'; none like the Gray
Dogs o' Kenmuir, bless 'em! And we'll win agin too——"
he broke off short; his eye had travelled down to the last
name on the list.

"'M'Adam's Wull!'" he read with unspeakable contempt, and put his great thumb across the name as though
to wipe it out. "'M'Adam's Wull!' Goo' gracious
sakes! P-h-g-h-r-r!"—and he made a motion as though
to spit upon the ground.

But a little shoulder was into his side, two small fists were beating at his chest, and a shrill voice was yelling: "Devil! devil! stan' awa'!"—and he was tumbled precipitately away from the mantelpiece, and brought up abruptly against the side-wall.

The precious Cup swayed on its ebony stand, the boy's hands, rudely withdrawn, almost overthrowing it. But the little man's first impulse, cursing and screaming though he was, was to steady it.

"'M'Adam's Wull'! I wish he was here to teach ye, ye snod-faced, ox-limbed profleegit!" he cried, standing in front of the Cup, his eyes blazing.

"Ay, 'M'Adam's Wull'! And why not 'M'Adam's Wull'? Ha' ye ony objections to the name?"

"I didn't know yo' was theer," said David, a thought sheepishly.

"Na; or ye'd not ha' said it."

"I'd ha thought it, though," muttered the boy.

Luckily, however, his father did not hear. He stretched his hands up tenderly for the Cup, lifted it down, and began reverently to polish the dimmed sides with his handkerchief.

"Ye're thinkin', nae doot," he cried, casting up a vicious glance at David, "that Wullie's no gude enough to ha' his name alongside o' they cursed Gray Dogs. Are ye no? Let's ha' the truth for aince—for a diversion."

"Reck'n he's good enough if there's none better," David replied dispassionately.

"And wha should there be better? Tell me that, ye muckle gowk."

David smiled.

"Eh, but that'd be long tellin," he said.

"And what wad ye mean by that?" his father cried.

"Nay; I was but thinkin' that Mr. Moore's Bob'll look gradely writ under yon." He pointed to the vacant space below Red Wull's name.

The little man put the Cup back on its pedestal with hurried hands. The handkerchief dropped unconsidered to the floor; he turned and sprang furiously at the boy, who stood against the wall, still smiling; and, seizing him by the collar of his coat, shook him to and fro with fiery energy.

"So ye're hopin', prayin', nae doot, that James Moore·—curse him!—will win ma Cup awa' from me, yer ain dad. I wonder ye're no 'shamed to crass ma door! Ye live on me; ye suck ma blood, ye foul-mouthed leech. Wullie and me brak' oorsel's to keep ye in hoose and hame—and what's yer gratitude? Ye plot to rob us of oor rights."

He dropped the boy's coat and stood back.

"No rights about it," said David, still keeping his temper.

"If I win is it no ma right as muckle as ony Englishman's?"

Red Wull, who had heard the rising voices, came trotting in, scowled at David, and took his stand beside his master.

"Ay, *if* yo' win it," said David, with significant emphasis on the conjunction.

"And wha's to beat us?"

David looked at his father in well-affected surprise.

"I tell yo' Owd Bob's rinin'," he answered.

"And what if he is?" the other cried.

"Why, even yo' should know so much," the boy sneered.

The little man could not fail to understand.

"So that's it!" he said.   Then, in a scream, with one finger pointing to the great dog:

"And what o' him?   What'll ma Wullie be doin' the while?   Tell me that, and ha' a care!   Mind ye, he stan's here hearkenin'!"   And, indeed, the Tailless Tyke was bristling for battle.

David did not like the look of things; and edged away toward the door.

"What'll Wullie be doin', ye chicken-hearted brock?" his father cried.

"'Im?" said the boy, now close on the door!   "'Im?" he said, with a slow contempt that made the red bristles quiver on the dog's neck.   "Lookin' on, I should think— lookin' on.   What else is he fit for?   I tell yo' oor Bob——"

"—'Oor Bob'!" screamed the little man, darting forward.   "'Oor Bob'!   Hark to him.   I'll 'oor——' At him, Wullie!   At him!"

But the Tailless Tyke needed no encouragement. With a harsh roar he sprang through the air, only to crash against the closing door!

The outer door banged, and in another second a mocking finger tapped on the window-pane.

"Better luck to the two on yo' next time!"   laughed a scornful voice; and David ran down the hill toward Kenmuir.

CHAPTER XII

HOW RED WULL HELD THE BRIDGE

FROM that hour the fire of M'Adam's jealousy blazed into a mighty flame. The winning of the Dale Cup had become a mania with him. He had won it once, and would again despite all the Moores, all the Gray Dogs, all the undutiful sons in existence; on that point he was resolved. The fact of his having tasted the joys of victory served to whet his desire. And now he felt he could never be happy till the Cup was his own—won outright.

At home David might barely enter the room. There the trophy stood.

"I'll not ha' ye touch ma Cup, ye dirty-fingered, ill-begotten wastrel. Wullie and me won it—you'd naught to do wi' it. Go you to James Moore and James Moore's dog."

"Ay, and shall I tak' Cup wi' me? or will ye bide till it's took from ye?"

So the two went on; and every day the tension approached nearer breaking-point.

In the Dale the little man met with no sympathy. The hearts of the Dalesmen were to a man with Owd Bob and his master.

Whereas once at the Sylvester Arms his shrill, ill tongue had been rarely still, now he maintained a sullen silence; Jem Burton, at least, had no cause of complaint. Crouched away in a corner, with Red Wull beside him, the little man would sit watching and listening as the Dalesman talked of Owd Bob's doings, his staunchness, sagacity, and coming victory.

Sometimes he could restrain himself no longer. Then he would spring to his feet, and stand, a little swaying figure, and denounce them passionately in almost pathetic eloquence. These orations always concluded in set fashion.

"Ye're all agin us!" the little man would cry in quivering voice.

"We are that," Tammas would answer complacently.

"Fair means or foul, ye're content sae lang as Wullie and me are beat. I wonder ye dinna poison him—a little arsenic, and the way's clear to your Bob."

"The way is clear enough wi'oot that," from Tammas caustically. Then a lengthy silence, only broken by that exceeding bitter cry: "Eh, Wullie, Wullie, they're all agin us!"

.   .   .   .   .

And always the rivals—red and gray—went about seeking their opportunity. But the Master, with his commanding presence and stern eyes, was ever ready for them. Toward the end, M'Adam, silent and sneering, would secretly urge on Red Wull to the attack; until one day in Grammoch-town, James Moore turned on him, his blue eyes glittering. "D'yo' think, yo' little fule," he cried in that hard voice of his, "that onst they got set we should iver git either of them off alive?" It seemed to strike the little man as a novel idea; for, from that moment, he was ever the first in his feverish endeavours to oppose his small form, buffer-like, between the would-be combatants.

.   .   .   .   .

Curse as M'Adam might, threaten as he might, when the time came Owd Bob won.

The styles of the rivals were well contrasted: the patience, the insinuating eloquence, combined with the splendid dash, of the one; and the fierce, driving fury of the other.

The issue was never in doubt. It may have been that the temper of the Tailless Tyke gave in the time of trial; it may have been that his sheep were wild, as M'Adam declared; certainly not. as the little man alleged in choking voice, that they had been chosen and purposely set aside to ruin his chance. Certain it is that his tactics scared them hopelessly: and he never had them in hand,

As for Owd Bob, his dropping, his driving, his penning, aroused the loud-tongued admiration of crowd and competitors alike. He was patient yet persistent, quiet yet firm, and seemed to coax his charges in the right way in that inimitable manner of his own.

When, at length, the verdict was given, and it was known that, after an interval of half a century, the Shepherds' Trophy was won again by a Gray Dog of Kenmuir, there was such a scene as has been rarely witnessed on the slope behind the Dalesman's Daughter.

Great fists were slapped on mighty backs; great feet were stamped on the sun-dried banks of the Silver Lea; stalwart lungs were strained to their uttermost capacity; and roars of "Moore!" "Owd Bob o' Kenmuir!" "The Gray Dogs!" thundered up the hillside, and were flung, thundering, back.

Even James Moore was visibly moved as he worked his way through the cheering mob; and Owd Bob, trotting alongside him in quiet dignity, seemed to wave his silvery brush in acknowledgment.

Master Jacky Sylvester alternately turned cart-wheels and felled the Hon. Launcelot Bilks to the ground. Lady Eleanour, her cheeks flushed with pleasure, waved her parasol, and attempted to restrain her son's exuberance. Parson Leggy danced an unclerical jig, and shook hands with the squire till both those fine old gentlemen were purple in the face. Long Kirby selected a small man in the crowd, and bashed his hat down over his eyes. While Tammas, Rob Saunderson, Tupper, Hoppin, Londesley, and the rest joined hands and went raving round like so many giddy girls.

Of them all, however, none was so uproarious in the mad heat of his enthusiasm as David M'Adam. He stood in the Kenmuir wagon beside Maggie, a conspicuous figure above the crowd, as he roared in hoarse ecstasy:

"Weel done, oor Bob! Weel done, Mr. Moore! Yo've knocked him! Knock him ag'n! Owd Bob o' Kenmuir! Moore! Moore o' Kenmuir! Hip! Hip!" until the noisy young giant attracted such attention in his boisterous delight that Maggie had to lay a hand upon his arm to restrain his violence.

Alone, on the far bank of the stream, stood the vanquished pair.

The little man was trembling slightly; his face was still hot from his exertions; and as he listened to the ovation accorded to his conqueror, there was a piteous set grin upon his face. In front stood the defeated dog, his lips wrinkling and hackles rising, as he, too, saw and heard and understood.

"It's a gran' thing to ha' a dutiful son, Wullie," the little man whispered, watching David's waving figure. "He's happy—and so are they a'—not sae much that James Moore has won, as that you and I are beat."

Then, breaking down for a moment:

"Eh, Wullie, Wullie! They're all agin us. It's you and I alane, lad."

Again, seeing the squire followed by Parson Leggy, Viscount Birdsaye, and others of the gentry, forcing their way through the press to shake hands with the victor, he continued:

"It's good to be in wi' the quality, Wullie. Niver mak' a friend of a man beneath ye in rank, nor an enemy of a man aboon ye: that's a soond principle, Wullie, if ye'd get on in honest England."

He stood there, alone with his dog, watching the crowd on the far slope as it surged upward in the direction of the committee tent. Only when the black mass had packed itself in solid phalanges about that ring, inside which, just a year ago, he had stood in very different circumstances, and was at length still, a wintry smile played for a moment about his lips. He laughed a mirthless laugh.

"Bide a wee, Wullie—he! he! Bide a wee.

"The best-laid schemes o' mice and men
Gang aft agley.'"

As he spoke, there came down to him, above the tumult a faint cry of mingled surprise and anger. The cheering ceased abruptly. There was silence; then there burst on the stillness a hurricane of indignation.

The crowd surged forward, then turned. Every eye was directed across the stream. A hundred damning fingers pointed at the solitary figure there. There were hoarse yells of: "There he be! Yon's him! What's he done wi' it? Thief! Throttle him!"

The mob came lumbering down the slope like one man, thundering their imprecations on a thousand throats. They looked dangerous, and their wrath was stimulated by the knot of angry Dalesmen who led the van. There was more than one white face among the women at the top of the slope as they watched the crowd blundering blindly down the hill. There were more men than Parson Leggy, the squire, James Moore, and the local constables in the thick of it all, striving frantically with voice and gesture, ay, and stick too, to stem the advance.

It was useless; on the dark wave rolled, irresistible.

On the far bank stood the little man, motionless, awaiting them with a grin upon his face. And a little farther in front was the Tailless Tyke, his back and neck like a newshorn wheat-field, as he rumbled a vast challenge.

"Come on, gentlemen!" the little man cried. "Come on! I'll bide for ye, never fear. Ye're a thousand to one and a dog. It's the odds ye like, Englishmen a'."

And the mob, with murder in its throat, accepted the invitation and came on.

At the moment, however, from the slope above, clear above the tramp of the multitude, a great voice bellowed:

"Way! Way! Way for Mr. Trotter!" The advancing host checked and opened out; and the secretary of the meeting bundled through.

He was a small, fat man, fussy at any time, and perpetually perspiring. Now his face was crimson with rage and running; he gesticulated wildly; vague words bubbled forth, as his short legs twinkled down the slope.

The crowd paused to admire. Some one shouted a witticism, and the crowd laughed. For the moment the situation was saved.

The fat secretary hurried on down the slope, unheeding of any insult but the one. He bounced over the plank-bridge: and as he came closer, M'Adam saw that in each hand brandished a brick.

"Hoots, man! dinna throw!" he cried, making a feint as though to turn in sudden terror.

"What's this? What's this?" gasped the secretary, waving his arms.

"Bricks 'twad seem," the other answered, staying his flight.

The secretary puffed up like a pudding in a hurry.

"Where's the Cup? Champion, Challenge, etc.," he jerked out. "Mind, sir, you're responsible! wholly responsible! Dents, damages, delays! What's it all mean, sir? These—these monstrous creations"—he brandished the bricks, and M'Adam started back— "wrapped, as I live, in straw, sir, in the Cup case, sir! the Cup case! No Cup! Infamous! Disgraceful! Insult me—meeting—committee—everyone! What's it mean, sir?" He paused to pant, his body filling and emptying like a bladder.

M'Adam approached him with one eye on the crowd,

which was heaving forward again, threatening still, but sullen and silent.

"I pit 'em there," he whispered; and drew back to watch the effect of his disclosure.

The secretary gasped.

"You—you not only do this—amazing thing—these monstrosities"—he hurled the bricks furiously on the unoffending ground—"but you dare to tell me so!"

The little man smiled.

"'Do wrang and conceal it, do right and confess it' that's Englishmen's motto, and mine, as a rule; but this time I had ma reasons."

"Reasons, sir! No reasons can justify such an extraordinary breach of all the—the decencies. Reasons? The reasons of a maniac. Not to say more, sir. Fraudulent detention—fraudulent, I say, sir! What were your precious reasons?"

The mob with Tammas and Long Kirby at their head had now well nigh reached the plank-bridge. They still looked dangerous, and there were isolated cries of:

"Duck him!"

"Chuck him in!"

"An' the dog!"

"Wi' one o' they bricks about their necks!"

"There are my reasons!" said M'Adam, pointing to the forest of menacing faces. "Ye see I'm no beloved amang yonder gentlemen, and"—in a stage whisper in the other's ear—"I thocht maybe I'd be 'tacked on the road.

Tammas foremost of the crowd, had now his foot upon the first plank.

"Ye robber! Ye thief! Wait till we set hands on ye, you and yer gorilla!" he called.

M'Adam half turned.

"Wullie," he said quietly, "keep the bridge."

At the order the Tailless Tyke shot gladly forward, and the leaders on the bridge as hastily back. The dog galloped on to the rattling plank, took his post fair and square in the centre of the narrow way, and stood facing the hostile crew like Cerberus guarding the gates of hell: his bull-head was thrust forward, hackles up, teeth glinting, and a distant rumbling in his throat, as though daring them to come on.

"Yo' first, ole lad!" said Tammas, hopping agilely behind Long Kirby.

"Nay; the old uns lead!" cried the big smith, his face gray-white. He wrenched round, pinned the old man by the arms, and held him forcibly before him as a covering shield. There ensued an unseemly struggle betwixt the two valiants, Tammas bellowing and kicking in the throes of mortal fear.

"Jim Mason'll show us," he suggested at last.

"Nay," said honest Jim; "I'm fear'd." He could say it with impunity; for the pluck of Postie Jim was a matter long past dispute.

Then Jem Burton'd go first?

Nay; Jem had a lovin' wife and dear little kids at 'ome.

Then Big Bell?

Big Bell'd see 'isself further first.

A tall figure came forcing through the crowd, his face a little paler than its wont, and a formidable knob-kerry in his hand.

"I'm goin'!" said David.

"But yo're not," answered burly Sam'l, gripping the boy from behind with arms like the roots of an oak.

"Your time'll coom soon enough by the look on yo' wi' niver no hurry." And the sense of the Dalesmen was with the big man; for, as old Rob Saunderson said:

"I reck'n he'd liefer claw on to your throat, lad, nor ony o' oors."

As there was no one forthcoming to claim the honour of the lead, Tammas came forward with cunning counsel.

"Tell yo' what, lads, we'd best let 'em as don't know nowt at all aboot him go first. And onst they're on, mind, we winna let 'em off; but keep a shovin' and a-bovin' on 'em forra'd. *Then* us'll foller."

By this time there was a little naked space of green round the bridge-head, like a fairy circle, into which the uninitiated might not penetrate. Round this the mob hedged: the Dalesmen in front, striving knavishly back and bawling to those behind to leggo that shovin'; and these latter urging valorously forward, yelling jeers and contumely at the front rank. "Come on! 'O's afraid? Lerrus through to 'em, then, ye Royal Stan'-backs!"—for well they knew the impossibility of their demand.

And as they wedged and jostled thus, there stole out from their midst as gallant a champion as ever trod the grass. He trotted out into the ring, the observed of all, and paused to gaze at the gaunt figure on the bridge. The sun lit the sprinkling of snow on the dome of his head; one forepaw was off the ground; and he stood there, royally alert, scanning his antagonist.

"Th' Owd Un!" went up in a roar fit to split the air as the hero of the day was recognized. And the Dalesmen gave a pace forward spontaneously as the gray knight-errant stole across the green.

"Oor Bob'll fetch him!" they roared, their blood leaping to fever heat, and gripped their sticks, determined in stern reality to follow now.

The gray champion trotted up on to the bridge, and paused again, the long hair about his neck rising like a ruff, and a strange glint in his eyes; and the holder of the bridge never moved.   Red and Gray stood thus, face to face: the one gay yet resolute, the other motionless, his great head slowly sinking between his forelegs, seemingly petrified.

There was no shouting now: it was time for deeds, not words.   Only, above the stillness, came a sound from the bridge like the snore of a giant in his sleep, and blending, with it, a low, deep, purring thunder like some monster cat well pleased.

"Wullie," came a solitary voice from the far side, "keep the bridge!"

One ear went back, one ear was still forward; the great head was low and lower between his forelegs and the glowing eyes rolled upward so that the watchers could see the murderous white.

Forward the gray dog stepped.

Then, for the second time that afternoon, a voice, stern and hard, came ringing down from the slope above over the heads of the many.

"Bob, lad, coom back!"

"He! he! I thocht that was comin'," sneered the small voice over the stream.

The gray dog heard, and checked.

"Bob, lad, coom in, I say!"

At that he swung round and marched slowly back, gallant as he had come, dignified still in his mortification.

And Red Wull threw back his head and bellowed a pæan of victory—challenge, triumph, scorn, all blended in that bull-like, blood-chilling blare.

.　　　.　　　.　　　.　　　.

In the mean time, M'Adam and the secretary had concluded their business. It had been settled that the Cup was to be delivered over to James Moore not later than the following Saturday.

"Saturday, see! at the latest!" the secretary cried as he turned and trotted off.

"Mr. Trotter," M'Adam called after him, "I'm sorry, but ye maun bide this side the Lea till I've reached the foot o' the Pass. Gin they gentlemen"—nodding toward the crowd—"should set hands on me, why——" and he shrugged his shoulders significantly. "Forbye, Wullie's keepin' the bridge."

With that the little man strolled off leisurely; now dallying to pick a flower, now to wave a mocking hand at the furious mob, and so slowly on to the foot of the Muirk Muir Pass.

There he turned and whistled that shrill, peculiar note. "Wullie, Wullie, to me!" he called.

At that, with one last threat thrown at the thousand souls he had held at bay for thirty minutes, the Tailless Tyke swung about and galloped after his lord.

CHAPTER XIII

THE FACE IN THE FRAME

ALL Friday M'Adam never left the kitchen. He sat opposite the Cup, in a coma, as it were: and Red Wull lay motionless at his feet.

Saturday came, and still the two never budged. Toward the evening the little man rose, all in a tremble, and took the Cup down from the mantelpiece; then he sat down again with it in his arms.

"Eh, Wullie, Wullie, is it a dream? Ha' they took her fra us? Eh, but it's you and I alane, lad."

He hugged it to him, crying silently, and rocking to and fro like a mother with a dying child. And Red Wull sat up on his haunches, and weaved from side to side in sympathy.

As the dark was falling, David looked in.

At the sound of the opening door the little man swung round noiselessly, the Cup nursed in his arms, and glared, sullen and suspicious, at the boy; yet seemed not to

recognize him.   In the half-light David could see the tears
coursing down the little wizened face.

"'Pon ma life, he's gaein' daft!" was his comment as he
turned away to Kenmuir.   And again the mourners were
left alone.

"A few hours noo, Wullie," the little man wailed, "and
she'll be gane.   We won her, Wullie, you and I, won her
fair: she's lit the hoose for us; she's softened a' for us—
and God kens we needed it; she was the ae thing we had to
look to and love.   And noo they're takin' her awa',
and 'twill be night agin.   We've cherished her, we've
garnished her, we've loved her like oor ain; and noo she
maun gang to strangers who know her not."

He rose to his feet, and the great dog rose with him.
His voice heightened to a scream, and he swayed with the
Cup in his arms till it seemed he must fall.

"Did they win her fair, Wullie? Na; they plotted,
they conspired, they worked ilka ain o' them agin us, and
they beat us.   Ay, and noo they're robbin' us—robbin'
us! But they shallna ha' her.   Oor's or naebody's,
Wullie!   We'll finish her sooner nor that."

He banged the Cup down on the table and rushed madly
out of the room, Red Wull at his heels.   In a moment he
came running back, brandishing a great axe about his
head.

"Come on, Wullie!" he cried. "'Scots wha hae'!
Noo's the day and noo's the hour!   Come on!"

On the table before him, serene and beautiful, stood the
target of his madness.   The little man ran at it, swinging
his murderous weapon like a flail.

"Oor's or naebody's Wullie! Come on! 'Lay the
proud usurpers low'!"   He aimed a mighty buffet: and

the Shepherds' Trophy—the Shepherds' Trophy which had won through the hardships of a hundred years—was almost gone. It seemed to quiver as the blow fell. But the cruel steel missed, and the axe-head sank into the wood, clean and deep, like a spade in snow.

Red Wull had leapt on to the table, and in his cavernous voice was grumbling a chorus to his master's yells. The little man danced up and down, tugging and straining at the axe-handle.

"You and I, Wullie!

> 'Tyrants fall in every foe!
> Liberty's in every blow!'"

The axe-head was as immoveable as the Muir Pike.

> "'Let us do or die!'"

The shaft snapped, and the little man tottered back. Red Wull jumped down from the table, and, in doing so, brushed against the Cup. It toppled* over on to the floor, and rolled tinkling away in the dust. And the little man fled madly out of the house, still screaming his war-song.

.   .   .   .   .

When, late that night, M'Adam returned home, the Cup was gone. Down on his hands and knees he traced out its path, plain to see, where it had rolled along the dusty floor. Beyond that there was no sign.

At first he was too much overcome to speak. Then he raved round the room like a derelict ship, Red Wull following uneasily behind. He cursed; he blasphemed; he screamed and beat the walls with feverish hands. A stranger, passing, might well have thought this was a

---

*N.B—You may see the dent in the Cup's white sides to this day.

private Bedlam. At last, exhausted, he sat down and cried.

"It's David, Wullie, ye may depend; David that's robbed his father's hoose. Oh, it's a grand thing to ha' a dutiful son!"—and he bowed his gray head in his hands.

David, indeed, it was. He had come back to the Grange during his father's absence, and, taking the Cup from its grimy bed, had marched it away to its rightful home. For that evening at Kenmuir, James Moore had said to him:

"David, your father's not sent the Cup. I shall come and fetch it to-morrow." And David knew he meant it. Therefore, in order to save a collision between his father and his friend—a collision the issue of which he dared hardly contemplate, knowing, as he did, the unalterable determination of the one and the lunatic passion of the other—the boy had resolved to fetch the Cup himself, then and there, in the teeth, if needs be, of his father and the Tailless Tyke. And he had done it.

When he reached home that night he marched, contrary to his wont, straight into the kitchen.

There sat his father facing the door, awaiting him, his hands upon his knees. For once the little man was alone; and David, brave though he was, thanked heaven devoutly that Red Wull was elsewhere.

For a while father and son kept silence, watching one another like two fencers.

"'Twas you as took ma Cup?" asked the little man at last, leaning forward in his chair.

"'Twas me as took Mr. Moore's Cup," the boy replied. "I thowt yo' mun ha' done wi' it—I found it all bashed upon the floor."

"You took it—pit up to it, nae doot, by James Moore."
David made a gesture of dissent.

"Ay, by James Moore," his father continued. "He
dursena come hissel' for his ill-gotten spoils, so he sent the
son to rob the father. The coward!"—his whole frame
shook with passion. "I'd ha' thocht James Moore'd ha'
bin man enough to come himself for what he wanted. I
see noo I did him a wrang—I misjudged him. I kent him
a heepocrite; ain o' yer unco gudes; a man as looks one
thing, says anither, and does a third; and noo I ken he's a
coward. He's fear'd o' me, sic as I am, five foot twa in
ma stockin's." He rose from his chair and drew himself
up to his full height.

"Mr. Moore had nowt to do wi' it," David persisted.

"Ye're lyin'. James Moore pit ye to it."

"I tell yo' he did not."

"Ye'd ha' bin willin' enough wi'oot him, if ye'd thocht
o't, I grant ye. But ye've no the wits. All there is o'
ye has gane to mak' yer muckle body. Hooiver, that's
no matter. I'll settle wi' James Moore anither time.
I'll settle wi' you noo, David M'Adam."

He paused, and looked the boy over from head to
foot.

"So, ye're not only an idler! a wastrel! a liar!"—
he spat the words out. "Ye're —God help ye—a thief!"

"I'm no thief!" the boy returned hotly. "I did but
give to a mon what ma feyther—shame on him!—wrong-
fully kept from him."

"Wrangfully?" cried the little man, advancing with
burning face.

"'Twas honourably done, keepin' what wasna your'n
to keep! Holdin' back his rights from a man! Ay, if

ony one's the thief, it's not me: it's you, I say, you!"—and he looked his father in the face with flashing eyes.

"I'm the thief, am I?" cried the other, incoherent with passion. "Though ye're three times ma size, I'll teach ma son to speak so to me."

The old strap, now long disused, hung in the chimney corner. As he spoke the little man sprang back, ripped it from the wall, and, almost before David realized what he was at, had brought it down with a savage slash across his son's shoulders; and as he smote he whistled a shrill, imperative note:

"Wullie, Wullie, to me!"

David felt the blow through his coat like a bar of hot iron laid across his back. His passion seethed within him; every vein throbbed; every nerve quivered. In a minute he would wipe out, once and for all, the score of years; for the moment, however, there was urgent business on hand. For outside he could hear the quick patter of feet hard-galloping, and the scurry of a huge creature racing madly to a call.

With a bound he sprang at the open door; and again the strap came lashing down, and a wild voice:

"Quick, Wullie! For God's sake, quick!"

David slammed the door to. It shut with a rasping snap; and at the same moment a great body from without thundered against it with terrific violence, and a deep voice roared like the sea when thwarted of its prey.

"Too late, agin!" said David, breathing hard; and shot the bolt home with a clang. Then he turned on his father.

"Noo," said he, "man to man!"

"Ay," cried the other, "father to son!"

The little man half turned and leapt at the old musketoon hanging on the wall. He missed it, turned again, and struck with the strap full at the other's face. David caught the falling arm at the wrist, hitting it aside with such tremendous force that the bone all but snapped. Then he smote his father a terrible blow on the chest, and the little man staggered back, gasping, into the corner; while the strap dropped from his numbed fingers.

Outside Red Wull whined and scratched; but the two men paid no heed.

David strode forward; there was murder in his face. The little man saw it: his time was come; but his bitterest foe never impugned Adam M'Adam's courage.

He stood huddled in the corner, all dishevelled, nursing one arm with the other, entirely unafraid.

"Mind, David," he said, quite calm, "murder 'twill be, not manslaughter."

"Murder 'twill be," the boy answered, in thick, low voice, and was across the room.

Outside Red Wull banged and clawed high up on the door with impotent pats.

The little man suddenly slipped his hand in his pocket, pulled out something, and flung it. The missile pattered on his son's face like a rain-drop on a charging bull, and David smiled as he came on. It dropped softly on the table at his side; he looked down and—it was the face of his mother which gazed up at him!

"Mither!" he sobbed, stopping short. "Mither! Ma God, ye saved him—and me!"

He stood there, utterly unhinged, shaking and whimpering.

It was some minutes before he pulled himself together;

then he walked to the wall, took down a pair of shears, and seated himself at the table, still trembling.   Near him lay the miniature, all torn and crumpled, and beside it the deep-buried axe-head.

He picked up the strap and began cutting it into little pieces.

"There!   and there!   and there!" he said with each snip.   "An' ye hit me agin there may be no mither to save ye."

M'Adam stood huddling in the corner.   He shook like an aspen leaf; his eyes blazed in his white face; and he still nursed one arm with the other.

"Honour yer father," he quoted in small low voice.

PART IV

THE BLACK KILLER

CHAPTER XIV

A MAD MAN

TAMMAS is on his feet in the tap-room of the Arms, brandishing a pewter mug.

"Gen'lemen!" he cries, his old face flushed; "I gie you a toast. Stan' oop!"

The knot of Dalesmen round the fire rises like one. The old man waves his mug before him, reckless of the good ale that drips on to the floor.

"The best sheep-dog i' th' North—Owd Bob o' Kenmuir!" he cries. In an instant there is uproar: the merry applause of clinking pewters; the stamping of feet; the rattle of sticks. Rob Saunderson and old Jonas are cheering with the best; Tupper and Ned Hoppin are bellowing in one another's ears; Long Kirby and Jem Burton are thumping each other on the back; even Sam'l Todd and Sexton Ross are roused from their habitual melancholy.

"Here's to Th' Owd Un! Here's to oor Bob!" yell

stentorian voices; while Rob Saunderson has jumped on
to a chair.

"Wi' the best sheep-dog i' th' North I gie yo' the
Shepherd's Trophy!—won outreet as will be!" he cries.
Instantly the clamour redoubles.

"The Dale Cup and Th' Owd Un! The Trophy and
oor Bob! 'Ip, 'ip, for the gray dogs! 'Ip, 'ip, for the
best sheep-dog as ever was or will be! 'Ooray, 'ooray!"

It is some minutes before the noise subsides; and slowly
the enthusiasts resume their seats with hoarse throats and
red faces.

"Gentlemen a'!"

A little unconsidered man is standing up at the back of
the room. His face is aflame, and his hands twitch spas-
modically; and, in front, with hackles up and eyes gleam-
ing, is a huge, bull-like dog.

"Noo," cries the little man, "I daur ye to repeat that
lie!"

"Lie!" screams Tammas; "lie! I'll gie 'im lie! Lem-
me at 'im, I say!"

The old man in his fury is half over the surrounding ring
of chairs before Jim Mason on the one hand and Jonas
Maddox on the other can pull him back.

"Coom, Mr. Thornton," soothes the octogenarian,
"let un be. Yo' surely bain't angered by the likes o'
'im!"—and he jerks contemptuously toward the solitary
figure at his back.

Tammas resumes his seat unwillingly.

The little man in the far corner of the room remains
silent, waiting for his challenge to be taken up. It is in
vain. And as he looks at the range of broad, impassive
backs turned on him, he smiles bitterly.

"They dursen't Wullie, not a man of them a'!" he cries. "They're one—two—three—four—eleven to one, Wullie, and yet they dursen't. Eleven of them, and every man a coward! Long Kirby—Thornton—Tupper—Todd —Hoppin—Ross—Burton—and the rest, and not one but's a bigger man nor me, and yet—— Weel, we might ha' kent it. We should ha' kent Englishmen by noo. They're aye the same and aye have bin. They tell lies, black lies——"

Tammas is again half out his chair, and only forcibly restrained by the men on either hand.

"——and then they ha' na the courage to stan' by em. Ye're English, ivery man o' ye, to yer marrow."

The little man's voice rises as he speaks. He seizes the tankard from the table at his side.

"Englishmen!" he cries waving it before him. "Here's a health! The best sheep-dog as iver penned a flock— Adam M'Adam's Red Wull!"

He pauses, the pewter at his lips, and looks at his audience with flashing eyes. There is no response from them.

"Wullie, here's to you!" he cries. "Luck and life to ye, ma trusty fier! Death and defeat to yer enemies!

> "'The warld's wrack we share o't,
>   The warstle and the care o't;'"

He raises the tankard and drains it to its uttermost dreg.

Then drawing himself up, he addresses his audience once more:

"An' noo I'll warn ye aince and for a', and ye may tell James Moore I said it: He may plot agin us, Wullie and me; he may threaten us; he may win the cup outright for his muckle favourite; but there was niver a man or dog yet as did Adam M'Adam and his Red Wull a hurt but in the end he wush't his mither hadna borne him."

A little later, and he walks out of the inn, the Tailless Tyke at his heels.

After he is gone it is Rob Saunderson who says: "The little mon's mad; he'll stop at nothin'"; and Tammas who answers:

"Nay; not even murder."

.   .   .   .   .

The little man had aged much of late. His hair was quite white, his eyes unnaturally bright, and his hands were never still, as though he were in everlasting pain. He looked the picture of disease.

After Owd Bob's second victory he had become morose and untalkative. At home he often sat silent for hours together, drinking and glaring at the place where the Cup had been. Sometimes he talked in low, eerie voice to Red Wull; and on two occasions, David, turning, suddenly had caught his father glowering stealthily at him with such an expression on his face as chilled the boy's blood. The two never spoke now; and David held this silent, deadly enmity far worse than the old-time perpetual warfare.

It was the same at the Sylvester Arms. The little man sat alone with Red Wull, exchanging words with no man, drinking steadily, brooding over his wrongs, only now and again galvanized into sudden action.

Other people than Tammas Thornton came to the conclusion that M'Adam would stop at nothing in the undoing of James Moore or the gray dog. They said drink and disappointment had turned his head; that he was mad and dangerous. And on New Year's day matters seemed coming to a crisis; for it was reported that in the gloom of a snowy evening he had drawn a knife on the Master in the High Street, but slipped before he could accomplish his fell purpose.

Most of them all, David was haunted with an ever-present anxiety as to the little man's intentions. The boy even went so far as to warn his friend against his father. But the Master only smiled grimly.

"Thank ye, lad," he said. "But 'I reck'n we can 'fend for oorsel's, Bob and I. Eh, Owd Un?"

Anxious as David might be, he was not so anxious as to be above taking a mean advantage of this state of strained apprehension to work on Maggie's fears.

One evening he was escorting her home from church, when, just before they reached the larch copse:

"Goo' sakes! What's that?" he ejaculated in horror-laden accents, starting back.

"What, Davie?" cried the girl, shrinking up to him all in a tremble.

"Couldna say for sure. It mought be owt, or agin it mought be nowt. But yo' grip my arm, I'll grip yo waist."

Maggie demurred.

"Canst see onythin'?" she asked, still in a flutter.

"Be'ind the 'edge."

"Wheer?"

"Theer!"—pointing vaguely.

"I canna see nowt."

"Why, theer, lass. Can yo' not see? Then yo' pi your head along o' mine—so—closer—closer." Then in aggrieved tones: "Whativer is the matter wi' yo', wench? I might be a leprosy."

But the girl was walking away with her head high as the snow-capped Pike.

"So long as I live, David M'Adam," she cried, "I'll niver go to church wi' you agin!"

"Iss but you will though—onst," he answered low.

Maggie whisked round in a flash, superbly indignant. "What d'yo' mean, sir-r-r?"

"Yo' know what I mean, lass," he replied sheepish and shuffling before her queenly anger.

She looked him up and down, and down and up again.

"I'll niver speak to you agin, Mr. M'Adam," she cried; "not if it was ever so—— Nay, I'll walk home by myself, thank you. I'll ha' nowt to do wi' you."

So the two must return to Kenmuir, one behind the other, like a lady and her footman.

David's audacity had more than once already all but caused a rupture between the pair. And the occurrence behind the hedge set the cap on his impertinences. That was past enduring and Maggie by her bearing let him know it.

David tolerated the girl's new attitude for exactly twelve minutes by the kitchen clock. Then: "Sulk wi' me, indeed! I'll teach her!" and he marched out of the door, "Niver to cross it agin, ma word!"

Afterward, however, he relented so far as to continue his visits as before; but he made it clear that he only came to see the Master and hear of Owd Bob's doings. On these occasions he loved best to sit on the window-sill outside the kitchen, and talk and chaff with Tammas and the men in the yard, feigning an uneasy bashfulness was reference made to Bessie Bolstock. And after sitting thus for some time, he would half turn, look over his shoulder, and remark in indifferent tones to the girl within: "Oh, good-evenin'! I forgot yo',"—and then resume his conversation. While the girl within, her face a little pinker, her lips a little tighter, and her chin a little higher, would go about her business, pretending neither to hear nor care.

The suspicions that M'Adam nourished dark designs against James Moore were somewhat confirmed in that, on several occasions in the bitter dusks of January afternoons, a little insidious figure was reported to have been seen lurking among the farm-buildings of Kenmuir.

Once Sam'l Todd caught the little man fairly, skulking away in the woodshed. Sam'l took him up bodily and carried him down the slope to the Wastrel, shaking him gently as he went.

Across the stream he put him on his feet.

"If I catches yo' cadgerin' aroun' the farm agin, little mon," he admonished, holding up a warning finger; "I'll tak' yo' and drap yo' in t' Sheep-wash, I warn yo' fair. I'd ha' done it noo an' yo'd bin a bigger and a younger mon. But theer! yo'm sic a scrappety bit. Noo, rin whoam." And the little man slunk silently away.

For a time he appeared there no more. Then, one evening when it was almost dark, James Moore, going the round of the outbuildings, felt Owd Bob stiffen against his side.

"What's oop, lad?" he whispered, halting; and, dropping his hand on the old dog's neck felt a ruff of rising hair beneath it.

"Steady, lad, steady," he whispered; "what is't?"

He peered forward into the gloom; and at length discerned a little familiar figure huddled away in the crevice between two stacks.

"It's yo', is it, M'Adam?" he said, and, bending, seized a wisp of Owd Bob's coat in a grip like a vise.

Then, in a great voice, moved to rare anger:

"Oot o' this afore I do ye a hurt, ye meeserable spyin' creetur!" he roared. "Yo' mun wait till dark cooms to hide yo', yo' coward, afore yo' daur coom crawlin' aboot ma hoose, frightenin' the women-folk and up to yer devilments. If yo've owt to say to me, coom like a mon in the open day. Noo git aff wi' yo', afore I lay hands to yo'!"

He stood there in the dusk, tall and mighty, a terrible figure, one hand pointing to the gate, the other still grasping the gray dog.

The little man scuttled away in the half-light, and out of the yard.

On the plank-bridge he turned and shook his fist at the darkening house.

"Curse ye, James Moore!" he sobbed, "I'll be even wi' ye yet."

CHAPTER XV

DEATH ON THE MARSHES

ON THE top of this there followed an attempt to poison Th' Owd Un. At least there was no other accounting for the affair.

In the dead of a long-remembered night James Moore was waked by a low moaning beneath his room. He leapt out of bed and ran to the window to see his favourite dragging about the moonlit yard, the dark head down, the proud tail for once lowered, the lithe limbs wooden, heavy, unnatural—altogether pitiful.

In a moment he was downstairs and out to his friend's assistance. "Whativer is't, Owd Un?" he cried in anguish.

At the sound of that dear voice the old dog tried to struggle to him, could not, and fell whimpering.

In a second the Master was with him, examining him tenderly, and crying for Sam'l, who slept above the stables.

There was every symptom of foul play: the tongue was swollen and almost black; the breathing laboured; the body twitched horribly; and the soft gray eyes all blood-shot and straining in agony.

With the aid of Sam'l and Maggie, drenching first and stimulants after, the Master pulled him around for the moment. And soon Jim Mason and Parson Leggy, hurriedly summoned, came running hot-foot to the rescue.

Prompt and stringent measures saved the victim—but only just. For a time the best sheep-dog in the North was pawing at the Gate of Death. In the end, as the gray dawn broke, the danger passed.

The attempt to get at him, if attempt it was, aroused passionate indignation in the countryside. It seemed the culminating point of the excitement long bubbling.

There were no traces of the culprit; not a vestige to lead to incrimination, so cunningly had the criminal accomplished his foul task. But as to the perpetrator, if there where no proofs there were yet fewer doubts.

At the Sylvester Arms Long Kirby asked M'Adam point-blank for his explanation of the matter.

"Hoo do I 'count for it?" the little man cried. "I dinna 'count for it ava."

"Then hoo did it happen?" asked Tammas with asperity.

"I dinna believe it did happen," the little man replied. "It's a lee, o' James Moore's—a characteristic lee." Whereon they chucked him out incontinently; for the Terror for once was elsewhere.

Now that afternoon is to be remembered for threefold causes. Firstly, because, as has been said, M'Adam was alone. Secondly, because, a few minutes after his ejectment, the window of the tap-room was thrown open from without, and the little man looked in. He spoke no word, but those dim, smouldering eyes of his wandered from face to face, resting for a second on each, as if to burn them on his memory. "I'll remember ye, gentlemen," he said at length quietly, shut the window, and was gone. Thirdly, for a reason now to be told.

Though ten days had elapsed since the attempt on him, the gray dog had never been his old self since. He had attacks of shivering; his vitality seemed sapped; he tired easily, and, great heart, would never own it. At length on this day, James Moore, leaving the old dog behind him, had gone over to Grammoch-town to consult Dingley, the vet. On his way home he met Jim Mason with Gyp, the faithful Betsy's unworthy successor, at the Dalesman's Daughter. Together they started for the long tramp home over the Marches. And that journey is marked with a red stone in this story.

All day long the hills had been bathed in impenetrable fog. Throughout there had been an accompanying drizzle; and in the distance the wind had moaned a storm-menace. To the darkness of the day was added the sombreness of falling night as the three began the ascent of the Murk Muir Pass. By the time they emerged into the Devil's Bowl it was altogether black and blind. But the threat of wind had passed, leaving utter stillness; and they could hear the splash of an otter on the far side of the Lone Tarn as they skirted that gloomy water's edge. When at length the last steep rise on to the Marches had been topped, a breath of soft air smote them lightly, and the curtain of fog began drifting away.

The two men swung steadily through the heather with that reaching stride the birthright of moor-men and high-landers. They talked but little, for such was their nature, a word or two on sheep and the approaching lambing-time; thence on to the coming Trials; the Shepherds' Trophy; Owd Bob and the attempt on him; and from that to M'Adam and the Tailless Tyke.

"D'yo' reck'n M'Adam had a hand in't?" the postman was asking.

"Nay; there's no proof."

"'Ceptin' he's mad to get shut o' Th' Owd Un afore Cup Day."

"'Im or me—it mak's no differ." For a dog is dis-qualified from competing for the Trophy who has changed hands during the six months prior to the meeting. And this holds good though the change be only from father to son on the decease of the former.

Jim looked up inquiringly at his companion.

"D'yo' think it'll coom to that?" he asked.

"What?"

"Why—murder."

"Not if I can help it," the other answered grimly.

The fog had cleared away by now, and the moon was up. To their right, on the crest of a rise some two hundred yards away, a low wood stood out black against the sky. As they passed it, a blackbird rose up screaming, and a brace of wood-pigeons winged noisily away.

"Hullo! hark to the yammerin'!" muttered Jim, stopping; "and at this time o' night too!"

Some rabbits, playing in the moonlight on the outskirts of the wood, sat up, listened, and hopped back into security. At the same moment a big hill-fox slunk out of the covert. He stole a pace forward and halted, listening with one ear back and one pad raised; then cantered silently away in the gloom, passing close to the two men and yet not observing them.

"What's up, I wonder?" mused the postman.

"The fox set 'em clackerin', I reck'n," said the Master.

"Not he; he was scared 'maist oot o' his skin," the other answered. Then in tones of suppressed excitement, with his hands on James Moore's arm: "And look'ee, there's ma Gyp a-beckonin' on us!"

There, indeed, on the crest of the rise beside the wood, was the little lurcher, now looking back at his master, now creeping stealthily forward.

"Ma word! theer's summat wrong yonder!" cried Jim, and jerked the post-bags off his shoulder. "Coom on, Master!"—and he set off running toward the dog; while James Moore, himself excited now, followed with an agility that belied his years.

Some score yards from the lower edge of the spinney, upon the farther side of the ridge, a tiny beck babbled through its bed of peat. The two men, as they topped the rise, noticed a flock of black-faced mountain-sheep clustered in the dip 'twixt wood and stream. They stood martialled in close array, facing half toward the wood, half toward the newcomers, heads up, eyes glaring, handsome as sheep only look when scared.

On the crest of the ridge the two men halted beside Gyp. The postman stood with his head a little forward, listening intently. Then he dropped in the heather like a dead man, pulling the other with him.

"Doon, mon!" he whispered, clutching at Gyp with his spare hand.

"What is't, Jim?" asked the Master, now thoroughly roused.

"Summat movin' i' th' wood," the other whispered, listening weasel-eared.

So they lay motionless for a while; but there came no sound from the copse.

"'Appen 'twas nowt," the postman at length allowed, peering cautiously about. "And yet I thowt!—I dunno reetly what I thowt."

Then, starting to his knees with a hoarse cry of terror: "Save us! what's yon theer?"

Then for the first time the Master raised his head and noticed, lying in the gloom between them and the array of sheep, a still, white heap.

James Moore was a man of deeds, not words.

"It's past waitin'!" he said, and sprang forward, his heart in his mouth.

The sheep stamped and shuffled as he came, and yet did not break.

"Ah, thanks be!" he cried, dropping beside the motionless body; "it's nob'but a sheep." As he spoke his hands wandered deftly over the carcase. "But what's this?" he called. "Stout[1] she was as me. Look at her fleece—crisp, close, strong; feel the flesh—firm as a rock. And ne'er a bone broke, ne'er a scrat on her body a pin could mak'. As healthy as a mon—and yet dead as mutton!"

[1] Stout—hearty.

Jim, still trembling from the horror of his fear, came up, and knelt beside his friend.

"Ah, but there's bin devilry in this!" he said; "I reck'ned they sheep had bin badly skeared, and not so long agone."

"Sheep-murder, sure enough!" the other answered. "No fox's doin'—a girt-grown two-shear as could 'maist knock a h'ox."

Jim's hands travelled from the body to the dead creature's throat. He screamed.

"By gob, Master! Look 'ee theer!" He held his hand up in the moonlight, and it dripped red. "And warm yet! warm!"

"Tear some bracken, Jim!" ordered the other, "and set a-light. We mun see to this."

The postman did as bid. For a moment the fern smouldered and smoked, then the flame ran crackling along and shot up in the darkness, weirdly lighting the scene: to the right the low wood, a block of solid blackness against the sky; in front the wall of sheep, staring out of the gloom with bright eyes; and as centre-piece that still, white body, with the kneeling men and lurcher sniffing tentatively round.

The victim was subjected to a critical examination. The throat, and that only, had been hideously mauled; from the raw wounds the flesh hung in horrid shreds; on the ground all about were little pitiful dabs of wool, wrenched off apparently in a struggle; and, crawling among the fern-roots, a snake-like track of red led down to the stream.

"A dog's doin', and no mistakin' thot," said Jim at length, after a minute inspection.

"Ay," declared the Master with slow emphasis, "and a sheep-dog's too, and an old un's, or I'm no shepherd."

The postman looked up.

"Why thot?" he asked, puzzled.

"Becos," the Master answered, "'im as did this killed for blood—and for blood only. If had bin ony other dog—greyhound, bull, tarrier, or even a young sheep-dog—d'yo' think he'd ha' stopped wi' the one? Not he; he'd ha' gone through 'em, and be runnin' 'em as like as not yet, nippin' 'em, pullin' 'em down, till he'd maybe killed the half. But 'im as did this killed for blood, I say. He got it—killed just the one, and nary touched the others, d'yo' see, Jim?"

The postman whistled, long and low.

"It's just what owd Wrottesley'd tell on," he said. "I never nob'but half believed him then—I do now though. D'yo' mind what th' owd lad'd tell, Master?"

James Moore nodded.

"Thot's it. I've never seen the like afore myself, but I've heard ma grandad speak o't mony's the time. An owd dog'll git the cravin' for sheep's blood on him, just the same as a mon does for the drink; he creeps oot o' nights, gallops afar, hunts his sheep, downs 'er, and satisfies the cravin'. And he nary kills but the one, they say, for he knows the vallie o' sheep same as you and me. He has his gallop, quenches the thirst, and then he's for home, maybe a score mile away, and no one the wiser i' th' mornin'. And so on, till he cooms to a bloody death, the murderin' traitor."

"If he does!" said Jim.

"And he does, they say, nigh always. For he gets bolder and bolder wi' not bein' caught, until one fine night a bullet lets light into him. And some mon gets knocked nigh endways when they bring his best tyke home i' th' mornin' dead, wi' the sheep's wool yet stickin' in his mouth."

The postman whistled again.

"It's what owd Wrottesley'd tell on to a tick. And he'd say, if ye mind, Master, as hoo the dog'd niver kill his master's sheep—kind o' conscience-like."

"Ay, I've heard that," said the Master. "Queer too, and 'im bein' such a bad un!"

Jim Mason rose slowly from his knees.

"Ma word," he said, "I wish Th' Owd Un was here. He'd 'appen show us summat!"

"I nob'but wish he was, pore owd lad!" said the Master.

As he spoke there was a crash in the wood above them; a sound as of some big body bursting furiously through brushwood.

The two men rushed to the top of the rise. In the darkness they could see nothing; only, standing still and holding their breaths, they could hear the faint sound, ever growing fainter, of some creature splashing in a hasty gallop over the wet moors.

"Yon's him! Yon's no fox, I'll tak' oath. And a main big un, too, hark to him!" cried Jim. Then to Gyp, who had rushed off in hot pursuit: "Coom back, chunk-'ead. What's use o' you agin a gallopin' 'potamus?"

Gradually the sounds died away and away, and were no more.

"Thot's 'im the devil!" said the Master at length.

"Nay; the devil has a tail, they do say," replied Jim thoughtfully. For already the light of suspicion was focussing its red glare.

"Noo I reck'n we're in for bloody times amang the sheep for a while," said the Master, as Jim picked up his bags.

"Better a sheep nor a mon," answered the postman, still harping on the old theme.

CHAPTER XVI

THE BLACK KILLER

THAT, as James Moore had predicted, was the first only of a long succession of such solitary crimes.

Those who have not lived in a desolate country like that about the Muir Pike, where sheep are paramount and every other man engaged in the profession pastoral, can barely imagine the sensation aroused. In market place, tavern, or cottage, the subject of conversation was always the latest sheep-murder and the yet-undetected criminal.

Sometimes there would be a lull, and the shepherds would begin to breathe more freely. Then there would come a stormy night, when the heavens were veiled in the cloak of crime, and the wind moaned fitfully over meres and marches, and another victim would be added to the lengthening list.

It was always such black nights, nights of wind and weather, when no man would be abroad, that the murderer chose for his bloody work; and that was how he became known from the Red Screes to the Muir Pike as the Black Killer. In the Daleland they still call a wild, wet night "A Black Killer's night"; for they say: "His ghaist'll be oot the night."

There was hardly a farm in the countryside but was marked with the seal of blood. Kenmuir escaped, and the Grange; Rob Saunderson at the Holt, and Tupper at Swinsthwaite; and they were about the only lucky ones.

As for Kenmuir, Tammas declared with a certain grim pride: "He knows better'n to coom wheer Th' Owd Un be." Whereat M'Adam was taken with a fit of internal spasms, rubbing his knees and cackling insanely for a half-hour afterward. And as for the luck of the Grange—well, there was a reason for that too, so the Dalesmen said.

Though the area of crime stretched from the Black Water to Grammoch-town, twenty-odd miles, there was never a sign of the perpetrator. The Killer did his bloody work with a thoroughness and a devilish cunning that defied detection.

It was plain that each murder might be set down to the same agency. Each was stamped with the same unmistakable sign-manual: one sheep killed, its throat torn into red ribands, and the others untouched.

It was at the instigation of Parson Leggy that the squire imported a bloodhound to track the Killer to his doom. Set on at a fresh killed carcase at the One Tree Knowe, he carried the line a distance in the direction of the Muir Pike; then was thrown out by a little bustling beck, and never acknowledged the scent again. Afterward he became unmanageable, and could be no further utilized. Then there was talk of inducing Tommy Dobson and his pack to come over from Eskdale, but that came to nothing.

The Master of the Border Hunt lent a couple of foxhounds, who effected nothing; and there were a hundred other attempts and as many failures. Jim Mason set a cunning trap or two and caught his own bob-tailed tortoise-shell and a terrible wigging from his missus; Ned Hoppin sat up with a gun two nights over a new slain victim and Londesley of the Home Farm poisoned a carcase. But the Killer never returned to the kill, and went about in the midst of them all, carrying on his infamous traffic and laughing up his sleeve.

In the meanwhile the Dalesmen raged and swore vengeance; their impotence, their unsuccess, and their losses heating their wrath to madness. And the bitterest sting of it all lay in this; that though they could not detect him, they were nigh to positive as to the culprit.

Many a time was the Black Killer named in low-voiced conclave; many a time did Long Kirby, as he stood in the Border Ram and watched M'Adam and the Terror walking down the High, nudge Jim Mason and whisper:

"Theer's the Killer—oneasy be his grave!" To which practical Jim always made the same retort:

"Ay, theer's the Killer; but wheer's the proof?"

And therein lay the crux. There was scarcely a man in the countryside who doubted the guilt of the Tailless Tyke; but, as Jim said, where was the proof? They could but point to his well-won nickname; his evil notoriety; say that, magnificent sheep-dog as he was, he was known even in his work as a rough handler of stock; and lastly remark significantly that the Grange was one of the few farms that had so far escaped unscathed. For with the belief that the Black Killer was a sheep-dog they held it as an article of faith that he would in honour spare his master's flock.

There may, indeed, have been prejudice in their judg-
ment. For each had his private grudge against the Terror;
and nigh every man bore on his own person, or his clothes,
or on the body of his dog, the mark of that huge savage.

Proof?

"Why, he near killed ma Lassie!" cries Londesley.

"And he did kill the Wexer!"

"And Wan Tromp!"

"And see pore old Wenus!" says John Swan, and pulls
out that fair Amazon, battered almost past recognition,
but a warrioress still.

"That's Red Wull—bloody be his end!"

"And he laid ma Rasper by for nigh three weeks!"
continues Tupper, pointing to the yet-unhealed scars on
the neck of the big bobtail. "See thisey—his work."

"And look here!" cries Saunderson, exposing a ragged
wound on Shep's throat; "thot's the Terror—black be his
fa'!"

"Ay," says Long Kirby with an oath; "the tykes love
him nigh as much as we do."

"Yes," says Tammas. "Yo' jest watch!"

The old man slips out of the tap-room; and in another
moment from the road without comes a heavy, regular
pat-pat-pat, as of some big creature approaching, and,
blending with the sound, little shuffling footsteps.

In an instant every dog in the room has risen to his feet
and stands staring at the door with sullen, glowing eyes;
lips wrinkling, bristles rising, throats rumbling.

An unsteady hand fumbles at the door; a reedy voice
calls, "Wullie, come here!" and the dogs move away, surly
to either side the fireplace, tails down, ears back, grumbling
still; the picture of cowed passion.

Then the door opens; Tammas enters, grinning; and each, after a moment's scrutiny, resumes his former position before the fire.

    .   .   .   .   .

Meanwhile over M'Adam, seemingly all unsuspicious of these suspicions, a change had come.   Whether it was that for the time he heard less of the best sheep-dog in the North, or for some more occult reason, certain it is that he became his old self.   His tongue wagged as gayly and bitterly as ever, and hardly a night passed but he infuriated Tammas almost to blows with his innuendoes and insidious sarcasms.

Old Jonas Maddox, one evening at the Sylvester Arms, inquired of him what his notion was as to the identity of the Killer.

"I hae ma suspicions, Mr. Maddox; I hae ma suspicions," the little man replied, cunningly wagging his head and giggling.   But more than that they could not elicit from him.   A week later, however, to the question:

"And what are yo' thinkin' o' this black Killer, Mr. M'Adam?"

"Why *black?*" the little man asked earnestly; "why *black* mair than white—or *gray*, we'll say?"   Luckily for him, however, the Dalesmen are slow of wit as of speech.

David, too, marked the difference in his father, who nagged at him now with all the old spirit.   At first he rejoiced in the change, preferring this outward and open warfare to that aforetime stealthy enmity.   But soon he almost wished the other back; for the older he grew the more difficult did he find it to endure calmly these everlasting bickerings.

For one reason he was truly glad of the altered condition of affairs; he believed that, for the nonce, at least, his father had abandoned any ill designs he might have cherished against James Moore; those sneaking night-visits to Kenmuir were, he hoped, discontinued.

Yet Maggie Moore, had she been on speaking terms with him, could have undeceived him. For, one night, when alone in the kitchen, on suddenly looking up, she had seen to her horror a dim, moonlike face glued against the window-pane. In the first mad panic of the moment she almost screamed, and dropped her work; then—a true Moore—controlled herself and sat feigning to work, yet watching all the while.

It was M'Adam, she recognized that: the face pale in its framework of black; the hair lying dank and dark on his forehead; and the white eyelids blinking, slow, regular, horrible. She thought of the stories she had heard of his sworn vengeance on her father, and her heart stood still, though she never moved. At length with a gasp of relief she discerned that the eyes were not directed on her. Stealthily following their gaze, she saw they rested on the Shepherds' Trophy; and on the Cup they remained fixed, immovable, while she sat motionless and watched.

An hour, it seemed to her, elapsed before they shifted their direction, and wandered round the room. For a second they dwelt upon her; then the face withdrew into the night.

Maggie told no one what she had seen. Knowing well how terrible her father was in anger, she deemed it wiser to keep silence. While as for David M'Adam, she would never speak to him again!

And not for a moment did that young man surmise

whence his father came when, on the night in question, M'Adam returned to the Grange, chuckling to himself. David was growing of late accustomed to these fits of silent, unprovoked merriment; and when his father began giggling and muttering to Red Wull, at first he paid no heed.

"He! he! Wullie. Aiblins we'll beat him yet. There's many a slip twixt Cup and lip—eh, Wullie, he! he!" And he made allusion to the flourishing of the wicked and their fall; ending always with the same refrain: "He! he! Wullie. Aiblins we'll beat him yet."

In this strain he continued until David, his patience exhausted, asked roughly:

"What is't yo' mumblin' aboot? Wha is it yo'll beat, you and yer Wullie?"

The lad's tone was as contemptuous as his words. Long ago he had cast aside any semblance of respect for his father.

M'Adam only rubbed his knees and giggled.

"Hark to the dear lad, Wullie! Listen hoo pleasantly he addresses his auld dad!" Then turning on his son, and leering at him: "Wha is it, ye ask? Wha should it be but the Black Killer? Wha else is there I'd be wushin' to hurt?"

"The Black Killer!" echoed the boy, and looked at his father in amazement.

Now David was almost the only man in Wastrel-dale who denied Red Wull's identity with the Killer. "Nay," he said once; "he'd kill me, given half a chance, but a sheep—no." Yet, though himself of this opinion, he knew well what the talk was, and was astonished accordingly at his father's remark.

"The Black Killer, is it? What d'you know o' the Killer?" he inquired.

"Why *black*, I wad ken? Why *black?*" the little man asked, leaning forward in his chair.

Now David, though repudiating in the village Red Wull's complicity with the crimes, at home was never so happy as when casting cunning innuendoes to that effect.

"What would you have him then?" he asked. "Red, yaller, muck-dirt colour?"—and he stared significantly at the Tailless Tyke, who was lying at his master's feet. The little man ceased rubbing his knees and eyed the boy. David shifted uneasily beneath that dim, persistent stare.

"Well?" he said at length gruffly.

The little man giggled, and his two thin hands took up their task again.

"Aiblins his puir auld doited fool of a dad kens mair than the dear lad thinks for, ay, or wushes—eh, Wullie, he! he!"

"Then what is it you do know, or think yo' know?" David asked irritably.

The little man nodded and chuckled.

"Naethin' ava, laddie, naethin' worth the mention. Only aiblins the Killer'll be caught afore sae lang."

David smiled incredulously, wagging his head in offensive scepticism.

"Yo'll catch him yo'self, I s'pose, you and yer Wullie? Tak' a chair on to the Marches, whistle a while, and when the Killer comes, why! pit a pinch o' salt upon his tail—, if he has one."

At the last words, heavily punctuated by the speaker, the little man stopped his rubbing as though shot.

"What wad ye mean by that?" he asked softly.

"What wad I?" the boy replied.

"I dinna ken for sure," the little man answered; "and it's aiblins just as well for you, dear lad"—in fawning accents—"that I dinna." He began rubbing and giggling afresh. "It's a gran' thing, Wullie, to ha' a dutiful son; a shairp lad wha has no silly sense o' shame aboot sharpen-in' his wits at his auld dad's expense. And yet, despite oor facetious lad there, aiblins we will ha' a hand in the Killer's catchin', you and I, Wullie—he! he!" And the great dog at his feet wagged his stump tail in reply.

David rose from his chair and walked across the room to where his father sat.

"If yo' know sic a mighty heap," he shouted, "happen yo'll just tell me what yo' do know!"

M'Adam stopped stroking Red Wull's massive head, and looked up.

"Tell ye? Ay, wha should I tell if not ma dear David? Tell? Ay, I'll tell ye this"—with a sudden snarl of bitterness—"that you'd be the vairy last person I wad tell."

CHAPTER XVII

A MAD DOG

DAVID and Maggie, meanwhile, were drifting further and further apart. He now thought the girl took too much upon herself; that this assumption of the woman and the mother was overdone. Once, on a Sunday, he caught her hearing Andrew his catechism. He watched the performance through a crack in the door, listened, giggling, to her simple teaching. At length his merriment grew so boisterous that she looked up, saw him, and, straightway rising to her feet, crossed the room and shut the door; tendering her unspoken rebuke with such a sweet dignity that he slunk away for once decently ashamed. And the incident served to add point to his hostility.

Consequently he was seldom at Kenmuir, and more often at home, quarrelling with his father.

Since that day, two years before, when the boy had been

an instrument in the taking of the Cup from him, father and son had been like two vessels charged with electricity, contact between which might result at any moment in a shock and a flash. This was the outcome not of a moment, but of years.

Of late the contest had raged markedly fierce; for M'Adam noticed his son's more frequent presence at home, and commented on the fact in his usual spirit of playful raillery.

"What's come to ye, David?" he asked one day. "Yer auld dad's head is nigh turned wi' yer condescension. Is James Moore feared ye'll steal the Cup fra him, as ye stole it from me, that he'll not ha' ye at Kenmuir? or what is it?"

"I thought I could maybe keep an eye on the Killer gin I stayed here," David answered, leering at Red Wull.

"Ye'd do better at Kenmuir—eh, Wullie!" the little man replied.

"Nay," the other answered, "he'll not go to Kenmuir. There's Th' Owd Un to see to him there o' nights."

The little man whipped round.

"Are ye so sure he is there o' nights, ma lad?" he asked with slow significance.

"He was there when some one—I dinna say who, though I have ma' thoughts—tried to poison him," sneered the boy, mimicking his father's manner.

M'Adam shook his head.

"If he was poisoned, and noo I think aiblins he was, he didna pick it up at Kenmuir, I tell ye that," he said, and marched out of the room.

In the mean time the Black Killer pursued his bloody trade unchecked. The public, always greedy of a new

sensation, took up the matter. In several of the great
dailies, articles on the "Agrarian Outrages" appeared,
followed by lengthy correspondence. Controversy raged
high; each correspondent had his own theory and his own
solution of the problem; and each waxed indignant as his
were discarded for another's.

The Terror had reigned already two months when,
with the advent of the lambing-time, matters took a yet
more serious aspect.

It was bad enough to lose one sheep, often the finest in
the pack; but the hunting of a flock at a critical moment,
which was incidental to the slaughter of the one, the
scaring of these woolly mothers-about-to-be almost out of
their fleeces, spelt for the small farmers something akin to
ruin, for the bigger ones a loss hardly bearable.

Such a woful season had never been known; loud were
the curses, deep the vows of revenge. Many a shepherd
at that time patrolled all night through with his dogs,
only to find in the morning that the Killer had slipped him
and havocked in some secluded portion of his beat.

It was heartrending work; and all the more so in that
though his incrimination seemed as far off as ever, there
was still the same positiveness as to the culprit's identity.

Long Kirby, indeed, greatly daring, went so far on one
occasion as to say to the little man: "And d'yo' reck'n
the Killer is a sheep-dog, M'Adam?"

"I do," the little man replied with conviction.

"And that he'll spare his own sheep?"

"Niver a doubt of it."

"Then," said the smith with a nervous cackle, "it
must lie between you and Tupper and Saunderson."

The little man leant forward and tapped the other on the arm.

"Or Kenmuir, ma friend," he said. "Ye've forgot Kenmuir."

"So I have," laughed the smith, "so I have."

"Then I'd not anither time," the other continued, still tapping. "I'd mind Kenmuir, d'ye see, Kirby?"

.   .   .   .   .

It was about the middle of the lambing-time, when the Killer was working his worst, that the Dalesmen had a lurid glimpse of Adam M'Adam as he might be were he wounded through his Wullie.

Thus it came about: It was market-day in Grammochtown, and in the Border Ram old Rob Saunderson was the centre of interest. For on the previous night Rob, who till then had escaped unscathed, had lost a sheep to the Killer: and—far worse—his flock of Herdwicks, heavy in lamb, had been galloped with disastrous consequences.

The old man, with tears in his eyes, was telling how on four nights that week he had been up with Shep to guard against mishap; and on the fifth, worn out with his double labour, had fallen asleep at his post. But a very little while he slumbered; yet when, in the dawn, he woke and hurried on his rounds, he quickly came upon a mangled sheep and the pitiful relic of his flock. A relic, indeed! For all about were cold wee lambkins and their mothers, dead and dying of exhaustion and their unripe travail—a slaughter of the innocents.

The Dalesmen were clustered round the old shepherd listening with lowering countenances, when a dark gray head peered in at the door and two wistful eyes dwelt for a moment on the speaker.

"Talk o' the devil!" muttered M'Adam, but no man heard him. For Red Wull, too, had seen that sad face, and, rising from his master's feet, had leapt with a roar at his enemy, toppling Jim Mason like a ninepin in the fury of his charge.

In a second every dog in the room, from the battered Venus to Tupper's big Rasper, was on his feet, bristling to have at the tyrant and wipe out past injuries, if the gray dog would but lead the dance.

It was not to be, however. For Long Kirby was standing at the door with a cup of hot coffee in his hand. Barely had he greeted the gray dog with—

"'Ullo, Owd Un!" when hoarse yells of "'Ware, lad! The Terror!" mingled with Red Wull's roar.

Half turning, he saw the great dog bounding to the attack. Straightway he flung the boiling contents of his cup full in that rage-wracked countenance. The burning liquid swished against the huge bull-head. Blinding, bubbling, scalding, it did its fell work well; nothing escaped that merciless torrent. With a cry of agony, half bellow, half howl, Red Wull checked in his charge. From without the door was banged to; and again the duel was postponed. While within the tap-room a huddle of men and dogs were left alone with a mad man and a madder brute.

Blind, demented, agonized, the Tailless Tyke thundered about the little room gnashing, snapping, oversetting; men, tables, chairs swirled off their legs as though they had been dolls. He spun round like a monstrous teetotum; he banged his tortured head against the wall; he burrowed into the unyielding floor. And all the while M'Adam pattered after him, laying hands upon him only to be flung aside as a terrier flings a rat. Now up, now down again, now tossed into a corner, now dragged upon the floor, yet always following on and crying in supplicating tones, "Wullie, Wullie, let me to ye! let yer man ease ye!" and then, with a scream and a murderous glance, "By -——, Kirby, I'll deal wi' you later!"

The uproar was like hell let loose. You could hear the noise of oaths and blows, as the men fought for the door, a half-mile away. And above it the horrid bellowing and the screaming of that shrill voice.

Long Kirby was the first man out of that murder-hole; and after him the others toppled one by one—men and dogs jostling one another in the frenzy of their fear. Big Bell, Londesley, Tupper, Hoppin, Teddy Bolstock, white-faced and trembling; and old Saunderson they pulled out by his heels. Then the door was shut with a clang, and the little man and mad dog were left alone.

In the street was already a big-eyed crowd, attracted by the uproar; while at the door was James Moore, seeking entrance. "Happen I could lend the little mon a hand," said he; but they withheld him forcibly.

Inside was pandemonium: bangings like the doors of hell; the bellowing of that great voice; the patter of little feet; the slithering of a body on the floor; and always that shrill, beseeching prayer: "Wullie, Wullie, let me to ye!" and, in a scream, "By——, Kirby, I'll be wi' ye soon!"

Jim Mason it was who turned, at length, to the smith and whispered, "Kirby, lad, yo'd best skip it."

The big man obeyed and ran. The stamp-stamp of his feet on the hard road rang above the turmoil. As the long legs vanished round the corner and the sound of the fugitive died away, a panic seized the listening crowd.

A woman shrieked; a girl fainted; and in two minutes the street was as naked of men as the steppes of Russia in winter: here a white face at a window; there a door ajar, and peering round a far corner a frightened boy. One man only scorned to run. Alone, James Moore stalked down the centre of the road, slow and calm, Owd Bob trotting at his heels.

It was a long half-hour before the door of the inn burst open, and M'Adam came out with a run, flinging the door behind him.

He rushed into the middle of the road; his sleeves were rolled at the wrist like a surgeon's; and in his right hand was a black-handled jack-knife.

"Noo, by ——!" he cried in a terrible voice, "where is he?"

He looked up and down the road, darting his fiery glances everywhere; and his face was whiter than his hair.

Then he turned and hunted madly down the whole length of the High, nosing like a weasel in every cranny, stabbing at the air as he went, and screaming, "By ——, Kirby, wait till I get ye!"

CHAPTER XVIII

HOW THE KILLER WAS SINGED

NO further harm came of the incident; but it served as a healthy object-lesson for the Dalesmen.

A coincidence it may have been, but, as a fact, for the fortnight succeeding Kirby's exploit there was a lull in the crimes. There followed, as though to make amends, the seven days still remembered in the Daleland as the Bloody Week.

On the Sunday the Squire lost a Cheviot ewe, killed not a hundred yards from the Manor wall. On the Monday a farm on the Black Water was marked with the red cross. On Tuesday—a black night—Tupper at Swinsthwaite came upon the murderer at his work; he fired into the darkness without effect; and the Killer escaped with a scaring. On the following night Viscount Birdsaye lost a shearling ram, for which he was reported to have paid a fabulous sum. Thursday was the one blank night of the week. On Friday Tupper was again visited and punished heavily, as though in revenge for that shot.

On the Saturday afternoon a big meeting was held at the Manor to discuss measures. The Squire presided; gentlemen and magistrates were there in numbers, and every farmer in the countryside.

To start the proceedings the Special Commissioner read a futile letter from the Board of Agriculture. After him Viscount Birdsaye rose and proposed that a reward more suitable to the seriousness of the case than the paltry £5 of the Police should be offered, and backed his proposal with a £25 cheque. Several others spoke, and, last of all, Parson Leggy rose.

He briefly summarized the history of the crimes; reiterated his belief that a sheep-dog was the criminal; declared that nothing had occurred to shake his conviction; and concluded by offering a remedy for their consideration. Simple it was, so he said, to laughableness; yet, if their surmise was correct, it would serve as an effectual preventive if not cure, and would at least give them time to turn round. He paused.

"My suggestion is: That every man-jack of you who owns a sheep-dog ties him up at night."

The farmers were given half an hour to consider the proposal, and clustered in knots talking it over. Many an eye was directed on M'Adam; but that little man appeared all unconscious.

"Weel, Mr. Saunderson," he was saying in shrill accents, "and shall ye tie Shep?"

"What d'yo' think?" asked Rob, eying the man at whom the measure was aimed.

"Why, it's this way, I'm thinkin'," the little man

replied. "Gin ye haud Shep's the guilty one I *wad*, by all
manner o' means—or shootin'd be aiblins better. If not,
why"—he shrugged his shoulders significantly; and having shown his hand and driven the nail well home, the
little man left the meeting.

James Moore stayed to see the Parson's resolution
negatived by a large majority, and then he too quitted the
hall. He had foreseen the result, and, previous to the
meeting, had warned the Parson how it would be.

"Tie up!" he cried almost indignantly, as Owd Bob
came galloping up to his whistle; "I think I see myself
chainin' yo', owd lad, like any murderer. Why, it's yo'
has kept the Killer off Kenmuir so far, I'll lay."

At the lodge-gate was M'Adam, for once without his
familiar spirit, playing with the lodge-keeper's child; for
the little man loved all children but his own, and was
beloved of them. As the Master approached he looked
up.

"Weel, Moore," he called, "and are you gaein' to tie
yer dog?"

"I will if you will yours," the Master answered grimly.

"Na," the little man replied, "it's Wullie as frichts the
Killer aff the Grange. That's why I've left him there
noo."

"It's the same wi' me," the Master said. "He's not
come to Kenmuir yet, nor he'll not so long as Th' Owd
Un's loose, I reck'n."

"Loose or tied, for the matter o' that," the little man
rejoined, "Kenmiur'll escape." He made the statement
dogmatically, snapping his lips.

The Master frowned.

"Why that?" he asked.

"Ha' ye no heard what they're sayin'?" the little man inquired with raised eyebrows.

"Nay; what?"

"Why, that the mere repitation o' th' best sheep-dog in the North should keep him aff. An' I guess they're reet," and he laughed shrilly as he spoke.

The Master passed on, puzzled.

"Which road are ye gaein' hame?" M'Adam called after him. "Because," with a polite smile, "I'll tak' t'ither."

"I'm off by the Windy Brae," the Master answered, striding on. "Squire asked me to leave a note wi' his shepherd t'other side o' the Chair." So he headed away to the left, making for home by the route along the Silver Mere.

It is a long sweep of almost unbroken moorland, the well-called Windy Brae; sloping gently down in mile on mile of heather from the Mere Marches on the top to the fringe of the Silver Mere below. In all that waste of moor the only break is the quaint-shaped Giant's Chair, puzzle of geologists, looking as though plumped down by accident in the heathery wild. The ground rises suddenly from the uniform grade of the Brae; up it goes, ever growing steeper, until at length it runs abruptly into a sheer curtain of rock—the Fall—which rises perpendicular some forty feet, on the top of which rests that tiny grassy bowl—not twenty yards across—they call the Scoop.

The Scoop forms the seat of the Chair and reposes on its collar of rock, cool and green and out of the world, like wine in a metal cup; in front is the forty-foot Fall; behind rising sheer again, the wall of rock which makes the back of the Chair. Inaccessible from above, the only means of

entrance to that little dell are two narrow sheep-tracks,
which crawl dangerously up between the sheer wall on the
one hand and the sheer Fall on the other, entering it at
opposite sides.

It stands out clear-cut from the gradual incline, that
peculiar eminence; yet as the Master and Owd Bob
debouched on to the Brae it was already invisible in the
darkening night.

Through the heather the two swung, the Master thinking now with a smile of David and Maggie; wondering
what M'Adam had meant; musing with a frown on the
Killer; pondering on his identity—for he was half of
David's opinion as to Red Wull's innocence; and thanking
his stars that so far Kenmuir had escaped, a piece of luck
he attributed entirely to the vigilance of Th' Owd Un,
who, sleeping in the porch, slipped out at all hours and
went his rounds, warding off danger.   And at the thought
he looked down for the dark head which should be travel
ling at his knee; yet could not see it, so thick hung the
pall of night.

So he brushed his way along, and ever the night grew
blacker; until, from the swell of the ground beneath his
feet, he knew himself skirting the Giant's Chair.

Now as he sped along the foot of the rise, of a sudden
there burst on his ear the myriad patter of galloping feet.
He turned, and at the second a swirl of sheep almost bore
him down.   It was velvet-black, and they fled furiously
by, yet he dimly discovered, driving at their trails, a
vague hound-like form.

"The Killer, by thunder!" he ejaculated, and, startled
though he was, struck down at that last pursuing shape to
miss and almost fall.

"Bob, lad!" he cried, "follow on!" and swung round; but in the darkness could not see if the gray dog had obeyed.

The chase swept on into the night, and, far above him on the hill-side, he could now hear the rattle of the flying feet. He started hotly in pursuit, and then, recognizing the futility of following where he could not see his hand, desisted. So he stood motionless, listening and peering into the blackness, hoping Th' Owd Un was on the villain's heels.

He prayed for the moon; and, as though in answer, the lantern of the night shone out and lit the dour face of the Chair above him. He shot a glance at his feet; and thanked heaven on finding the gray dog was not beside him.

Then he looked up. The sheep had broken, and were scattered over the steep hill-side, still galloping madly. In the rout one pair of darting figures caught and held his gaze: the foremost dodging, twisting, speeding upward, the hinder hard on the leader's heels, swift, remorseless, never changing. He looked for a third pursuing form; but none could be discern.

"He mun ha' missed him in the dark," the Master muttered, the sweat standing on his brow, as he strained his eyes upward.

Higher and higher sped those two dark specks, far outtopping the scattered remnant of the flock. Up and up, until of a sudden the sheer Fall dropped its relentless barrier in the path of the fugitive. Away, scudding along the foot of the rock-wall struck the familiar track leading to the Scoop, and up it, bleating pitifully, nigh spent the Killer hard on her now.

"He'll doon her in the Scoop!" cried the Master hoarsely, following with fascinated eyes. "Owd Un! Owd Un! wheer iver are yo' gotten to?" he called in agony; but no Owd Un made reply.

As they reached the summit, just as he had prophesied, the two black dots were one; and down they rolled together into the hollow of the Scoop, out of the Master's ken. At the same instant the moon, as though loth to watch the last act of the bloody play, veiled her face.

It was his chance. "Noo!"—and up the hillside he sped like a young man, girding his loins for the struggle. The slope grew steep and steeper; but on and on he held in the darkness, gasping painfully, yet running still, until the face of the Fall blocked his way too.

There he paused a moment, and whistled a low call. Could he but dispatch the old dog up the one path to the Scoop, while he took the other, the murderer's one road to safety would be blocked.

He waited, all expectant; but no cold muzzle was shoved into his hand. Again he whistled. A pebble from above almost dropped on him, as if the criminal up there had moved to the brink of the Fall to listen; and he dared no more.

He waited till all was still again, then crept, cat-like, along the rock-foot, and hit, at length, the track up which a while before had fled Killer and victim. Up that ragged way he crawled on hands and knees. The perspiration rolled off his face; one elbow brushed the rock perpetually; one hand plunged ever and anon into that naked emptiness on the other side.

He prayed that the moon might keep in but a little longer; that his feet might be saved from falling, where a slip might well mean death, certain destruction to any chance of success. He cursed his luck that Th' Owd Un had somehow missed him in the dark; for now he must trust to chance, his own great strength, and his good oak stick. And as he climbed, he laid his plan: to rush in on the Killer as he still gorged and grapple with him. If in the darkness he missed—and in that narrow arena the contingency was improbable!—the murderer might still, in the panic of the moment, forget the one path to safety and leap over the Fall to his destruction.

At length he reached the summit and paused to draw breath. The black void before him was the Scoop, and in its bosom—not ten yards away—must be lying the Killer and the killed.

He crouched against the wet rock-face and listened. In that dark silence, poised 'twixt heaven and earth, he seemed a million miles apart from living soul.

No sound, and yet the murderer must be there. Ay, there was the tinkle of a dislodged stone; and again, the tread of stealthy feet.

The Killer was moving; alarmed; was off.

Quick!

He rose to his full height; gathered himself, and leapt

Something collided with him as he sprang; something wrestled madly with him; something wrenched from beneath him; and in a clap he heard the thud of a body striking ground far below, and the slithering and splattering of some creature speeding furiously down the hillside and away.

"Who the blazes?" roared he.

"What the devil?" screamed a little voice.

The moon shone out.

"Moore!"

"M'Adam!"

And there they were still struggling over the body of a dead sheep.

In a second they had disengaged and rushed to the edge of the Fall.   In the quiet they could still hear the scrambling hurry of the fugitive far below them.   Nothing was to be seen, however, save an array of startled sheep on the hill-side, mute witnesses of the murderer's escape.

The two men turned and eyed each other; the one grim, the other sardonic: both dishevelled and suspicious.

"Well?"

"Weel?"

A pause and, careful scrutiny.

"There's blood on your coat."

"And on yours."

Together they walked back into the little moon-lit hollow.   There lay the murdered sheep in a pool of blood. Plain it was to see whence the marks on their coats came. M'Adam touched the victim's head with his foot.   The movement exposed its throat.   With a shudder he replaced it as it was.

The two men stood back and eyed one another.

"What are yo' doin' here?"

"After the Killer.   What are you?"

"After the Killer?"

"Hoo did you come?"

"Up this path,"   pointing to the one behind him.   "Hoo did you?"

"Up this."

Silence; then again:

"I'd ha' had him but for yo'."

"I did have him, but ye tore me aff."

A pause again.

"Where's yer gray dog?" This time the challenge was unmistakable.

"I sent him after the Killer. Wheer's your Red Wull?"

"At hame, as I tell't ye before."

"Yo' mean yo' left him there?"

M'Adam's fingers twitched.

"He's where I left him."

James Moore shrugged his shoulders. And the other began:

"When did yer dog leave ye?"

"When the Killer came past."

"Ye wad say ye missed him then?"

"I say what I mean."

"Ye say he went after the Killer. Noo the Killer was here," pointing to the dead sheep. "Was your dog here, too?"

"If he had been he'd been here still."

"Onless he went over the Fall!"

"That was the Killer, yo' fule."

"Or your dog."

"There was only *one* beneath me. I felt him."

"Just so," said M'Adam, and laughed. The other's brow contracted.

"An' that was a big un," he said slowly. The little man stopped his cackling.

"There ye lie," he said smoothly. "He was small."

They looked one another full in the eyes.

"That's a matter of opinion," said the Master.

"It's a matter of fact," said the other.

The two stared at one another, silent and stern, each

trying to fathom the other's soul; then they turned again to the brink of the Fall. Beneath them, plain to see, was the splash and furrow in the shingle marking the Killer's line of retreat. They looked at one another again, and then each departed the way he had come to give his version of the story.

"We mucked it atween us," said the Master. "If Th' Owd Un had kept wi' me, I should ha' had him."

And—

"I tell ye I did have him, but James Moore pulled me aff. Strange, too, his dog not bein' wi' him!"

CHAPTER XIX

LAD AND LASS

AN immense sensation this affair of the Scoop created in the Daleland. It spurred the Dalesmen into fresh endeavours. James Moore and M'Adam were examined and re-examined as to the minutest details of the matter. The whole country-side was placarded with huge bills, offering £100 reward for the capture of the criminal dead or alive. While the vigilance of the watchers was such that in a single week they bagged a donkey, an old woman, and two amateur detectives.

In Wastrel-dale the near escape of the Killer, the collision between James Moore and Adam, and Owd Bob's unsuccess, who was not wont to fail, aroused intense excitement, with which was mingled a certain anxiety as to their favourite.

For when the Master had reached home that night, he had found the old dog already there, and he must have wrenched his foot in the pursuit or run a thorn into it, for he was very lame. Whereat, when it was reported at the Sylvester Arms, M'Adam winked at Red Wull and muttered, "Ah, forty foot is an ugly tumble."

A week later the little man called at Kenmuir. As he entered the yard, David was standing outside the kitchen window, looking very glum and miserable. On seeing his father, however, the boy started forward, all alert.

"What d'yo' want here?" he cried roughly.

"Same as you, dear lad," the little man giggled, advancing. "I come on a visit."

"Your visits to Kenmuir are usually paid by night, so I've heard," David sneered.

The little man affected not to hear.

"So they dinna allow ye indoors wi' the Cup," he laughed. "They know yer little ways then, David."

"Nay, I'm not wanted in there," David answered bitterly, but not so loud that his father could hear. Maggie within the kitchen heard, however, but paid no heed; for her heart was hard against the boy, who of late, though he never addressed her, had made himself as unpleasant in a thousand little ways as only David M'Adam could.

At that moment the Master came stalking into the yard, Owd Bob preceding him; and as the old dog recognized his visitor he bristled involuntarily.

At the sight of the Master M'Adam hurried forward.

"I did but come to ask after the tyke," he said. "Is he gettin' over his lameness?"

James Moore looked surprised; then his stern face relaxed into a cordial smile. Such generous anxiety as to the welfare of Red Wull's rival was a wholly new characteristic in the little man.

"I tak' it kind in yo', M'Adam," he said, "to come and inquire."

"Is the thorn oot?" asked the little man with eager interest, shooting his head forward to stare closely at the other.

"It came oot last night wi' the poulticin'," the Master answered, returning the other's gaze, calm and steady.

"I'm glad o' that," said the little man, still staring. But his yellow grinning face said as plain as words, "What a liar ye are, James Moore."

The days passed on. His father's taunts and gibes, always becoming more bitter, drove David almost to distraction.

He longed to make it up with Maggie; he longed for that tender sympathy which the girl had always extended to him when his troubles with his father were heavy on him. The quarrel had lasted for months now, and he was well weary of it, and utterly ashamed. For, at least, he had the good grace to acknowledge that no one was to blame but himself; and that it had been fostered solely by his ugly pride.

At length he could endure it no longer, and determined to go to the girl and ask forgiveness. It would be a bitter ordeal to him; always unwilling to acknowledge a fault, even to himself, how much harder would it be to confess it to this strip of a girl. For a time he thought it was almost more than he could do. Yet, like his father, once set upon a course, nothing could divert him. So, after a week of doubts and determinations, of cowardice and courage, he pulled himself together and off he set.

An hour it took him from the Grange to the bridge over

the Wastrel—an hour which had wont to be a quarter. Now, as he walked on up the slope from the stream, very slowly, heartening himself for his penance, he was aware of a strange disturbance in the yard above him: the noisy cackling of hens, the snorting of pigs disturbed, and above the rest the cry of a little child ringing out in shrill distress.

He set to running, and sped up the slope as fast as his long legs would carry him. As he took the gate in his stride, he saw the white-clad figure of Wee Anne fleeing with unsteady, toddling steps, her fair hair streaming out behind, and one bare arm striking wildly back at a great pursuing sow.

David shouted as he cleared the gate, but the brute paid no heed, and was almost touching the fugitive when Owd Bob came galloping round the corner, and in a second had flashed between pursuer and pursued. So close were the two that as he swung round on the startled sow, his tail brushed the baby to the ground; and there she lay kicking fat legs to heaven and calling on all her gods.

David, leaving the old dog to secure the warrior pig, ran round to her; but he was anticipated. The whole matter had barely occupied a minute's time; and Maggie, rushing from the kitchen, now had the child in her arms and was hurrying back with her to the house.

"Eh, ma pet, are yo' hurted, dearie?" David could hear her asking tearfully, as he crossed the yard and established himself in the door.

"Well," he said, in bantering tones, "yo'm a nice wench to ha' charge o' oor Annie!"

It was a sore subject with the girl, and well he knew it. Wee Anne, that golden-haired imp of mischief, was forever evading her sister-mother's eye and attempting to immolate herself. More than once she had only been saved from serious hurt by the watchful devotion of Owd Bob, who always found time, despite his many labours, to keep a guardian eye on his well-loved lassie. In the previous winter she had been lost on a bitter night on the Muir Pike; 'once she had climbed into a field with the Highland bull, and barely escaped with her life, while the gray dog held the brute in check; but a little while before she had been rescued from drowning by the Tailless Tyke; there had been numerous other mischances; and now the present mishap. But the girl paid no heed to her tormentor in her joy at finding the child all unhurt.

"Theer! yo' bain't so much as scratted, ma precious, is yo'?" she cried. "Rin oot agin, then," and the baby toddled joyfully away.

Maggie rose to her feet and stood with face averted. David's eyes dwelt lovingly upon her, admiring the pose of the neat head with its thatch of pretty brown hair; the slim figure, and slender ankles, peeping modestly from beneath her print frock.

"Ma word! if yo' dad should hear tell o' hoo his Anne ——" he broke off into a long-drawn whistle.

Maggie kept silence; but her lips quivered, and the flush deepened on her cheek.

"I'm fear'd I'll ha' to tell him," the boy continued. "'Tis but ma duty."

"Yo' may tell wham yo' like what yo' like," the girl replied coldly; yet there was a tremour in her voice.

"First yo' throws her in the stream," David went on remorselessly; "then yo' chucks her to the pig, and if it had not bin for me——"

"Yo', indeed!" she broke in contemptuously. "Yo'l,

'twas Owd Bob reskied her. Yo'd nowt' to do wi' it, 'cept lookin' on—'bout what yo're fit for."

"I tell yo'," David pursued stubbornly, "an it had not bin for me yo' wouldn't have no sister by noo. She'd be lyin', she would, pore little lass, cold as ice, pore mite, wi' no breath in her. An' when yo' dad coom home there'd be no Wee Anne to rin to him, and climb on his knee, and yammer to him, and beat his face. And he'd say, 'What's gotten to oor Annie, as I left wi' yo'?' And then yo'd have to tell him, 'I never took no manner o' fash after her, dad; d'reckly yo' back was turned, I——'"

The girl sat down, buried her face in her apron, and indulged in the rare luxury of tears.

"Yo're the cruellest mon as iver was, David M'Adam," she sobbed, rocking to and fro.

He was at her side in a moment, tenderly bending over her.

"Eh, Maggie, but I am sorry, lass——"

She wrenched away from beneath his hands.

"I hate yo'," she cried passionately.

He gently removed her hands from before her tear-stained face.

"I was nob'but laffin', Maggie," he pleaded; "say yo' forgie me."

"I don't," she cried, struggling. "I think yo're the hatefullest lad as iver lived."

The moment was critical; it was a time for heroic measures.

"No, yo' don't, lass," he remonstrated; and, releasing her wrists, lifted the little drooping face, wet as it was, like the earth after a spring shower, and, holding it between his two big hands, kissed it twice.

"Yo' coward!" she cried, a flood of warm red crimsoning her cheeks; and she struggled vainly to be free.

"'Yo' used to let me," he reminded her in aggrieved tones.

"I niver did!" she cried, more indignant than truthful.

"Yes, yo' did, when we was little uns; that is, yo' was allus for kissin' and I was allus agin it. And noo," with whole-souled bitterness, "I mayn't so much as keek at yo' over a stone wall."

However that might be, he was keeking at her from closer range now; and in that position—for he held her firmly still—she could not help but keek back. He looked so handsome—humble for once; penitent yet reproachful; his own eyes a little moist; and, withal, his old audacious self—that, despite herself, her anger grew less hot.

"Say yo' forgie me and I'll let yo' go."

"I don't, nor niver shall," she answered firmly; but there was less conviction in her heart than voice.

"Iss yo' do, lass," he coaxed, and kissed her again.

She struggled faintly.

"Hoo daur yo'?" she cried through her tears. But he was not to be moved.

"Will yo' noo?" he asked.

She remained dumb, and he kissed her again.

"Impidence!" she cried.

"Ay," said he, closing her mouth.

"I wonder at ye, Davie!" she said, surrendering.

After that Maggie must needs give in; and it was well understood, though nothing definite had been said, that the boy and girl were courting. And in the Dale the

unanimous opinion was that the young couple would make
"a gradely pair, surely."

M'Adam was the last person to hear the news, long after
it had been common knowledge in the village. It was in
the Sylvester Arms he first heard it, and straightway fell
into one of those foaming frenzies characteristic of him.

"The dochter o' Moore o' Kenmuir, d'ye say? sic a
dochter o' sic a man! The dochter o' th' one man in the
warld that's harmed me aboon the rest! I'd no ha'
believed it gin ye'd no tell't me. Oh, David, David!
I'd no ha' thocht it even o' you, ill son as ye've aye bin to
me. I think he might ha' waited till his auld dad was gone
and he'd no had to wait lang the noo." Then the little
man sat down and burst into tears. Gradually, however,
he resigned himself, and the more readily when he realized
that David by his act had exposed a fresh wound into
which he might plunge his barbed shafts. And he
availed himself to the full of his new opportunities. Often
and often David was sore pressed to restrain himself.

"Is't true what they're sayin' that Maggie Moore's
nae better than she should be?" the little man asked one
evening with anxious interest.

"They're not sayin' so, and if they were 'twad be a lie,"
the boy answered angrily.

M'Adam leant back in his chair and nodded his head

"Ay, they tell't me that gin ony man knew 'twad be
David M'Adam."

David strode across the room.

"No, no mair o' that," he shouted. "Y'ought to be
'shamed, an owd mon like you, to speak so o' a lass."
The little man edged close up to his son, and looked up
into the fair flushed face towering above him.

"David," he said in smooth soft tones, "I'm 'stonished ye dinna strike yer auld dad." He stood with his hands clasped behind his back as if daring the young giant to raise a finger against him. "Ye maist might noo," he continued suavely. "Ye maun be sax inches taller, and a good four stane heavier. Hooiver, aiblins ye're wise to wait. Anither year twa I'll be an auld man, as ye say, and feebler, and Wullie here'll be gettin' on, while you'll be in the prime o' yer strength. Then I think ye might hit me wi' safety to your person, and honour to yourself."

He took a pace back, smiling.

"Feyther," said David, huskily, "one day yo'll drive me too far."

CHAPTER XX

THE SNAPPING OF THE STRING

THE spring was passing, marked throughout with the
bloody trail of the Killer.   The adventure in the
Scoop scared him for a while into innocuousness; then he
resumed his game again with redoubled zest.   It seemed
likely he would harry the district till some lucky accident
carried him off, for all chance there was of arresting him.

You could still hear nightly in the Sylvester Arms and
elsewhere the assertion, delivered with the same dogmatic
certainty as of old, "It's the Terror, I tell yo'!" and that
irritating, inevitable reply.   "Ay; but wheer's the proof?"
While often, at the same moment, in a house not far away,
a little lonely man was sitting before a low-burnt fire,
rocking to and fro, biting his nails, and muttering to the
great dog whose head lay between his knees: "If we had
but the proof, Wullie! if we had but the proof!   I'd give
ma right hand aff my arm gin we had the proof to-morrow."

Long Kirby, who was always for war when some one else

was to do the fighting, suggested that David should be requested in the name of the Dalesmen, to tell M'Adam, that he must make an end to Red Wull.   But Jim Mason quashed the proposal, remarking truly enough that there was too much bad blood as it was between father and son; while Tammas proposed with a sneer that the smith should be his own agent in the matter.

Whether it was this remark of Tammas's which stung the big man into action, or whether it was that the intensity of his hate gave him unusual courage, anyhow, a few days later, M'Adam caught him lurking in the granary of the Grange.

The little man may not have guessed his murderous intent; yet the blacksmith's white-faced terror, as he crouched away in the darkest corner, could have hardly escaped remark; though—and Kirby may thank his stars for it—the treacherous gleam of a gun-barrel, ill-concealed behind him, did.

"Hullo, Kirby!" said M'Adam cordially, "ye'll stay the night wi' me?"   And the next thing the big man heard was a giggle on the far side the door, lost in the clank of padlock and rattle of chain.   Then—through a crack—"Good-night to ye. Hope ye'll be comfie." And there he stayed that night, the following day and next night—thirty-six hours in all, with swedes for his hunger and the dew off the thatch for his thirst.

Meanwhile the struggle between David and his father seemed coming to a head. The little man's tongue wagged more bitterly than ever; now it was never at rest—searching out sores, stinging, piercing.

Worst of all, he was continually dropping innuendoes, seemingly innocent enough, yet with a world of subtile

meaning at their back, respecting Maggie. The leer and
wink with which, when David came home from Kenmuir
at nights, he would ask the simple question, "And was
she kind, David—eh, eh?" made the boy's blood boil
within him.

And the more effective the little man saw his shots to be,
the more persistently he plied them. And David re-
taliated in kind. It was a war of reprisals. There was
no peace; there were no truces in which to bury the dead
before the opponents set to slaying others. And every
day brought the combatants nearer to that final struggle,
the issue of which neither cared to contemplate.

There came a Saturday, toward the end of the spring,
long to be remembered by more than David in the Dale.

For that young man the day started sensationally.
Rising before cock-crow, and going to the window, the
first thing he saw in the misty dawn was the gaunt, gigantic figure of Red Wull, hounding up the hill from the
Stony Bottom; and in an instant his faith was shaken to
its foundation.

The dog was travelling up at a long, slouching trot; and
as he rapidly approached the house, David saw that his
flanks were all splashed with red mud, his tongue out, and
the foam dripping from his jaws, as though he had come
far and fast.

He slunk up to the house, leapt on to the sill of the
unused back-kitchen, some five feet from the ground,
pushed with his paw at the cranky old hatchment, which
was its only covering; and, in a second, the boy, straining
out of the window the better to see, heard the rattle of the
boards as the dog dropped within the house.

For the moment, excited as he was, David held his peace. Even the Black Killer took only second place in his thoughts that morning. For this was to be a momentous day for him.

That afternoon James Moore and Andrew would, he knew, be over at Grammoch-town, and, his work finished for the day, he was resolved to tackle Maggie and decide his fate. If she would have him—well, he would go next morning and thank God for it, kneeling beside her in the tiny village church; if not, he would leave the Grange and all its unhappiness behind, and straightway plunge out into the world.

All through a week of stern work he had looked forward to this hard-won half-holiday. Therefore, when, as he was breaking off at noon, his father turned to him and said abruptly:

"David, ye're to tak' the Cheviot lot o'er to Grammoch-town at once," he answered shortly:

"Yo' mun tak' 'em yo'sel', if yo' wish 'em to go to-day."

"Na," the little man answered; "Wullie and me, we're busy. Ye're to tak' 'em, I tell ye."

"I'll not," David replied. "If they wait for me, they wait till Monday," and with that he left the room.

"I see what 'tis," his father called after him; "she's give ye a tryst at Kenmuir. Oh, ye randy David!"

"Yo' tend yo' business; I'll tend mine," the boy answered hotly.

Now it happened that on the previous day Maggie had given him a photograph of herself, or, rather, David had taken it and Maggie had demurred. As he left the room it dropped from his pocket.   He failed to notice his loss, but directly he was gone M'Adam pounced on it.

"He! he! Wullie, what's this?" he giggled, holding the photograph into his face.   "He! he! it's the jade hersel', I war'nt; it's Jezebel!"

He peered into the picture.

"She kens what's what, I'll tak' oath, Wullie.   See her eyes—sae saft and languishin'; and her lips—such lips, Wullie!"   He held the picture down for the great dog to see: then walked out of the room, still sniggering, and chucking the face insanely beneath its cardboard chin.

Outside the house he collided against David.   The boy had missed his treasure and was hurrying back for it.

"What yo' got theer?" he asked suspiciously.

"Only the pictur' o' some randy quean," his father answered, chucking away at the inanimate chin.

"Gie it me!" David ordered fiercely.   "It's mine."

"Na, na," the little man replied.   "It's no for sic douce lads as dear David to ha' ony touch wi' leddies sic as this."

"Gie it me, I tell ye, or I'll tak' it!" the boy shouted.

"Na, na; it's ma duty as yer dad to keep ye from sic limmers."   He turned, still smiling, to Red Wull.

"There ye are, Wullie!"   He threw the photograph to the dog.   "Tear her, Wullie, the Jezebel!"

The Tailless Tyke sprang on the picture, placed one big paw in the very centre of the face, forcing it into the muck, and tore a corner off; then he chewed the scrap with unctious, slobbering gluttony, dropped it, and tore a fresh piece.

David dashed forward.

"Touch it, if ye daur, ye brute!" he yelled; but his father seized him and held him back.

"'And the dogs o' the street,'" he quoted.

David turned furiously on him.

"I've half a mind to brak' ivery bone in yer body!" he shouted, "robbin' me o' what's mine and throwin' it to yon black brute!"

"Whist, David, whist!" soothed the little man. "'Twas but for yer ain good yer auld dad did it. 'Twas that he had at heart as he aye has. Rin aff wi' ye noo to Kenmuir. She'll mak' it up to ye, I war'nt. She's leeberal wi' her favours, I hear. Ye've but to whistle and she'll come."

David seized his father by the shoulder.

"An' yo' gie me much more o' your sauce," he roared.

"Sauce, Wullie," the little man echoed in gentle voice.

"I'll twist yer neck for yo'!"

"He'll twist my neck for me."

"I'll gang reet awa', I warn yo', and leave you and yer Wullie to yer lone."

The little man began to whimper.

"It'll brak' yer auld dad's heart, lad," he said.

"Nay; yo've got none. But 'twill ruin yo', please God. For yo' and yer Wullie'll get ne'er a soul to work for yo'—yo' cheeseparin', dirty-tongued rascal."

The little man burst into an agony of affected tears, rocking to and fro, his face in his hands.

"Waesucks, Wullie! d'ye hear him? He's gaein' to leave us—the son o' my bosom! my Benjamin! my little Davie! he's gaein' awa'!"

David turned away down the hill; and M'Adam lifted his stricken face and waved a hand at him.

"'Adieu, dear amiable youth!'" he cried in broken voice: and straightway set to sobbing again.

Half-way down to the Stony Bottom David turned.

"'I'll gie yo' a word o' warnin','" he shouted back, "I'd advise yo' to keep a closer eye to yer Wullie's goings on, 'specially o' nights, or happen yo'll wake to a surprise one mornin'.'"

In an instant the little man ceased his fooling.

"And why that?" he asked, following down the hill.

"I'll tell yo'.   When I wak' this mornin' I walked to the window, and what d'yo' think I see?   Why, your Wullie gallopin' like a good un up from the Bottom, all foamin', too, and red-splashed, as if he'd coom from the Screes. What had he bin up to, I'd like to know?"

"What should he be doin'," the little man replied, "but havin' an eye to the stock? and that when the Killer might be oot."

David laughed harshly.

"Ay, the Killer was oot, I'll go bail, and yo' may hear o't afore the evenin', ma man," and with that he turned away again.

As he had foreseen, David found Maggie alone.   But in the heat of his indignation against his father he seemed to have forgotten his original intent, and instead poured his latest troubles into the girl's sympathetic ear.

"There's but one mon in the world he wishes worse nor me," he was saying.   It was late in the afternoon, and he was still inveighing against his father and his fate. Maggie sat in her father's chair by the fire, knitting;

while he lounged on the kitchen table, swinging his long legs.

"And who may that be?" the girl asked.

"Why, Mr. Moore, to be sure, and Th' Owd Un, too. He'd do either o' them a mischief if he could."

"But why, David?" she asked anxiously. "I'm sure dad niver hurt him, or ony ither mon for the matter o' that."

David nodded toward the Dale Cup which rested on the mantelpiece in silvery majesty.

"It's yon done it," he said. "And if Th' Owd Un wins agin, as win he will, bless him! why, look out for 'me and ma Wullie'; that's all."

Maggie shuddered, and thought of the face at the window.

"'Me and ma Wullie,'" David continued; "I've had about as much of them as I can swaller. It's aye the same—'Me and ma Wullie,' and 'Wullie and me,' as if I never put ma hand to a stroke! Ugh!"—he made a gesture of passionate disgust—"the two on 'em fair madden me. I could strike the one and throttle t'other," and he rattled his heels angrily together.

"Hush, David," interposed the girl; "yo' munna speak so o' your dad; it's agin' the commandments."

"'Tain't agin human nature," he snapped in answer. "Why ,'twas nob'but yester' morn' he says in his nasty way, 'David, ma gran' fellow, hoo ye work! ye 'stonish me!' And on ma word, Maggie"—there were tears in the great boy's eyes—"ma back was nigh broke wi' toilin'. And the Terror, he stands by and shows his teeth, and looks at me as much as to say, 'Some day, by the grace o' goodness, I'll ha' my teeth in your throat, young mon.'"

Maggie's knitting dropped into her lap and she looked up, her soft eyes for once flashing.

"It's cruel, David; so 'tis!" she cried. "I wonder yo' bide wi' him. If he treated me so, I'd no stay anither minute. If it meant the House for me I'd go," and she looked as if she meant it.

David jumped off the table.

"Han' yo' niver guessed why I stop, lass, and me so happy at home?" he asked eagerly.

Maggie's eyes dropped again.

"Hoo should I know?" she asked innocently.

"Nor care, neither, I s'pose," he said in reproachful accents. "Yo' want me to go and leave yo', and go reet awa'; I see hoo 'tis. Yo' wouldna mind, not yo', if yo' was niver to see pore David agin. I niver thowt yo' welly like me, Maggie; and noo I know it."

"Yo' silly lad," the girl murmured, knitting steadfastly.

"Then yo' do," he cried, triumphant, "I knew yo' did." He approached close to her chair, his face clouded with eager anxiety.

"But d'yo' like me more'n just *likin'*, Maggie? d'yo'," he bent and whispered in the little ear.

The girl cuddled over her work so that he could not see her face.

"If yo' won't tell me yo' can show me," he coaxed. "There's other things besides words."

He stood before her, one hand on the chair-back on either side. She sat thus, caged between his arms, with drooping eyes and heightened colour.

"Not so close, David, please," she begged, fidgeting uneasily; but the request was unheeded.

"Do'ee move away a wee," she implored.

"Not till yo've showed me," he said, relentless.

"I canna, Davie," she cried with laughing petulance.

"Yes, yo' can, lass."

"Tak' your hands away, then."

"Nay; not till yo've showed me."

A pause.

"Do'ee, Davie," she supplicated.

And—

"Do'ee," he pleaded.

She tilted her face provokingly, but her eyes were still down.

"It's no manner o' use, Davie."

"Iss, 'tis," he coaxed.

"Niver."

"Please."

A lengthy pause.

"Well, then——" She looked up, at last, shy, trustful, happy; and the sweet lips were tilted further to meet his.

And thus they were situated, lover-like, when a low, rapt voice broke in on them,—

> "'A dear-lov'd lad, convenience snug,
>   A treacherous inclination.'

Oh, Wullie, I wush you were here!"

It was little M'Adam. He was leaning in at the open window, leering at the young couple, his eyes puckered, an evil expression on his face.

"The creetical moment! and I interfere! David, ye'll never forgie me."

The boy jumped round with an oath; and Maggie, her

face flaming, started to her feet.   The tone, the words, the look of the little man at the window were alike insufferable.

"By thunder! I'll teach yo' to come spyin' on me!" roared David.   Above him on the mantel-piece blazed the Shepherds' Trophy.   Searching any missile in his fury, he reached up a hand for it.

"Ay, gie it me back.   Ye robbed me o't," the little man cried, holding out his arms as if to receive it.

"Dinna, David," pleaded Maggie, with restraining hand on her lover's arm.

"By the Lord!   I'll give him something!" yelled the boy.   Close by there stood a pail of soapy water.   He seized it, swung it, and slashed its contents at the leering face in the window.

The little man started back, but the dirty torrent caught him and soused him through.   The bucket followed, struck him full on the chest, and rolled him over in the mud.   After it with a rush came David.

"I'll let yo' know, spyin' on me!" he yelled.   "I'll ——" Maggie, whose face was as white now as it had been crimson, clung to him, hampering him.

"Dinna, David, dinna!" she implored.   "He's yer ain dad."

"I'll dad him!   I'll learn him!" roared David half through the window.

At the moment Sam'l Todd came floundering furiously round the corner, closely followed by 'Enry and oor Job.

"Is he dead?" shouted Sam'l seeing the prostrate form.

"Ho! ho!" went the other two.

They picked up the draggled little man and hustled him out of the yard like a thief, a man on either side and a man behind.

As they forced him through the gate, he struggled round.

"By Him that made ye! ye shall pay for this, David M'Adam, you and yer——"

But Sam'l's big hand descended on his mouth, and he was borne away before that last ill word had flitted into being.

CHAPTER XXI

HORROR OF DARKNESS

IT was long past dark that night when M'Adam stag-gered home.

All that evening at the Sylvester Arms his imprecations against David had made even the hardest shudder. James Moore, Owd Bob, and the Dale Cup were for once forgotten as, in his passion, he cursed his son.

The Dalesmen gathered fearfully away from the little dripping madman. For once these men, whom, as a rule, no such geyser outbursts could quell, were dumb before him; only now and then shooting furtive glances in his direction, as though on the brink of some daring enterprise of which he was the objective. But M'Adam noticed nothing, suspected nothing.

When, at length, he lurched into the kitchen of the Grange, there was no light and the fire burnt low. So dark was the room that a white riband of paper pinned on to the table escaped his remark.

The little man sat down heavily, his clothes still sodden, and resumed his tireless anathema.

"I've tholed mair fra him, Wullie, than Adam M'Adam ever thocht to thole from ony man. And noo it's gane past bearin'. He struck me, Wullie! struck his ain father. Ye see it yersel', Wullie. Na, ye werena there. Oh, gin ye had but bin, Wullie! Him and his madam! But I'll gar him ken Adam M'Adam. I'll stan' nae mair!"

He sprang to his feet and, reaching up with trembling hands, pulled down the old bell-mouthed blunderbuss that hung above the mantelpiece.

"We'll mak' an end to't, Wullie, so we will, aince and for a'!" And he banged the weapon down upon the table. It lay right athwart that slip of still condemning paper, yet the little man saw it not.

Resuming his seat, he prepared to wait. His hand sought the pocket of his coat, and fingered tenderly a small stone bottle, the fond companion of his widowhood. He pulled it out, uncorked it, and took a long pull; then placed it on the table by his side.

Gradually the gray head lolled; the shrivelled hand dropped and hung limply down, the finger-tips brushing the floor; and he dozed off into a heavy sleep, while Red Wull watched at his feet.

It was not till an hour later that David returned home.

As he approached the lightless house, standing in the darkness like a body with the spirit fled, he could but contrast this dreary home of his with the bright kitchen and cheery faces he had left.

Entering the house, he groped to the kitchen door and opened it; then struck a match and stood in the doorway peering in.

"Not home, bain't he?" he muttered, the tiny light above his head. "Wet inside as well as oot by noo, I'll lay. By gum! But 'twas a lucky thing for him I didna get ma hand on him this evenin'. I could ha' killed him." He held the match above his head.

Two yellow eyes, glowing in the darkness like cairngorms, and a small dim figure bunched up in a chair, told him his surmise was wrong. Many a time had he seen his father in such case before, and now he muttered contemptuously:

"Drunk; the leetle swab! Sleepin' it off, I reck'n."

Then he saw his mistake. The hand that hung above the floor twitched and was still again.

There was a clammy silence. A mouse, emboldened by the quiet, scuttled across the hearth. One mighty paw lightly moved; a lightning tap, and the tiny beast lay dead.

Again that hollow stillness: no sound, no movement; only those two unwinking eyes fixed cn him immovable.

At length a small voice from the fireside broke the quiet.

"Drunk—the—leetle—swab!"

Again a clammy silence, and a life-long pause.

"I thowt yo' was sleepin'," said David, at length, lamely.

"Ay, so ye said. 'Sleepin' it aff'; I heard ye." Then, still in the same small voice, now quivering imperceptibly,

"Wad ye obleege me, sir, by leetin' the lamp? Or, d'ye think, Wullie, 'twad be soilin' his dainty fingers? They're mair used, I'm told, to danderin' wi' the bonnie brown hair o' his——"

"I'll not ha' ye talk o' ma Maggie so," interposed the boy passionately.

"*His* Maggie, mark ye, Wullie—*his*! I thocht 'twad soon get that far."

"Tak' care, dad! I'll stan' but little more," the boy warned him in choking voice; and began to trim the lamp with trembling fingers.

M'Adam forthwith addressed himself to Red Wull.

"I suppose no man iver had sic a son as him, Wullie. Ye ken what I've done for him, an' ye ken hoo he's repaid it. He's set himsel' agin me; he's misca'd me; he's robbed me o' ma Cup; last of all, he struck me—struck me afore them a'. We've toiled for him, you and I, Wullie; we've slaved to keep him in hoose an' hame, an' he's passed his time, the while, in riotous leevin', carousin' at Kenmuir, amusin' himsel' wi' his——" He broke off short. The lamp was lit, and the strip of paper, pinned on to the table, naked and glaring, caught his eye.

"What's this?" he muttered; and unloosed the nail that clamped it down.

This is what he read:

"Adam Mackadam yer warned to mak' an end to yer Red Wull will be best for him and the Sheep. This is the first yoll have two more the third will be the last —+"

It was written in pencil, and the only signature was a dagger, rudely limned in red.

M'Adam read the paper once, twice, thrice. As he slowly assimilated its meaning, the blood faded from his face. He stared at it and still stared, with whitening face and pursed lips. Then he stole a glance at David's broad back.

"What d'ye ken o' this, David?" he asked, at length, in a dry thin voice, reaching forward in his chair.

"O' what?"

"O' this," holding up the slip. "And ye'd obleege me by the truth for once."

David turned, took up the paper, read it, and laughed harshly.

"It's coom to this, has it?" he said, still laughing, and yet with blanching face.

"Ye ken what it means. I daresay ye pit it there; aiblins writ it. Ye'll explain it." The little man spoke in the same small, even voice, and his eyes never moved off his son's face.

"It's plain as day. Ha' ye no heard?"

"I've heard naethin'. . . . I'd like the truth, David, if ye can tell it."

The boy smiled a forced, unnatural smile, looking from his father to the paper in his hand.

"Yo' shall have it, but yo'll not like it. It's this: Tupper lost a sheep to the Killer last night."

"And what if he did?" The little man rose smoothly to his feet. Each noticed the other's face—dead-white.

"Why, he—lost—it—on——Wheer d'yo' think?" He drawled the words out, dwelling almost lovingly on each.

"Where?"

"On—the—Red—Screes."

The crash was coming—inevitable now. David knew it, knew that nothing could avert it, and braced himself to meet it. The smile had fled from his face, and his breath fluttered in his throat like the wind before a thunderstorm.

"What of it?" The little man's voice was calm as a summer sea.

"Why, your Wullie—as I told yo'—was on the Screes ast night."

"Go on, David."

"And this," holding up the paper, "tells you that they ken as I ken noo, as maist o' them ha' kent this mony a day, that your Wullie, Red Wull—the Terror——"

"Go on."

"Is——"

"Yes."

"The Black Killer."

It was spoken.

The frayed string was snapped at last. The little man's hand flashed to the bottle that stood before him.

"Ye—liar!" he shrieked, and threw it with all his strength at the boy's head. David dodged and ducked, and the bottle hurtled over his shoulder.

Crash! it whizzed into the lamp behind, and broke on the wall beyond, its contents trickling down the wall to the floor.

For a moment, darkness. Then the spirits met the lamp's smouldering wick and blazed into flame.

By the sudden light David saw his father on the far side the table, pointing with crooked forefinger. By his side Red Wull was standing alert, hackles up, yellow fangs bared, eyes lurid; and, at his feet, the wee brown mouse lay still and lifeless.

"Ooot o' ma hoose! Back to Kenmuir! Back to yer——" The unpardonable word, unmistakable, hovered for a second on his lips like some foul bubble, and never burst.

"No mither this time!" panted David, racing round the table.

"Wullie!"

The Terror leapt to the attack; but David overturned

the table as he ran, the blunderbuss crashing to the
floor; it fell, opposing a momentary barrier in the dog's
path.

"Stan' off, ye——!" screeched the little man, seizing
a chair in both hands; "stan' off, or I'll brain ye!"

But David was on him.

"Wullie, Wullie, to me!"

Again the Terror came with a roar like the sea. But
David, with a mighty kick catching him full on the jaw,
repelled the attack.

Then he gripped his father round the waist and lifted
him from the ground. The little man, struggling in those
iron arms, screamed, cursed, and battered at the face
above him, kicking and biting in his frenzy.

"The Killer! wad ye ken wha's the Killer? Go and
ask 'em at Kenmuir! Ask yer——"

David swayed slightly, crushing the body in his arms
till it seemed every rib must break; then hurled it from
him with all the might of passion. The little man fell with
a crash and a groan.

The blaze in the corner flared, flickered, and died.
There was hell-black darkness, and silence of the dead.

David stood against the wall, panting, every nerve
tightstrung as the hawser of a straining ship.

In the corner lay the body of his father, limp and still;
and in the room one other living thing was moving.

He clung close to the wall, pressing it with wet hands.
The horror of it all, the darkness, the man in the corner,
that moving something, petrified him.

"Feyther!" he whispered.

There was no reply. A chair creaked at an invisible
touch. Something was creeping, stealing, crawling closer.

David was afraid.

"Feyther!" he whispered in hoarse agony, "are yo' hurt?"

The words were stifled in his throat. A chair over-turned with a crash; a great body struck him on the chest, a hot, pestilent breath volleyed in his face, and wolfish teeth were reaching for his throat.

"Come on, Killer!" he screamed.

The horror of suspense was past. It had come, and with it he was himself again.

Back, back, back, along the wall he was borne. His hands entwined themselves around a hairy throat; he forced the great head with its horrid lightsome eyes from him; he braced himself for the effort, lifted the huge body at his breast, and heaved it from him. It struck the wall and fell with a soft thud.

As he recoiled a hand clutched his ankle and sought to trip him. David kicked back and down with all his strength. There was one awful groan, and he staggered against the door and out.

There he paused, leaning against the wall to breathe.

He struck a match and lifted his foot to see where the hand had clutched him.

God! there was blood on his heel.

Then a great fear laid hold on him. A cry was suff-ocated in his breast by the panting of his heart.

He crept back to the kitchen door and listened.

Not a sound.

Fearfully he opened it a crack.

Silence of the tomb.

He banged it to. It opened behind him, and the fact lent wings to his feet.

He turned and plunged out into the night, and ran ran through the blackness for his life. And a great owl swooped softly by and hooted mockingly:

"For your life! For your life! For your life!"

PART V
OWD BOB O' KENMUIR

CHAPTER XXII

A MAN AND A MAID

IN the village even the Black Killer and the murder on
the Screes were forgotten in this new sensation. The
mystery in which the affair was wrapped, and the ig-
norance as to all its details, served to whet the general
interest. There had been a fight; M'Adam and the
Terror had been mauled; and David had disappeared—
those were the facts. But what was the origin of the
affray no one could say.

One or two of the Dalesmen had, indeed, a shrewd
suspicion. Tupper looked guilty; Jem Burton muttered,
"I knoo hoo 'twould be"; while as for Long Kirby, he vanished entirely not to reappear till three months had sped.

Injured as he had been, M'Adam was yet sufficiently
recovered to appear in the Sylvester Arms on the Saturday
following the battle. He entered the tap-room silently
with never a word to a soul; one arm was in a sling and
his head bandaged. He eyed every man present critically

and all, except Tammas, who was brazen, and Jim
Mason, who was innocent, fidgeted beneath the stare.
Maybe it was well for Long Kirby he was not there.

"Onythin' the matter?" asked Jem, at length, rather
lamely, in view of the plain evidences of battle.

"Na, na; naethin' oot o' the ordinar'," the little
man replied, giggling. "Only David set on me, and me
sleepin'. And," with a shrug, "here I am noo." He
sat down, wagging his bandaged head and grinning.
"Ye see he's sae playfu', is Davie. He wangs ye o'er the
head wi' a chair, kicks ye in the jaw, stamps on yer wame,
and all as merry as May." And nothing further could
they get from him, except that if David reappeared it was
his [M'Adam's] firm resolve to hand him over to the police
for attempted parricide.

"'Brutal assault on an auld man by his son!' 'Twill
look well in the *Argus*; he! he! They couldna let him
aff under two years, I'm thinkin'."

M'Adam's version of the affair was received with quiet
incredulity. The general verdict was that he had brought
his punishment entirely on his own head. Tammas, indeed,
who was always rude when he was not witty, and, in fact,
the difference between the two things is only one of degree,
told him straight: "It served yo' well reet. An' I nob'
but wish he'd made an end to yo'."

"He did his best, puir lad," M'Adam reminded him
gently.

"We've had enough o' yo'," continued the uncom-
promising old man. "I'm fair grieved he didna slice yer
throat while he was at it."

At that M'Adam raised his eyebrows, stared, and then
broke into a low whistle.

"That's it, is it?" he muttered, as though a new light was dawning on him. "Ah, noo I see."

The days passed on. There was still no news of the missing one, and Maggie's face became pitifully white and haggard.

Of course she did not believe that David had attempted to murder his father, desperately tried as she knew he had been. Still, it was a terrible thought to her that he might at any moment be arrested; and her girlish imagination was perpetually conjuring up horrid pictures of a trial, conviction, and the things that followed.

Then Sam'l started a wild theory that the little man had murdered his son, and thrown the mangled body down the dry well at the Grange. The story was, of course, preposterous, and, coming from such a source, might well have been discarded with the ridicule it deserved. Yet it served to set the cap on the girl's fears; and she resolved, at whatever cost, to visit the Grange, beard M'Adam, and discover whether he could not or would not allay her gnawing apprehension.

Her intent she concealed from her father, knowing well that were she to reveal it to him, he would gently but firmly forbid the attempt; and on an afternoon some fortnight after David's disappearance, choosing her opportunity, she picked up a shawl, threw it over her head, and fled with palpitating heart out of the farm and down the slope to the Wastrel.

The little plank-bridge rattled as she tripped across it; and she fled faster lest any one should have heard and come to look. And, indeed, at the moment it rattled again behind her, and she started guiltily round. It proved, however, to be only Owd Bob, sweeping after, and she was glad.

"Comin' wi' me, lad?" she asked as the old dog cantered up, thankful to have that gray protector with her.

Round Langholm now fled the two conspirators; over the summer-clad lower slopes of the Pike, until, at length, they reached the Stony Bottom. Down the bramble-covered bank of the ravine the girl slid; picked her way from stone to stone across the streamlet tinkling in that rocky bed; and scrambled up the opposite bank.

At the top she halted and looked back. The smoke from Kenmuir was winding slowly up against the sky; to her right the low gray cottages of the village cuddled in the bosom of the Dale; far away over the Marches towered the gaunt Scaur; before her rolled the swelling slopes of the Muir Pike; while behind—she glanced timidly over her shoulder—was the hill, at the top of which squatted the Grange, lifeless, cold, scowling.

Her heart failed her. In her whole life she had never spoken to M'Adam. Yet she knew him well enough from all David's accounts—ay, and hated him for David's sake. She hated him and feared him, too; feared him mortally—this terrible little man. And, with a shudder, she recalled the dim face at the window, and thought of his notorious hatred of her father. But even M'Adam could hardly harm a girl coming, broken-hearted, to seek her lover. Besides, was not Owd Bob with her?

And, turning, she saw the old dog standing a little way up the hill, looking back at her as though he wondered why she waited. "Am I not enough?" the faithful gray eyes seemed to say.

"Lad, I'm fear'd," was her answer to the unspoken question.

Yet that look determined her. She clenched her little teeth, drew the shawl about her, and set off running up the hill.

Soon the run dwindled to a walk, the walk to a crawl, and the crawl to a halt. Her breath was coming painfully, and her heart pattered against her side like the beatings of an imprisoned bird. Again her gray guardian looked up, encouraging her forward.

"Keep close, lad," she whispered, starting forward afresh. And the old dog ranged up beside her, shoving into her skirt, as though to let her feel his presence.

So they reached the top of the hill; and the house stood before them, grim, unfriendly.

The girl's face was now quite white, yet set; the resemblance to her father was plain to see. With lips compressed and breath quick-coming, she crossed the threshold, treading softly as though in a house of the dead. There she paused and lifted a warning finger at her companion, bidding him halt without; then she turned to the door on the left of the entrance and tapped.

She listened, her head buried in the shawl, close to the wood panelling. There was no answer; she could only hear the drumming of her heart.

She knocked again. From within came the scraping of a chair cautiously shoved back, followed by a deep-mouthed cavernous growl.

Her heart stood still, but she turned the handle and entered, leaving a crack open behind.

On the far side the room a little man was sitting. His head was swathed in dirty bandages, and a bottle was on the table beside him. He was leaning forward; his face was gray, and there was a stare of naked horror in his eyes. One hand grasped the great dog who stood at his side, with yellow teeth glinting, and muzzle hideously wrinkled; with the other he pointed a palsied finger at her.

"Ma God! wha are ye?" he cried hoarsely.

The girl stood hard against the door, her fingers still on the handle; trembling like an aspen at the sight of that uncannie pair.

That look in the little man's eyes petrified her: the swollen pupils; lashless lids, yawning wide; the broken range of teeth in that gaping mouth, froze her very soul. Rumours of the man's insanity tided back on her memory.

"I'm—I——" the words came in trembling gasps.

At the first utterance, however, the little man's hand dropped; he leant back in his chair and gave a soul-bursting sigh of relief.

No woman had crossed that threshold since his wife died; and, for a moment, when first the girl had entered silent-footed, aroused from dreaming of the long ago, he had thought this shawl-clad figure with the pale face and peeping hair no earthly visitor; the spirit, rather, of one he had loved long since and lost, come to reproach him with a broken troth.

"Speak up, I canna hear," he said, in tones mild compared with those last wild words.

"I—I'm Maggie Moore," the girl quavered.

"Moore! Maggie Moore, d'ye say?" he cried, half rising from his chair, a flush of colour sweeping across his face, "the dochter o' James Moore?" He paused for an answer, glowering at her; and she shrank, trembling, against the door.

The little man leant back in his chair. Gradually a grim smile crept across his countenance.

"Weel, Maggie Moore," he said, half-amused, "ony gate ye're a good plucked un."   And his wizened countenance looked at her almost kindly from beneath its dirty crown of bandages.

At that the girl's courage returned with a rush. After all this little man was not so very terrible. Perhaps he would be kind. And in the relief of the moment, the blood swept back into her face.

There was not to be peace yet, however. The blush was still hot upon her cheeks, when she caught the patter of soft steps in the passage without. A dark muzzle flecked with gray pushed in at the crack of the door; two anxious gray eyes followed.

Before she could wave him back, Red **Wull had marked** the intruder. With a roar he tore himself from his master's restraining hand, and dashed across the room.

"Back, Bob!" screamed Maggie, and the dark head withdrew. The door slammed with a crash as the great dog flung himself against it, and Maggie was hurled, breathless and white-faced, into a corner.

M'Adam was on his feet, pointing with a shrivelled finger, his face diabolical.

"Did you bring him? Did you bring *that* to ma door?"

Maggie huddled in the corner in a palsy of trepidation. Her eyes gleamed big and black in the white face peering from the shawl. Red Wull was now beside her snarling horribly. With nose to the bottom of the door and busy paws he was trying to get out; while, on the other side, Owd Bob, snuffling also at the crack, scratched and pleaded to get in. Only two miserable wooden inches separated the pair.

"I brought him to protect me. I—I was afraid."

M'Adam sat down and laughed abruptly.

"Afraid! I wonder ye were na afraid to bring him here. It's the first time iver he's set foot on ma land, and 't had best be the last." He turned to the great dog. "Wullie, Wullie, wad ye?" he called. "Come here. Lay ye doon—so—under ma chair—good lad. Noo's no the time to settle wi' him"—nodding toward the door. "We can wait for that, Wullie; we can wait." Then, turning to Maggie, "Gin ye want him to mak' a show at the Trials two months hence, he'd best not come here agin. Gin he does, he'll no leave ma land alive; Wullie'll see to that. Noo, what is 't ye want o' me?"

The girl in the corner, scared almost out of her senses by this last occurrence, remained dumb.

M'Adam marked her hesitation, and grinned sardonically.

"I see hoo 'tis," said he; "yer dad's sent ye. Aince before he wanted somethin' o' me, and did he come to fetch it himself like a man? Not he. He sent the son to rob the father." Then, leaning forward in his chair and glaring at the girl, "Ay, and mair than that! The night the lad set on me he cam'"—with hissing emphasis—"straight from Kenmuir!" He paused and stared at her intently, and she was still dumb before him. "Gin I'd ben killed, Wullie'd ha' bin disqualified from competin' for the Cup. With Adam M'Adam's Red Wull oot o' the way—noo d'ye see? Noo d'ye onderstan'?"

She did not, and he saw it and was satisfied. What he had been saying she neither knew nor cared. She only remembered the object of her mission; she only saw before her the father of the man she loved; and a wave of emotion surged up in her breast.

She advanced timidly toward him, holding out her hands.

"Eh, Mr. M'Adam," she pleaded, "I come to ask ye after David." The shawl had slipped from her head, and lay loose upon her shoulders; and she stood before him with her sad face, her pretty hair all tossed, and her eyes big with unshed tears—a touching suppliant.

"Will ye no tell me wheer he is? I'd not ask it, I'd not :rouble yo', but I've bin waitin' a waefu' while, it seems, and I'm wearyin' for news o' him."

The little man looked at her curiously. "Ah, noo 1 mind me,"—this to himself. "You're the lass as is thinkin' o' marryin' him?"

"We're promised," the girl answered simply.

"Weel," the other remarked, "as I said afore, ye're a good plucked un." Then, in a tone in which, despite the cynicism, a certain indefinable sadness was blended, "Gin he mak's you as good husband as he mad' son to me, ye'll ha' made a maist remairkable match, my dear."

Maggie fired in a moment.

"A good feyther makes a good son," she answered almost pertly; and then, with infinite tenderness, "and I'm prayin' a good wife'll make a good husband."

He smiled scoffingly.

"I'm feared that'll no help ye much," he said.

But the girl never heeded this last sneer, so set was she on her purpose. She had heard of the one tender place in the heart of this little man with the tired face and mocking tongue, and she resolved to attain her end by appealing to it.

"Yo' loved a lass yo'sel' aince, Mr. M'Adam," she

said. "Hoo would yo' ha' felt had she gone away and left yo'? Yo'd ha' bin mad; yo' know yo' would. And, Mr. M'Adam, I love the lad yer wife loved." She was kneeling at his feet now with both hands on his knees, looking up at him. Her sad face and quivering lips pleaded for her more eloquently than any words.

The little man was visibly touched.

"Ay, ay, lass, that's enough," he said, trying to avoid those big beseeching eyes which would not be avoided.

"Will ye no tell me?" she pleaded.

"I canna tell ye, lass, for why, I dinna ken," he answered querulously. In truth, he was moved to the heart by her misery.

The girl's last hopes were dashed. She had played her last card and failed. She had clung with the fervour of despair to this last resource, and now it was torn from her. She had hoped, and now there was no hope. In the anguish of her disappointment she remembered that this was the man who, by his persistent cruelty, had driven her love into exile.

She rose to her feet and stood back.

"Nor ken, nor care!" she cried bitterly.

At the words all the softness fled from the little man's face.

"Ye do me a wrang, lass; ye do indeed," he said, looking up at her with an assumed ingenuousness which, had she known him better, would have warned her to beware. "Gin I kent where the lad was I'd be the vairy first to let you, and the p'lice, ken it too; eh, Wullie! he! he!" He chuckled at his wit and rubbed his knees, regardless of the contempt blazing in the girl's face.

"I canna tell ye where he is now, but ye'd aiblins care

to hear o' when I saw him last." He turned his chair the better to address her. "'Twas like so: I was sittin' in this vairy chair it was, asleep, when he crep' up behind an' lep' on ma back. I knew naethin' o't till I found masel' on the floor an' him kneelin' on me. I saw by the look on him he was set on finishin' me, so I said——"

The girl waved her hand at him, superbly disdainful.

"Yo' ken yo're lyin', ivery word o't," she cried.

The little man hitched his trousers, crossed his legs, and yawned.

"An honest lee for an honest purpose is a matter ony man may be proud of, as you'll ken by the time you're my years, ma lass."

The girl slowly crossed the room. At the door she turned.

"Then ye'll no tell me wheer he is?" she asked with a heart-breaking trill in her voice.

"On ma word, lass, I dinna ken," he cried half passionately.

"On your word, Mr. M'Adam!" she said with a quiet scorn in her voice that might have stung Iscariot.

The little man spun round in his chair, an angry red dyeing his cheeks. In another moment he was suave and smiling again.

"I canna tell ye where he is noo," he said, unctuously; "but aiblins, I could let ye know where' hes gaein' to."

"Can yo'? will yo'?" cried the simple girl all unsuspecting. In a moment she was across the room and at his knees.

"Closer, and I'll whisper." The little ear, peeping from its nest of brown, was tremblingly approached to his lips. The little man leant forward and whispered one short.

sharp word, then sat back, grinning, to watch the effect of his disclosure.

He had his revenge, an unworthy revenge on such a victim. And, watching the girl's face, the cruel disappointment merging in the heat of her indignation, he had yet enough nobility to regret his triumph.

She sprang from him as though he were unclean.

"An' yo' his father!" she cried, in burning tones.

She crossed the room, and at the door paused. Her face was white again and she was quite composed.

"If David did strike you, you drove him to it," she said, speaking in calm, gentle accents. "Yo' know, none so well, whether yo've bin a good feyther to him, and him no mither, poor laddie! Whether yo've bin to him what she'd ha' had yo' be. Ask yer conscience, Mr. M'Adam. An' if he was a wee aggravatin' at times, had he no reason? He'd a heavy cross to bear, had David, and yo' know best if yo' helped to ease it for him."

The little man pointed to the door; but the girl paid no heed.

"D'yo' think when yo' were cruel to him, jeerin' and fleerin', he never felt it, because he was too proud to show ye? He'd a big saft heart, had David, beneath the varnish. Mony's the time when mither was alive, I've seen him throw himsel' into her arms, sobbin', and cry, 'Eh, if I had but mither! 'Twas different when mither was alive; he was kinder to me then. An' noo I've no one; I'm alone.' An' he'd sob and sob in mither's arms, and she, weepin' hersel', would comfort him, while he, wee laddie, would no be comforted, cryin' broken-like, 'There's none to care for me noo; I'm alone. Mither's left me and eh! I'm prayin' to be wi' her!'"

The clear, girlish voice shook. M'Adam, sitting with face averted, waved to her, mutely ordering her to be gone. But she held on, gentle, sorrowful, relentless.

"An' what'll yo' say to his mither when yo meet her, as yo' must soon noo, and she asks yo': 'An what o' David? What o' th' lad I left wi' yo', Adam, to guard and keep for me, faithful and true, till this Day?' And then yo'll ha' to speak the truth, God's truth; and yo'll ha' to answer: 'Sin' the day yo' left me I niver said a kind word to the lad. I niver bore wi' him, and niver tried to. And in the end I drove him by persecution to try and murder me'. Then maybe she'll look at yo'—yo' best ken hoo—and she'll say: 'Adam, Adam! is this what I deserved fra yo'?'"

The gentle, implacable voice ceased. The girl turned and slipped softly out of the room; and M'Adam was left alone to his thoughts and his dead wife's memory.

"Mither and father, baith! Mither and father, baith!" rang remorselessly in his ears.

CHAPTER XXIII

TH' OWD UN

THE Black Killer still cursed the land. Sometimes there would be a cessation in the crimes; then a shepherd, going his rounds would notice his sheep herding together, packing in unaccustomed squares; a raven, gorged to the crop, would rise before him and flap wearily away, and he would come upon the murderer's latest victim.

The Dalesmen were in despair, so utterly futile had their efforts been. There was no proof; no hope, no apparent probability that the end was near. As for the Tailless Tyke, the only piece of evidence against him had flown with David, who, as it chanced, had divulged what he had seen to no man.

The £100 reward offered had brought no issue. The police had done nothing. The Special Commissioner had been equally successful. After the affair in the Scoop the Killer never ran a risk, yet never missed a chance.

Then, as a last resource, Jim Mason made his attempt. He took a holiday from his duties and disappeared into the wilderness. Three days and three nights no man saw him. On the morning of the fourth he reappeared, haggard, unkempt, a furtive look haunting his eyes, sullen for once, irritable, who had never been irritable before—to confess his failure. Cross-examined further, he answered with unaccustomed fierceness: "I seed nowt, I tell ye. Who's the liar as said I did?"

But that night his missus heard him in his sleep conning over something to himself in slow, fearful whisper, "Two on 'em; one ahint t'other. The first big—bull-like; t'ither——" At which point Mrs. Mason smote him a smashing blow in the ribs, and he woke in a sweat, crying terribly, "Who said I seed——"

.　　　.　　　.　　　.

The days were slipping away; the summer was hot upon the land, and with it the Black Killer was forgotten; David was forgotton; everything sank into oblivion before the all-absorbing interest of the coming Dale trials.

The long-anticipated battle for the Shepherds' Trophy was looming close; soon everything that hung upon the issue of that struggle would be decided finally. For ever the justice of Th' Owd Un' claim to his proud title would be settled. If he won, he won outright—a thing unprecedented in the annals of the Cup; if he won, the place of Owd Bob o' Kenmuir as first in his profession was assured for all time. Above all, it was the last event in the six years' struggle 'twixt Red and Gray. It was the last time those two great rivals would meet in battle.

The supremacy of one would be decided once and for all.
For win or lose, it was the last public appearance of the
Gray Dog of Kenmuir.

And as every hour brought the great day nearer, nothing
else was talked of in the country-side. The heat of the
Dalesmen's enthusiasm was only intensified by the fever
of their apprehension. Many a man would lose more
than he cared to contemplate were Th' Owd Un beat.
But he'd not be! Nay; owd, indeed, he was—two years
older than his great rival; there were a hundred risks, a
hundred chances; still: "What's the odds agin Owd
Bob o' Kenmuir? I'm takin' 'em. Who'll lay agin Th'
Owd Un?"

And with the air saturated with this perpetual talk of
the old dog, these everlasting references to his certain
victory; his ears drumming with the often boast that the
gray dog was the best in the North, M'Adam became the
silent, ill-designing man of six months since—morose,
brooding, suspicious, muttering of conspiracy, plotting
revenge.

The scenes at the Sylvester Arms were replicas of those
of previous years. Usually the little man sat isolated in a
far corner, silent and glowering, with Red Wull at his
feet. Now and then he burst into a paroxysm of insane
giggling, slapping his thigh, and muttering, "Ay, it's
likely they'll beat us, Wullie. Yet aiblins there's a wee
somethin'—a somethin' we ken and they dinna, Wullie,—
eh! Wullie, he! he!" And sometimes he would leap to his
feet and address his pot-house audience, appealing to them
passionately, satirically, tearfully, as the mood might be
on him; and his theme was always the same: James
Moore, Owd Bob, the Cup, and the plots agin him and his

Wullie; and always he concluded with that hint of the
surprise to come.

Meantime, there was no news of David; he had gone as
utterly as a ship foundered in mid-Atlantic. Some said
he'd 'listed; some, that he'd gone to sea. And "So he
'as," corroborated Sam'l, "floatin', 'eels uppards."

With no gleam of consolation, Maggie's misery was such
as to rouse compassion in all hearts. She went no longer
blithely singing about her work; and all the springiness
had fled from her gait. The people of Kenmuir vied with
one another in their attempts to console their young
mistress.

.   .   .   .   .

Maggie was not the only one in whose life David's
absence had created a void. Last as he would have been
to own it, M'Adam felt acutely the boy's loss. It may
have been he missed the ever-present butt; it may have
been a nobler feeling. Alone with Red Wull, too late he
felt his loneliness. Sometimes, sitting in the kitchen by
himself, thinking of the past, he experienced sharp pangs
of remorse; and this was all the more the case after
Maggie's visit. Subsequent to that day the little man,
to do him justice, was never known to hint by word or
look an ill thing of his enemy's daughter. Once, indeed,
when Melia Ross was drawing on a dirty imagination with
Maggie for subject, M'Adam shut her up with: "Ye're
a maist amazin' big liar, Melia Ross."

Yet, though for the daughter he had now no evil thought
his hatred for the father had never been so uncompromis-
ing.

He grew reckless in his assertions. His life was one
long threat against James Moore's. Now he openly

stated his conviction that, on the eventful night of the fight, James Moore, with object easily discernible, had egged David on to murder him.

"Then why don't yo' go and tell him so, yo' muckle liar?" roared Tammas at last, enraged to madness.

"I will!" said M'Adam. And he did.

.   .   .   .   .

It was on the day preceding the great summer sheep fair at Grammoch-town that he fulfilled his vow.

That is always a big field-day at Kenmuir; and on this occasion James Moore and Owd Bob had been up and working on the Pike from the rising of the sun. Throughout the straggling lands of Kenmuir the Master went with his untiring adjutant, rounding up, cutting out, drafting. It was already noon when the flock started from the yard.

On the gate by the stile, as the party came up, sat M'Adam.

"I've a word to say to you, James Moore," he announced, as the Master approached.

"Say it then, and quick. I've no time to stand gossipin' here, if yo' have," said the Master.

M'Adam strained forward till he nearly toppled off the gate.

"Queer thing, James Moore, you should be the only one to escape this Killer."

"Yo' forget yoursel', M'Adam."

"Ay, there's me," acquiesced the little man. "But you—hoo d'yo' 'count for *your* luck?"

James Moore swung round and pointed proudly at the gray dog, now patrolling round the flock.

"There's my luck!" he said.

M'Adam laughed unpleasantly.

"So I thought," he said, "so I thought! And I s'pose ye're thinkin' that yer luck," nodding at the gray dog, "will win you the Cup for certain a month hence."

"I hope so!" said the Master.

"Strange if he should not after all," mused the little man.

James Moore eyed him suspiciously.

"What d'yo' mean?" he asked sternly.

M'Adam shrugged his shoulders.

"There's mony a slip 'twixt Cup and lip, that's a'. I was thinkin' some mischance might come to him."

The Master's eyes flashed dangerously. He recalled the many rumours he had heard, and the attempt on the old dog early in the year.

"I canna think ony one would be coward enough to murder him," he said drawing himself up.

M'Adam leant forward. There was a nasty glitter in his eye, and his face was all a-tremble.

"Ye'd no think ony one'd be cooard enough to set the son to murder the father. Yet some one did—set the lad on to 'sassinate me. He failed at me, and next, I suppose, he'll try at Wullie!" There was a flush on the sallow face, and a vindictive ring in the thin voice. "One way or t'ither, fair or foul, Wullie or me, ain or baith, has got to go afore Cup Day, eh, James Moore! eh?"

The Master put his hand on the latch of the gate, "That'll do, M'Adam," he said. "I'll stop to hear no more, else I might get angry wi' yo'. Noo git off this gate, yo're trespassin' as 'tis."

He shook the gate. M'Adam tumbled off, and went sprawling into the sheep clustered below. Picking himself up, he dashed on through the flock, waving his arms, kicking fantastically, and scattering confusion everywhere.

"Just wait till I'm thro' wi' 'em, will yo'?" shouted the Master, seeing the danger.

It was a request which, according to the etiquette of shepherding, one man was bound to grant another. But M'Adam rushed on regardless, dancing and gesticulating. Save for the lightning vigilance of Owd Bob, the flock must have broken.

"I think yo' might ha' waited!" remonstrated the Master, as the little man burst his way through.

"Noo, I've forgot somethin'!" the other cried, and back he started as he had gone.

It was more than human nature could tolerate.

"Bob, keep him off!"

A flash of teeth; a blaze of gray eyes; and the old dog had leapt forward to oppose the little man's advance.

"Shift oot o' ma light!" cried he, striving to dash past. "Hold him, lad!"

And hold him the old dog did, while his master opened the gate and put the flock through, the opponents dodging in front of one another like opposing three-quarter-backs at the Rugby game.

"Oot o' ma path, or I'll strike!" shouted the little man in a fury, as the last sheep passed through the gate.

"I'd not," warned the Master.

"But I will!" yelled M'Adam; and, darting forward as the gate swung to, struck furiously at his opponent.

He missed, and the gray dog charged at him like a mail-train.

"Hi! James Moore——" but over he went like a toppled wheelbarrow, while the old dog turned again, raced at the gate, took it magnificently in his stride, and galloped up the lane after his master.

At M'Adam's yell, James Moore had turned.

"Served yo' properly!" he called back. "He'll larn ye yet it's not wise to tamper wi' a gray dog or his sheep. Not the first time he's downed ye, I'm thinkin'!"

The little man raised himself painfully to his elbow and crawled toward the gate. The Master, up the lane, could hear him cursing as he dragged himself. Another moment and a head was poked through the bars of the gate, and a devilish little face looked after him.

"Downed me, by ——, he did!" the little man cried passionately. "I owed ye baith somethin' before this, and noo, by ——, I owe ye somethin' more. An' mind ye, Adam M'Adam pays his debts!"

"I've heard the contrary," the Master replied drily, and turned away up the lane toward the Marches.

CHAPTER XXIV

A SHOT IN THE NIGHT

IT WAS only three short weeks before Cup Day that one afternoon Jim Mason brought a letter to Kenmuir. James Moore opened it as the postman still stood in the door.

It was from Long Kirby—still in retirement—begging him for mercy's sake to keep Owd Bob safe within doors at nights; at all events till after the great event was over. For Kirby knew, as did every Dalesman, that the old dog slept in the porch, between the two doors of the house, of which the outer was only loosely closed by a chain, so that the ever-watchful guardian might slip in and out and go his rounds at any moment of the night.

This was how the smith concluded his ill-spelt note: "Look out for M'Adam i tell you i *know* hel tri at thowd un afore cup day—failin im you. if the ole dog's bete i'm a ruined man i say so for the luv o' God keep yer eyes wide."

The Master read the letter, and handed it to the postman, who perused it carefully.

"I tell yo' what," said Jim at length, speaking with an earnestness that made the other stare, "I wish yo'd do what he asks yo': keep Th' Owd Un in o' nights, I mean, just for the present."

The Master shook his head and laughed, tearing the etter to pieces.

"Nay," said he; "M'Adam or no M'Adam, Cup or no Cup, Th' Owd Un has the run o' ma land same as he's had since a puppy. Why, Jim, the first night I shut him up that night the Killer comes, I'll lay."

The postman turned wearily away, and the Master stood looking after him, wondering what had come of late to his former cheery friend.

Those two were not the only warnings James Moore received. During the weeks immediately preceding the Trials, the danger signal was perpetually flaunted beneath his nose.

Twice did Watch, the black cross-bred chained in the straw-yard, hurl a brazen challenge on the night air. Twice did the Master, with lantern, Sam'l and Owd Bob, sally forth and search every hole and corner on the premises—to find nothing. One of the dairy-maids gave notice, avowing that the farm was haunted; that, on several occasions in the early morning, she had seen a bogie flitting down the slope to the Wastrel—a sure portent, Sam'l declared, of an approaching death in the house. While once a shearer, coming up from the village, reported having seen, in the twilight of dawn, a little ghostly figure, haggard and startled, stealing silently from tree to tree in the larch-copse by the lane. The Master, however, irritated by these constant alarms, dismissed the story summarily.

"One thing I'm sartin o'," said he. "There's not a critter moves on Kenmuir at nights but Th' Owd Un knows it."

Yet, even as he said it, a little man, draggled, weary-eyed, smeared with dew and dust, was limping in at the door of a house barely a mile away. "Nae luck, Wullie, curse it!" he cried throwing himself into a chair, and addressing some one who was not there—"nae luck. An' yet I'm sure o't as I am that there's a Godin heaven."

. . . . .

M'Adam had become an old man of late. But little more than fifty, yet he looked to have reached man's allotted years. His sparse hair was quite white; his body shrunk and bowed; and his thin hand shook like an aspen as it groped to the familiar bottle.

In another matter, too, he was altogether changed. Formerly, whatever his faults, there had been no harder-working man in the country-side. At all hours, in all weathers, you might have seen him with his gigantic attendant going his rounds. Now all that was different: he never put his hand to the plough, and with none to help him the land was left wholly untended; so that men said that, of a surety, there would be a farm to let on the March Mere Estate come Michaelmas.

Instead of working, the little man sat all day in the kitchen at home, brooding over his wrongs, and brewing vengeance. Even the Sylvester Arms knew him no more; for he stayed where he was with his dog and his bottle. Only, when the shroud of night had come down to cover him, he slipped out and away on some errand on which not even Red Wull accompanied him.

.   .   .   .   .

So the time glided on, till the Sunday before the Trials came round.

All that day M'Adam sat in his kitchen, drinking, muttering, hatching revenge.

"Curse it, Wullie! curse it! The time's slippin'—slippin'—slippin'! Thursday next—but three days mair! and I haena the proof—I haena the proof!"—and he rocked to and fro, biting his nails in the agony of his impotence.

All day long he never moved. Long after sunset he sat on; long after dark had eliminated the features of the room.

"They're all agin us, Wullie. It's you and I alane, lad. M'Adam's to be beat somehow, onyhow; and Moore's to win. So they've settled it, and so 'twill be—onless, Wullie, onless—but curse it! I've no the proof!"—and he hammered the table before him and stamped on the floor.

At midnight he rose, a mad, desperate plan looming through his fuddled brain.

"I swore I'd pay him, Wullie, and I will. If I hang for it I'll be even wi' him. I haena the proof, but I *know*—I *know!*" He groped his way to the mantelpiece with blind eyes and swirling brain. Reaching up with fumbling hands, he took down the old blunderbuss from above the fireplace.

"Wullie," he whispered, chuckling hideously, "Wullie, come on! You and I—he! he!" But the Tailless Tyke was not there.   At nightfall he had slouched silently out of the house on business he best wot of.   So his master crept out of the room alone—on tiptoe, still chuckling.

The cool night air refreshed him, and he stepped stealthily along, his quaint weapon over his shoulder: down the hill; across the Bottom; skirting the Pike; till he reached the plank-bridge over the Wastrel.

He crossed it safely, that Providence whose care is drunkards placing his footsteps.   Then he stole up the slope like a hunter stalking his prey.

Arrived at the gate, he raised himself cautiously, and peered over into the moonlit yard.   There was no sign or sound of living creature.   The little gray house slept peacefully in the shadow of the Pike, all unaware of the man with murder in his heart laboriously climbing the yard-gate.

The door of the porch was wide, the chain hanging limply down, unused; and the little man could see within, the moon shining on the iron studs of the inner door, and the blanket of him who should have slept there, *and did not.*

"He's no there, Wullie!   He's no there!"

He jumped down from the gate.   Throwing all caution to the winds, he reeled recklessly across the yard.   The drunken delirium of battle was on him.   The fever of anticipated victory flushed his veins.   At length he would take toll for the injuries of years.

Another moment, and he was in front of the good oak door, battering at it madly with clubbed weapon, yelling, dancing, screaming vengeance.

"Where is he?   What's he at?   Come and tell me that, James Moore!   Come doon, I say, ye coward! Come and meet me like a man!"

"'Scots wha hae wi' Wallace bled,
    Scots wham Bruce has aften led—
    Welcome to your gory bed
        Or to victorie!'"

The soft moonlight streamed down on the white-haired madman thundering at the door, screaming his war-song.

The quiet farmyard, startled from its sleep, awoke in an uproar. Cattle shifted in their stalls; horses whinnied; fowls chattered, aroused by the din and dull thudding of the blows: and above the rest, loud and piercing, the shrill cry of a terrified child.

Maggie, wakened from a vivid dream of David chasing the police, hurried a shawl around her, and in a minute had the baby in her arms and was comforting her—vaguely fearing the while that the police were after David.

James Moore flung open a window, and, leaning out, looked down on the dishevelled figure below him.

M'Adam heard the noise, glanced up, and saw his enemy. Straightway he ceased his attack on the door, and, running beneath the window, shook his weapon up at his foe.

"There ye are, are ye? Curse ye for a coward! curse ye for a liar! Come doon, I say, James Moore! Come doon —I daur ye to it! Aince and for a' let's settle oor account."

The Master, looking down from above, thought that at length the little man's brain had gone.

"What is't yo' want?" he asked as calmly as he could, hoping to gain time.

"What is't I want?" screamed the madman. "Hark to him! He crosses me in ilka thing; he plots agin me; he robs me o' ma Cup; he sets ma son agin me and pits him on to murder me! And in the end he——"

"Coom, then coom! I'll——"

"Gie me back the Cup ye stole, James Moore! **Gie me** back ma son ye've took from me!   And there's anither thing.   What's yer gray dog doin'?   Where's yer——"

The Master interposed again:

"I'll coom doon and talk things over wi' yo'," he said soothingly.   But before he could withdraw, M'Adam had jerked his weapon to his shoulder and aimed it full at his enemy's head.

The threatened man looked down the gun's great quivering mouth, wholly unmoved.

"Yo' mon hold it steadier, little mon, if yo'd hit!" he said grimly.   "There, I'll coom help yo'!"   He withdrew slowly; and all the time was wondering where the gray dog was.

In another moment he was downstairs, undoing the bolts and bars of the door.   On the other side stood M'Adam, his blunderbuss at his shoulder, his finger trembling on the trigger, waiting.

"Hi, Master!   Stop, or yo're dead!" roared a voice from the loft on the other side the yard.

"Feyther! feyther! git yo' back!" screamed Maggie, who saw it all from the window above the door.

Their cries were too late!   The blunderbuss went off with a roar, belching out a storm of sparks and smoke. The shot peppered the door like hail, and the whole yard seemed for a moment wrapped in flame.

"Aw! oh! ma gummy!   A'm waounded!   A'm a goner! A'm shot! 'Elp! Murder! Eh! Oh!" bellowed a lusty voice—and it was not James Moore's.

The little man, the cause of the uproar, lay quite still with another figure standing over him.   As he had stood finger on trigger, waiting for that last bolt to be drawn, a gray form, shooting whence no one knew, had suddenly and silently attacked him from behind, and jerked him backward to the ground. With the shock of the fall the blunderbuss had gone off.

The last bolt was thrown back with a clatter, and the Master emerged. In a glance he took in the whole scene: the fallen man; the gray dog; the still-smoking weapon.

"Yo', was't Bob lad?" he said. "I was wonderin' wheer yo' were. Yo' came just at the reet moment, as yo' aye do!" Then, in a loud voice, addressing the darkness: "Yo're not hurt, Sam'l Todd—I can tell that by yer noise; it was nob'but the shot off the door warmed yo'. Coom away doon and gie me a hand."

He walked up to M'Adam, who still lay gasping on the ground. The shock of the fall and recoil of the weapon had knocked the breath out of the little man's body; beyond that he was barely hurt.

The Master stood over his fallen enemy and looked sternly down at him.

"I've put up wi' more from you, M'Adam, than I would from ony other man," he said. "But this is too much—comin' here at night wi' loaded arms, scarin' the wimmen and childer oot o' their lives, and I can but think meanin' worse. If yo' were half a man I'd gie yo' the finest thrashin' iver yo' had in yer life. But, as yo' know well, I could no more hit yo' than I could a woman. Why yo've got this down on me yo' ken best. I niver did yo' or ony ither mon a harm. As to the Cup, I've got it and I'm goin' to do ma best to keep it—it's for yo' to win it from me if yo' can o' Thursday. As for what yo' say o David, yo' know it's a lie. And as for what yo're drivin' at wi' yer hints and mysteries, I've no more idee than a babe unborn. Noo I'm goin' to lock yo' up, yo're not safe abroad. I'm thinkin' I'll ha' to hand ye o'er to the p'lice."

With the help of Sam'l he half dragged, half supported the stunned little man across the yard; and shoved him into a tiny semi-subterraneous room, used for the storage of coal, at the end of the farm-buildings.

"Yo' think it over that side, ma lad," called the Master grimly, as he turned the key, "and I will this." And with that he retired to bed.

.   .   .   .   .

Early in the morning he went to release his prisoner. But he was a minute too late. For scuttling down the slope and away was a little black-begrimed, tottering figure with white hair blowing in the wind. The little man had broken away a wooden hatchment which covered a manhole in the wall of his prison-house, squeezed his small body through, and so escaped.

"Happen it's as well," thought the Master, watching the flying figure. Then, "Hi, Bob, lad!" he called; for the gray dog, ears back, tail streaming, was hurling down the slope after the fugitive.

On the bridge M'Adam turned, and, seeing his pursuer hot upon him, screamed, missed his footing, and fell with a loud splash into the stream—almost in that identical spot into which, years before, he had plunged voluntarily to save Red Wull.

On the bridge Owd Bob halted and looked down at the man struggling in the water below. He made a half move as though to leap in to the rescue of his enemy; then, seeing it was unnecessary, turned and trotted back to his master.

"Yo' nob 'but served him right, I'm thinkin'," said the Master. "Like as not he came here wi' the intent to mak' an end to yo'. Well, after Thursday, I pray God, we'll ha' peace. It's gettin' above a joke." The two turned back into the yard.

But down below them, along the edge of the stream, for the second time in this story, a little dripping figure was tottering homeward. The little man was crying—the hot tears mingling on his cheeks with the undried waters of the Wastrel—crying with rage, mortification, weariness.

CHAPTER XXV

THE SHEPHERDS' TROPHY

CUP Day.

It broke calm and beautiful, no cloud on the horizon, no threat of storm in the air; a fitting day on which the Shepherds' Trophy must be won outright.

And well it was so. For never since the founding of the Dale Trials had such a concourse been gathered together on the north bank of the Silver Lea. From the Highlands they came; from the far Campbell country; from the Peak; from the county of many acres; from all along the silver fringes of the Solway; assembling in that quiet corner of the earth to see the famous Gray Dog of Kenmuir fight his last great battle for the Shepherds' Trophy.

By noon the gaunt Scaur looked down on such a gathering as it had never seen. The paddock at the back of the Dalesman's Daughter was packed with a clammering, chattering multitude: animated groups of farmers; bevies of solid rustics; sharp-faced townsmen; loud-voiced bookmakers; giggling girls; amorous boys,—thrown together like toys in a sawdust bath; whilst here and there on the outskirts of the crowd, a lonely man and wise-faced dog, come from afar to wrest his proud title from the best sheep-dog in the North.

At the back of the enclosure was drawn up a formidable array of carts and carriages, varying as much in quality and character as did their owners. There was the squire's landau rubbing axle-boxes with Jem Burton's modest moke-cart; and there Viscount Birdsaye's flaring barouche side by side with the red-wheeled wagon of Kenmuir.

In the latter, Maggie, sad and sweet in her simple summer garb, leant over to talk to Lady Eleanour; while golden-haired wee Anne, delighted with the surging crowd around, trotted about the wagon, waving to her friends, and shouting from very joyousness.

Thick as flies clustered that motley assembly on the north bank of the Silver Lea. While on the other side the stream was a little group of judges, inspecting the course.

The line laid out ran thus: the sheep must first be found in the big enclosure to the right of the starting flag; then up the slope and away from the spectators; around a flag and obliquely down the hill again; through a gap in the wall; along the hillside, parallel to the Silver Lea; abruptly to the left through a pair of flags—the trickiest turn of them all; then down the slope to the pen, which was set up close to the bridge over the stream.

The proceedings began with the Local Stakes, won by Rob Saunderson's veteran, Shep. There followed the Open Juveniles, carried off by Ned Hoppin's young dog. It was late in the afternoon when, at length, the great event of the meeting was reached.

In the enclosure behind the Dalesman's Daughter the clamour of the crowd increased tenfold, and the yells of the bookmakers were redoubled.

"Walk up, gen'lemen, walk up! the ole firm! Rasper? Yessir—twenty to one bar two! Twenty to one bar two! Bob? What price, Bob? Even money, sir—no, not a penny longer, couldn't do it! Red Wull? 'oo says Red Wull?"

On the far side the stream is clustered about the starting flag the finest array of sheep-dogs ever seen together.

"I've never seen such a field, and I've seen fifty," is Parson Leggy's verdict.

There, beside the tall form of his master, stands Owd Bob o' Kenmuir, the observed of all. His silvery brush fans the air, and he holds his dark head high as he scans his challengers, proudly conscious that to-day will make or mar his fame. Below him, the mean-looking, smooth-coated black dog is the unbeaten Pip, winner of the re-nowned Cambrian Stakes at Llangollen—as many think the best of all the good dogs that have come from sheep-dotted Wales. Beside him that handsome sable collie, with the tremendous coat and slash of white on throat and face, is the famous MacCallum More, fresh from his victory at the Highland meeting. The cobby, brown dog, seeming of many breeds, is from the land o' the Tykes—Merry, on whom the Yorkshiremen are laying as though they loved him. And Jess, the wiry black-and-tan, is the favourite of the men of the Derwent and Dove. Tupper's big blue Rasper is there; Londesley's Lassie; and many more—too many to mention: big and small, grand and mean, smooth and rough—and not a bad dog there.

And alone, his back to the others, stands a little bowed,

conspicuous figure—Adam M'Adam; while the great dog beside him, a hideous incarnation of scowling defiance, is Red Wull, the Terror o' the Border.

The Tailless Tyke had already run up his fighting colours. For MacCallum More, going up to examine this forlorn great adversary, had conceived for him a violent antipathy, and, straightway, had spun at him with all the fury of the Highland cateran, who attacks first and explains afterward. Red Wull, forthwith, had turned on him with savage, silent gluttony; bob-tailed Rasper was racing up to join in the attack; and in another second the three would have been locked inseparably—but just in time M'Adam intervened.

One of the judges came hurrying up.

"Mr. M'Adam," he cried angrily, "if that brute of yours gets fighting again, hang me if I don't disqualify him! Only last year at the Trials he killed the young Cossack dog."

A dull flash of passion swept across M'Adam's face. "Come here, Wullie!" he called. "Gin yon Hielant tyke attacks ye agin, ye're to be disqualified."

He was unheeded. The battle for the Cup had begun— little Pip leading the dance.

On the opposite slope the babel had subsided now. Hucksters left their wares, and bookmakers their stools, to watch the struggle. Every eye was intent on the moving figures of man and dog and three sheep over the stream.

One after one the competitors ran their course and penned their sheep—there was no single failure. And all received their just meed of applause, save only Adam M'Adam's Red Wull.

Last of all, when Owd Bob trotted out to uphold his

title, there went up such a shout as made Maggie's wan cheeks to blush with pleasure, and wee Anne to scream right lustily.

His was an incomparable exhibition. Sheep should be humoured rather than hurried; coaxed rather than co-erced. And that sheep-dog has attained the summit of his art who subdues his own personality and leads his sheep in pretending to be led. Well might the bosoms of the Dalesmen swell with pride as they watched their favourite at his work; well might Tammas pull out that hackneyed phrase, "The brains of a mon and the way of a woman"; well might the crowd bawl their enthusiasm, and Long Kirby puff his cheeks and rattle the money in his trouser pockets.

But of this part it is enough to say that Pip, Owd Rob, and Red Wull were selected to fight out the struggle afresh.

The course was altered and stiffened. On the far side the stream it remained as before; up the slope; round a flag; down the hill again; through the gap in the wall; along the hillside; down through the two flags; turn; and to the stream again. But the pen was removed from its former position, carried over the bridge, up the near slope, and the hurdles put together at the very foot of the spectators.

The sheep had to be driven over the plank-bridge, and the penning done beneath the very nose of the crowd. A stiff course, if ever there was one; and the time allowed, ten short minutes.

The spectators hustled and elbowed in their endeavours to obtain a good position. And well they might; for

about to begin was the finest exhibition of sheep-handling any man there was ever to behold.

.   .   .   .   .

Evan Jones and little Pip led off.

Those two, who had won on many a hard-fought field, worked together as they had never worked before. Smooth and swift, like a yacht in Southampton Water; round the flag, through the gap, they brought their sheep. Down between the two flags—accomplishing right well that awkward turn; and back to the bridge.

There they stopped: the sheep would not face that narrow way. Once, twice, and again, they broke; and each time the gallant little Pip, his tongue out and tail quivering, brought them back to the bridge-head.

At length one faced it; then another, and—it was too late. Time was up. The judges signalled; and the Welshman called off his dog and withdrew.

Out of sight of mortal eye, in a dip of the ground, Evan Jones sat down and took the small dark head between his knees—and you may be sure the dog's heart was heavy as the man's. "We did our pest, Pip," he cried brokenly, "but we're peat—the first time ever we've been!"

.   .   .   .   .

No time to dally.

James Mcore and Owd Bob were off on their last run.

No applause this time; not a voice was raised; anxious faces; twitching fingers; the whole crowd tense as a stretched wire. A false turn, a wilful sheep, a cantankerous judge, and the gray dog would be beat. And not a man there but knew it.

Yet over the stream master and dog went about their husiness never so quiet, never so collected; for all the world as though they were rounding up a flock on the Muir Pike.

The old dog found his sheep in a twinkling and a wild, scared trio they proved. Rounding the first flag, one bright-eyed wether made a dash for the open. He was quick; but the gray dog was quicker: a splendid recover, and a sound like a sob from the watchers on the hill.

Down the slope they came for the gap in the wall. A little below the opening, James Moore took his stand to stop and turn them; while a distance behind his sheep loitered Owd Bob, seeming to follow rather than drive, yet watchful of every movement and anticipating it. On he came, one eye on his master, the other on his sheep; never hurrying them, never flurrying them, yet bringing them rapidly along.

No word was spoken; barely a gesture made; yet they worked, master and dog, like one divided.

Through the gap, along the hill parallel to the spectators, playing into one another's hands like men at polo.

A wide sweep for the turn at the flags, and the sheep wheeled as though at the word of command, dropped through them, and travelled rapidly for the bridge.

"Steady!" whispered the crowd.

"Steady, man!" muttered Parson Leggy.

"Hold 'em, for God's sake!" croaked Kirby huskily. "D——n! I knew it! I saw it coming!"

The pace down the hill had grown quicker—too quick. Close on the bridge the three sheep made an effort to break. A dash—and two were checked; but the third went away like the wind, and after him Owd Bob, a gray streak against the green.

Tammas was cursing silently; Kirby was white to the

lips; and in the stillness you could plainly hear the Dales-men's sobbing breath, as it fluttered in their throats.

"Gallop! they say he's old and slow!" muttered the Parson. "Dash! Look at that!" For the gray dog, racing like the nor'easter over the sea, had already retrieved the fugitive.

Man and dog were coaxing the three a step at a time toward the bridge.

One ventured—the others followed.

In the middle the leader stopped and tried to turn—and time was flying, flying, and the penning alone must take minutes. Many a man's hand was at his watch, but no one could take his eyes off the group below him to look.

"We're beat! I've won bet, Tammas!" groaned Sam'l (The two had a long-standing wager on the matter.) "I allus knoo hoo 'twould be. I allus told yo' th' owd tyke——" Then breaking into a bellow, his honest face crimson with enthusiasm: "Come on, Master! Good for yo', Owd Un! Yon's the style!"

For the gray dog had leapt on the back of the hindmost sheep; it had surged forward against the next, and they were over, and making up the slope amidst a thunder of applause.

At the pen it was a sight to see shepherd and dog working together. The Master, his face stern and a little whiter than its wont, casting forward with both hands, herding the sheep in; the gray dog, his eyes big and bright, dropping to hand; crawling and creeping, closer and closer.

"They're in!—Nay—Ay—dang me! Stop 'er. Good Owd Un! Ah-h-h, they're in!" And the last sheep reluctantly passed through—on the stroke of time.

A roar went up from the crowd; Maggie's white face turned pink; and the Dalesmen mopped their wet brows. The mob surged forward, but the stewards held them back.

"Back, please! Don't encroach! M'Adam's to come!"

From the far bank the little man watched the scene. His coat and cap were off, and his hair gleamed white in the sun; his sleeves were rolled up; and his face was twitching but set as he stood—ready.

The hubbub over the stream at length subsided. One of the judges nodded to him.

"Noo, Wullie—noo or niver!—'Scots wha hae'!"—and they were off.

"Back, gentlemen! Back! He's off—he's coming! M'Adam's coming!"

They might well shout and push; for the great dog was on to his sheep before they knew it; and they went away with a rush, with him right on their backs. Up the slope they swept and round the first flag, already galloping. Down the hill for the gap, and M'Adam was flying ahead to turn them. But they passed him like a hurricane, and Red Wull was in front with a rush and turned them alone.

"M'Adam wins! Five to four M'Adam! I lay agin Owd Bob!" rang out a clear voice in the silence.

Through the gap they rattled, ears back, feet twinkling like the wings of driven grouse.

"He's lost 'em! They'll break! They're away!" was the cry.

Sam'l was half up the wheel of the Kenmuir wagon; every man was on his toes; ladies were standing in their carriages; even Jim Mason's face flushed with momentary excitement.

The sheep were tearing along the hillside, all together,

like a white scud. After them, galloping like a Waterloo winner, raced Red Wull. And last of all, leaping over the ground like a demoniac, making not for the two flags, but the plank-bridge, the white-haired figure of M'Adam.

"He's beat! The Killer's beat!" roared a strident voice.

"M'Adam wins! Five to four M'Adam! I lay agin Owd Bob!" rang out the clear reply.

Red Wull was now racing parallel to the fugitives and above them. All four were travelling at a terrific rate; while the two flags were barely twenty yards in front, below the line of flight and almost parallel to it. To effect the turn a change of direction must be made almost through a right angle.

"He's beat! he's beat! M'Adam's beat! Can't make it nohow!" was the roar.

From over the stream a yell—

"Turn 'em, Wullie!"

At the word the great dog swerved down on the flying three. They turned, still at the gallop, like a troop of cavalry, and dropped, clean and neat, between the flags; and down to the stream they rattled, passing M'Adam on the way as though he was standing.

"Weel done, Wullie!" came the scream from the far bank; and from the crowd went up an involuntary burst of applause.

"Ma word!"

"Did yo' see that?"

"By gob!"

It was a turn, indeed, of which the smartest team in the galloping horse-gunners might well have been proud. A shade later, and they must have overshot the mark; a shade sooner, and a miss.

"He's not been two minutes so far. We're beaten—don't you think so, Uncle Leggy?" asked Muriel Sylvester, looking up piteously into the parson's face.

"It's not what I think, my dear; it's what the judges think," the parson replied; and what he thought their verdict would be was plainly writ on his face for all to read.

Right on to the centre of the bridge the leading sheep galloped and—stopped abruptly.

Up above in the crowd there was utter silence; staring eyes; rigid fingers. The sweat was dripping off Long Kirby's face; and, at the back, a green-coated bookmaker slipped his notebook in his pocket, and glanced behind him. James Moore, standing in front of them all, was the calmest there.

Red Wull was not to be denied. Like his forerunner he leapt on the back of the hindmost sheep. But the red dog was heavy where the gray was light. The sheep staggered, slipped, and fell.

Almost before it had touched the water, M'Adam, his face afire and eyes flaming, was in the stream. In a second he had hold of the struggling creature, and, with an almost superhuman effort, had half thrown, half shoved it on to the bank.

Again a tribute of admiration, led by James Moore.

The little man scrambled, panting, on to the bank and raced after sheep and dog. His face was white beneath the perspiration; his breath came in quavering gasps; his trousers were wet and clinging to his legs; he was trembling in every limb, and yet indomitable.

They were up to the pen, and the last wrestle began. The crowd, silent and motionless, craned forward to watch the uncanny, white-haired little man and the huge dog, working so close below them. M'Adam's face was white; his eyes staring, unnaturally bright; his bent body projected forward; and he tapped with his stick on the ground like a blind man, coaxing the sheep in. And the Tailless Tyke, his tongue out and flanks heaving, crept and crawled and worked up to the opening, patient as he had never been before.

They were in at last.

There was a lukewarm, half-hearted cheer; then silence.

Exhausted and trembling, the little man leant against the pen, one hand on it; while Red Wull, his flanks still heaving, gently licked the other. Quite close stood James Moore and the gray dog; above was the black wall of people, utterly still; below, the judges comparing notes. In the silence you could almost hear the panting of the crowd.

Then one of the judges went up to James Moore and shook him by the hand.

The gray dog had won. Owd Bob o' Kenmuir had won the Shepherds' Trophy outright.

A second's palpitating silence; a woman's hysterical laugh—and a deep-mouthed bellow rent the expectant air: shouts, screams, hat-tossings, back-clappings blending in a din that made the many-winding waters of the Silver Lea quiver and quiver again.

Owd Bob o' Kenmuir had won the Shepherds' Trophy outright.

Maggie s face flushed a scarlet hue. Wee Anne flung fat arms toward her triumphant Bob, and screamed with the best. Squire and parson, each red-cheeked, were boisterously shaking hands. Long Kirby, who had not prayed for thirty years, ejaculated with heartfelt earnestness, "Thank God!" Sam'l Todd bellowed in Tammas's ear, and almost slew him with his mighty buffets. Among the Dalesmen some laughed like drunken men; some cried like children; all joined in that roaring song of victory.

To little M'Adam, standing with his back to the crowd, that storm of cheering came as the first announcement of defeat.

A wintry smile, like the sun over a March sea, crept across his face.

"We might a kent it, Wullie," he muttered, soft and low. The tension loosed, the battle lost, the little man almost broke down. There were red dabs of colour in his face; his eyes were big; his lips pitifully quivering; he was near to sobbing.

An old man—utterly alone—he had staked his all on a throw—and lost.

Lady Eleanour marked the forlorn little figure, standing solitary on the fringe of the uproarious mob. She noticed the expression on his face; and her tender heart went out to the lone man in his defeat.

She went up to him and laid a hand upon his arm.

"Mr. M'Adam," she said timidly, "won't you come and sit down in the tent? You look *so* tired! I can find you a corner where no one shall disturb you."

The little man wrenched roughly away. The unexpected kindness, coming at that moment, was almost too much for him. A few paces off he turned again.

"It's reel kind o' yer ladyship," he said huskily; and tottered away to be alone with Red Wull.

．　　　　．　　　　‘　　　　．　　　　．

Meanwhile the victors stood like rocks in the tideway. About them surged a continually changing throng, shaking the man's hand, patting his dog.

Maggie had carried wee Anne to tender her congratulations; Long Kirby had come; Tammas, Saunderson, Hoppin, Tupper, Londesley—all but Jim Mason; and now elbowing through the press, came squire and parson.

"Well done, James! well done, indeed! Knew you'd win! Told you so—eh, eh!" Then facetiously to Owd Bob: "Knew you would, Robert, old man! Ought to—Robert the Dev—musn't be a naughty boy—eh, eh!"

"The first time ever the Dale Cup's been won outright!" said the parson; "and I dare say it never will again. And I think Kenmuir's the very fittest place for its final home, and a Gray Dog of Kenmuir for its winner."

"Oh, by the by!" burst in the squire. "I've fixed the Manor dinner for to-day fortnight, James. Tell Saunderson and Tupper, will you? Want all the tenants there." He disappeared into the crowd, but in a minute had fought his way back. "I'd forgotten something!" he shouted. "Tell your Maggie perhaps you'll have news for her after it—eh! eh!"—and he was gone again.

Last of all, James Moore was aware of a white, blotchy, grinning face at his elbow.

"I maun congratulate ye, Mr. Moore. Ye've beat us—you and the gentlemen—judges."

"'Twas a close thing, M'Adam," the other answered. "An' yo' made a gran' fight. In ma life I niver saw a finer turn than yours by the two flags yonder. I hope yo' bear no malice."

"Malice! Me? Is it likely? Na, na. 'Do onto ivery man as he does onto you—and somethin' over,' that's my motter. I owe ye mony a good turn, which I'll pay ye yet. Na na; there's nae good fechtin' agin fate—and the judges. Weel, I wush you well o' yer victory. Aiblins 'twill be oor turn next."

Then a rush, headed by Sam'l, roughly hustled the one away and bore the other off on its shoulders in boisterous triumph.

.   .   .   .   .

In giving the Cup away, Lady Eleanour made a prettier speech than ever. Yet all the while she was haunted by a white, miserable face; and all the while she was conscious of two black moving dots in the Murk Muir Pass opposite her—solitary, desolate, a contrast to the huzzaing crowd around.

.   .   .   .   .

That is how the champion challenge Dale Cup, the world-known Shepherds' Trophy, came to wander no more; won outright by the last of the Gray Dogs of Kenmuir—Owd Bob.

Why he was the last of the Gray Dogs is now to be told.

PART VI

THE BLACK KILLER

CHAPTER XXVI

RED-HANDED

THE sun was hiding behind the Pike. Over the lowlands the feathery breath of night hovered still. And the hillside was shivering in the chillness of dawn.

Down on the silvery sward beside the Stony Bottom there lay the ruffled body of a dead sheep. All about the victim the dewy ground was dark and patchy like dishevelled velvet; bracken trampled down; stones displaced as though by straggling feet; and the whole spotted with the all-pervading red.

A score yards up the hill, in a writhing confusion of red and gray, two dogs at death-grips. While yet higher, a pack of wild-eyed hill-sheep watched, fascinated, the bloody drama.

The fight raged. Red and gray, blood-spattered, murderous-eyed; the crimson froth dripping from their jaws; now rearing high with arching crests and wrestling paws; now rolling over in tumbling, tossing, worrying disorder—the two fought out their blood-feud.

Above, the close-packed flock huddled and stamped, ever edging nearer to watch the issue. Just so must the women of Rome have craned round the arenas to see two men striving in death-struggle.

The first cold flicker of dawn stole across the green. The red eye of the morning peered aghast over the shoulder of the Pike. And from the sleeping dale there arose the yodling of a man driving his cattle home.

Day was upon them.

 . . . . .

James Moore was waked by a little whimpering cry beneath his window. He leapt out of bed and rushed to look; for well he knew 'twas not for nothing that the old dog was calling.

"Lord o' mercy! whativer's come to yo', Owd Un?" he cried in anguish. And, indeed, his favourite, war-daubed almost past recognition, presented a pitiful spectacle.

In a moment the Master was downstairs and out, examining him.

"Poor old lad, yo' have caught it this time!" he cried. There was a ragged tear on the dog's cheek; a deep gash in his throat from which the blood still welled, staining the white escutcheon on his chest; while head and neck were clotted with the red.

Hastily the Master summoned Maggie. After her, Andrew came hurrying down. And a little later a tiny, night-clad, naked-footed figure appeared in the door, wide-eyed, and then fled, screaming.

They doctored the old warrior on the table in the

kitchen. Maggie tenderly washed his wounds and dressed them with gentle, pitying fingers; and he stood all the while grateful yet fidgeting, looking up into his master's face as if imploring to be gone.

"He mun a had a rare tussle wi' some one—eh, dad?" said the girl, as she worked.

"Ay; and wi' whom? 'Twasn't for nowt he got fightin', I war'nt. Nay; he's a tale to tell, has Th' Owd Un, and——Ah-h-h! I thowt as much. Look 'ee!" For bathing the bloody jaws, he had come upon a cluster of tawny red hair, hiding in the corners of the lips.

The secret was out. Those few hairs told their own accusing tale. To but one creature in the Daleland could they belong—"The Tailless Tyke."

"He mun a bin trespassin'!" cried Andrew.

"Ay, and up to some o' his bloody work, I'll lay my life," the Master answered. "But Th' Owd Un shall show us."

The old dog's hurts proved less severe than had at first seemed possible. His good gray coat, forest-thick about his throat, had never served him in such good stead. And at length, the wounds washed and sewn up, he jumped down all in a hurry from the table and made for the door.

"Noo, owd lad, yo' may show us," said the Master, and, with Andrew, hurried after him down the hill, along the stream, and over Langholm How. And as they neared the Stony Bottom, the sheep, herding in groups, raised frightened heads to stare.

Of a sudden a cloud of poisonous flies rose, buzzing, up before them; and there in a dimple of the ground lay a murdered sheep. Deserted by its comrades, the glazed eyes staring helplessly upward, the throat horribly worried, it slept its last sleep.

The matter was plain to see. At last the Black Killer had visited Kenmuir.

"I guessed as much," said the Master, standing over the mangled body. "Well, it's the worst night's work ever the Killer done. I reck'n Th' Owd Un come on him while he was at it; and then they fought. And, ma word! it mun ha' ben a fight too." For all around were traces of that terrible struggle: the earth torn up and tossed, bracken uprooted, and throughout little dabs of wool and tufts of tawny hair, mingling with dark-stained iron-gray wisps.

James Moore walked slowly over the battlefield, stooping down as though he were gleaning. And gleaning he was.

A long time he bent so, and at length raised himself.

"The Killer has killed his last," he muttered; "Red Wull has run his course." Then, turning to Andrew: "Run yo' home, lad, and fetch the men to carry yon away," pointing to the carcass. "And Bob, lad, yo've done your work for to-day, and right well too; go yo' home wi' him. I'm off to see to this!"

He turned and crossed the Stony Bottom. His face was set like a rock. At length the proof was in his hand. Once and for all the hill-country should be rid of its scourge.

As he stalked up the hill, a dark head appeared at his knee. Two big gray eyes, half doubting, half penitent, wholly wistful, looked up at him, and a silvery brush signalled a mute request.

"Eh, Owd Un, but yo' should ha' gone wi' Andrew," the Master said. "Hooiver, as yo' are here, come along.'

And he strode away up the hill, gaunt and menacing, with the gray dog at his heels.

As they approached the house, M'Adam was standing in the door, sucking his eternal twig. James Moore eyed him closely as he came, but the sour face framed in the door betrayed nothing. Sarcasm, surprise, challenge, were all writ there, plain to read; but no guilty consciousness of the other's errand, no storm of passion to hide a failing heart. If it was acting it was splendidly done.

As man and dog passed through the gap in the hedge, the expression of the little man's face changed again. He started forward.

"James Moore, as I live!" he cried, and advanced with with both hands extended, as though welcoming a long-lost brother. "'Deed and it's a weary while sin' ye've honoured ma puir hoose." And, in fact, it was nigh twenty years. "I tak' it gey kind in ye to look in on a lonely auld man. Come ben and let's ha' a crack. James Moore kens weel hoo welcome he aye is in ma bit biggin'."

The Master ignored the greeting.

"One o' ma sheep been killed back o' t' Dyke," he announced shortly, jerking his thumb over his shoulder.

"The Killer?"

"The Killer."

The cordiality beaming in every wrinkle of the little man's face was absorbed in a wondering interest: and that again gave place to sorrowful sympathy.

"Dear, dear! it's come to that, has it—at last?" he said gently, and his eyes wandered to the gray dog and dwelt mournfully upon him. "Man, I'm sorry—I canna tell ye I'm surprised. Masel', I kent it all alang. But gin Adam M'Adam had tell't, ye'd no ha' believed him. Weel,

weel, he's lived his life, gin ony dog iver did; and noo he maun gang where he's sent a many before him. Puir mon! puir tyke!" He heaved a sigh, profoundly melancholy, tenderly sympathetic. Then, brightening up a little: "Ye'll ha' come for the gun?"

James Moore listened to his harangue at first puzzled. Then he caught the other's meaning, and his eyes flashed.

"Ye fool, M'Adam! did ye hear iver tell o' a sheep-dog worryin' his master's sheep?"

The little man was smiling and suave again now, rubbing his hands softly together.

"Ye're right, I never did. But your dog is not as ither dogs—'There's none like him—none,' I've heard ye say so yersel, mony a time. An' I'm wi' ye. There's none like him—for devilment." His voice began to quiver and his face to blaze. "It's his cursed cunning that's deceived ivery one but me—whelp o' Satan that he is!" He shouldered up to his tall adversary. "If not him, wha else had done it?" he asked, looking up into the other's face as if daring him to speak.

The Master's shaggy eyebrows lowered. He towered above the other like the Muir Pike above its surrounding hills.

"Wha, ye ask?" he replied coldly, "and I answer you. Your Red Wull, M'Adam, your Red Wull. It's your Wull's the Black Killer! It's your Wull's bin the plague o' the land these months past! It's your Wull's killed ma sheep back o' yon!"

At that all the little man's affected good-humour fled.

"Ye lee, mon! ye lee!" he cried in a dreadful scream, dancing up to his antagonist. "I knoo hoo 'twad be. I said so. I see what ye're at. Ye've found at last—

blind that ye've been!—that it's yer ain hell's tyke that's the Killer; and noo ye think by yer leein' impitations to throw the blame on ma Wullie. Ye rob me o' ma Cup, ye rob me o' ma son, ye wrang me in ilka thing; there's but ae thing left me—Wullie. And noo ye're set on takin' him awa'. But ye shall not—I'll kill ye first!"

He was all a-shake, bobbing up and down like a stopper in a soda-water bottle, and almost sobbing.

"Ha' ye no wranged me enough wi' oot that? Ye lang-leggit liar, wi' yer skulkin murderin' tyke!" he cried. "Ye say it's Wullie. Where's yer proof?"—and he snapped his fingers in the other's face.

The Master was now as calm as his foe was passionate. "Where?" he replied sternly; "why, there!" holding out his right hand. "Yon's proof enough to hang a hunner'd." For lying in his broad palm was a little bundle of that damning red hair.

"Where?"

"There!"

"Let's see it!" The little man bent to look closer.

"There's for yer proof!" he cried, and spat deliberately down into the other's naked palm. Then he stood back, facing his enemy in a manner to have done credit to a nobler deed.

James Moore strode forward. It looked as if he was about to make an end of his miserable adversary, so strongly was he moved. His chest heaved, and the blue eyes blazed. But just as one had thought to see him take his foe in the hollow of his hand and crush him, who should come stalking round the corner of the house but the Tailless Tyke.

A droll spectacle he made, laughable even at that

moment. He limped sorely, his head and neck were swathed in bandages, and beneath their ragged fringe the little eyes gleamed out fiery and bloodshot.

Round the corner he came, unaware of strangers; then straightway recognizing his visitors, halted abruptly. His hackles ran up, each individual hair stood on end till his whole body resembled a new-shorn wheat-field; and a snarl, like a rusty brake shoved hard down, escaped from between his teeth. Then he trotted heavily forward, his head sinking low and lower as he came.

And Owd Bob, eager to take up the gage of battle, advanced, glad and gallant, to meet him. Daintily he picked his way across the yard, head and tail erect, perfectly self-contained. Only the long gray hair about his neck stood up like the ruff of a lady of the court of Queen Elizabeth.

But the war-worn warriors were not to be allowed their will.

"Wullie, Wullie, wad ye!" cried the little man.

"Bob, lad, coom in!" called the other. Then he turned and looked down at the man beside him, contempt flaunting in every feature.

"Well?" he said shortly.

M'Adam's hands were opening and shutting; his face was quite white beneath the tan; but he spoke calmly.

"I'll tell ye the whole story, and it's the truth," he said slowly. "I was up there the morn"—pointing to the window above—"and I see Wullie crouchin' down alangside the Stony Bottom. (Ye ken he has the run o' ma land o' neets, the same as your dog.) In a minnit I see anither dog squatterin' alang on your side the Bottom. He creeps up to the sheep on th' hillside, chases 'em, and doons one. The sun was risen by then, and I see the dog clear as I see you noo. It was that dog there—I swear it!" His voice rose as he spoke, and he pointed an accusing finger at Owd Bob.

"Noo, Wullie! thinks I. And afore ye could clap yer hands, Wullie was over the Bottom and on to him as he gorged—the bloody-minded murderer! They fought and fought—I could hear the roarin' a't where I stood. I watched till I could watch nae langer, and, all in a sweat, I rin doon the stairs and oot. When I got there, there was yer tyke makin' fu' split for Kenmuir, and Wullie comin' up the hill to me. It's God's truth, I'm tellin' ye. Tak' him hame, James Moore, and let his dinner be an ounce o' lead. 'Twill be the best day's work iver ye done."

The little man must be lying—lying palpably. Yet he spoke with an earnestness, a seeming belief in his own story, that might have convinced one who knew him less well. But the Master only looked down on him with a great scorn.

"It's Monday to-day," he said coldly. "I gie yo' till Saturday. If yo've not done your duty by then—and well you know what 'tis—I shall come do it for ye. Ony gate, I shall come and see. I'll remind ye agin o' Thursday—yo'll be at the Manor dinner, I suppose. Noo I've warned yo,' and you know best whether I'm in earnest or no. Boy, lad!"

He turned away, but turned again.

"I'm sorry for ye, but I've ma duty to do—so've you. Till Saturday I shall breathe no word to ony soul o' this business, so that if you see good to put him oot o' the way wi'oot bother, no one need iver know as hoo Adam M'Adam's Red Wull was the Black Killer."

He turned away for the second time. But the little man sprang after him, and clutched him by the arm.

"Look ye here, James Moore!" he cried in thick, shaky horrible voice. "Ye're big, I'm sma'; ye're strang, I'm weak; ye've ivery one to your back, I've niver a one; you tell your story, and they'll believe ye—for you gae to church; I'll tell mine, and they'll think I lie—for I dinna. But a word in your ear! If iver agin I catch ye on ma land, by—!"—he swore a great oath—"I'll no spare ye. You ken best if I'm in earnest or no." And his face was dreadful to see in its hideous determinedness.

CHAPTER XXVII

FOR THE DEFENCE

THAT night a vague story was whispered in the Sylvester Arms. But Tammas, on being inter-rogated, pursed his lips and said: "Nay, I'm sworn to say nowt." Which was the old man's way of putting that he knew nowt.

.   .   .   .   .

On Thursday morning, James Moore and Andrew came down arrayed in all their best. It was the day of the squire's annual dinner to his tenants.

The two, however, were not allowed to start upon their way until they had undergone a critical inspection by Maggie; for the girl liked her mankind to do honour to Kenmuir on these occasions. So she brushed up Andrew, tied his scarf, saw his boots and hands were clean, and titivated him generally till she had converted the ungainly hobbledehoy into a thoroughly "likely young mon."

And all the while she was thinking of that other boy for whom on such gala days she had been wont to perform like offices. And her father, marking the tears in her eyes, and mindful of the squire's mysterious hint, said gently:

"Cheer up, lass. Happen I'll ha' news for you the night!"

The girl nodded, and smiled wanly.

"Happen so, dad," she said. But in her heart she doubted.

Nevertheless it was with a cheerful countenance that, a little later, she stood in the door with wee Anne and Owd Bob and waved the travellers Godspeed; while the golden-haired lassie, fiercely gripping the old dog's tail with one hand and her sister with the other, screamed them a wordless farewell.

.   .   .   .   .

The sun had reached its highest when the two wayfarers passed through the gray portals of the Manor.

In the stately entrance hall, imposing with all the evidences of a long and honourable line, were gathered now the many tenants throughout the wide March Mere Estate. Weather-beaten, rent-paying sons of the soil; most of them native-born, many of them like James Moore, whose fathers had for generations owned and farmed the land they now leased at the hands of the Sylvesters—there in the old hall they were assembled, a mighty host. And apart from the others, standing as though in irony beneath the frown of one of those steel-clad warriors who held the door, was little M'Adam, puny always, paltry now, mocking his manhood.

The door at the far end of the hall opened, and the squire entered, beaming on everyone.

"Here you are—eh, eh! How are you all? Glad to see ye! Good-day, James! Good-day, Saunderson! Good-day to you all! Bringin' a friend with me—eh, eh!" and he stood aside to let by his agent, Parson Leggy, and last of all, shy and blushing, a fair-haired young giant.

"If it bain't David!" was the cry. "Eh, lad, we's fain to see yo'! And yo'm lookin' stout, surely!" And they thronged about the boy, shaking him by the hand, and asking him his story.

'Twas but a simple tale. After his flight on the eventful night he had gone south, drovering. He had written to Maggie, and been surprised and hurt to receive no reply. In vain he had waited, and too proud to write again, had remained ignorant of his father's recovery, neither caring nor daring to return. Then by mere chance, he had met the squire at the York cattle-show; and that kind man, who knew his story, had eased his fears and obtained from him a promise to return as soon as the term of his engagement had expired. And there he was.

The Dalesmen gathered round the boy, listening to his tale, and in return telling him the home news, and chaffing him about Maggie.

Of all the people present, only one seemed unmoved, and that was M'Adam. When first David had entered he had started forward, a flush of colour warming his thin cheeks; but no one had noticed his emotion; and now, back again beneath his armour, he watched the scene, a sour smile playing about his lips.

"I think the lad might ha' the grace to come and

say he's sorry for 'temptin' to murder me. Hooiver"—
with a characteristic shrug—"I suppose I'm onraison-
able."

Then the gong rang out its summons, and the squire led
the way into the great dining-hall. At the one end of the
long table, heavy with all the solid delicacies of such a
feast, he took his seat with the Master of Kenmuir upon
his right. At the other end was Parson Leggy. While
down the sides the stalwart Dalesmen were arrayed, with
M'Adam a little lost figure in the centre.

At first they talked but little, awed like children:
knives plied, glasses tinkled, the carvers had all their work,
only the tongues were at rest. But the squire's ringing
laugh and the parson's cheery tones soon put them at
their ease; and a babel of voices rose and waxed.

Of them all, only M'Adam sat silent. He talked to no
man, and you may be sure no one talked to him. His
hand crept oftener to his glass than plate, till the sallow
face began to flush, and the dim eyes to grow unnaturally
bright.

Toward the end of the meal there was loud tapping on
the table, calls for silence, and men pushed back their
chairs. The squire was on his feet to make his annual
speech.

He started by telling them how glad he was to see
them there. He made an allusion to Owd Bob and the
Shepherds' Trophy which was heartily applauded. He
touched on the Black Killer, and said he had a remedy to
propose: that Th' Owd Un should be set upon the criminal's track—a suggestion which was received with
enthusiasm, while M'Adam's cackling laugh could be
heard high above the rest.

From that he dwelt upon the existing condition of agriculture, the depression in which he attributed to the late Radical Government. He said that now with the Conservatives in office, and a ministry composed of "honourable men and gentlemen" he felt convinced that things would brighten. The Radicals' one ambition was to set class against class, landlord against tenant. Well, during the last five hundred years, the Sylvesters had rarely been—he was sorry to have to confess it—good men [laughter and dissent]; but he never yet heard of the Sylvester—though he shouldn't say it—who was a bad landlord [loud applause].

This was a free country, and any tenant of his who was not content [a voice, " 'Oo says we bain't?"]—"thank you, thank you!"—well, there was room for him outside. [Cheers.] He thanked God from the bottom of his heart that during the forty years he had been responsible for the March Mere Estate, there had never been any friction between him and his people [cheers], and he didn't think there ever would be. [Loud cheers.]

"Thank you, thank you!" And his motto was "Shun a Radical as you do the devil!"—and he was very glad to see them all there—very glad; and he wished to give them a toast, "The Queen! God bless her!" and —wait a minute!—with her Majesty's name to couple—he was sure that gracious lady would wish it—that of "Owd Bob o' Kenmuir!" Then he sat down abruptly amid thundering applause.

The toasts duly honoured, James Moore, by prescriptive right as Master of Kenmuir, rose to answer.

He began by saying that he spoke "as representing all the tenants,"—but he was interrupted.

"Na," came a shrill voice from half-way down the table. "Ye'll except me, James Moore. I'd as lief be represented by Judas!"

There were cries of "Hold ye gab, little mon!" and the squire's voice, "That'll do, Mr. M'Adam!"

The little man restrained his tongue, but his eyes gleamed like a ferret's; and the Master continued his speech.

He spoke briefly and to the point, in short phrases. And all the while M'Adam kept up a low-voiced, running commentary. At length he could control himself no longer. Half rising from his chair, he leant forward with hot face and burning eyes, and cried: "Sit doon, James Moore! Hoo daur ye stan' there like an honest man, ye whitewashed sepulchre? Sit doon, I say, or"—threateningly—"wad ye hae me come to ye?"

At that the Dalesmen laughed uproariously, and even the Master's grim face relaxed. But the squire's voice rang out sharp and stern.

"Keep silence and sit down, Mr. M'Adam! D'you hear me, sir? If I have to speak to you again it will be to order you to leave the room."

The little man obeyed, sullen and vengeful, like a beaten cat.

The Master concluded his speech by calling on all present to give three cheers for the squire, her ladyship, and the young ladies.

The call was responded to enthusiastically, every man standing. Just as the noise was at its zenith, Lady Eleanour herself, with her two fair daughters, glided into the gallery at the end of the hall; whereat the cheering became deafening.

Slowly the clamour subsided. One by one the tenants sat down. At length there was left standing only one solitary figure—M'Adam.

His face was set, and he gripped the chair in front of him with thin, nervous hands.

"Mr. Sylvester," he began in low yet clear voice, "ye said this is a free country and we're a' free men. And that bein' so, I'll tak' the liberty, wi 'yer permission, to say a word. It's maybe the last time I'll be wi' ye, so I hope ye'll listen to me."

The Dalesmen looked surprised, and the squire uneasy Nevertheless he nodded assent.

The little man straightened himself. His face was tense as though strung up to a high resolve. All the passion had fled from it, all the bitterness was gone; and left behind was a strange, ennobling earnestness. Standing there in the silence of that great hall, with every eye upon him, he looked like some prisoner at the bar about to plead for his life.

"Gentlemen," he began, "I've bin amang ye noo a score years, and I can truly say there's not a man in this room I can ca' 'Friend.'" He looked along the ranks of upturned faces. "Ay, David, I see ye, and you, Mr. Hornbut, and you, Mr. Sylvester—ilka one o' you, and not one as'd back me like a comrade gin a trouble came upon me." There was no rebuke in the grave little voice —it merely stated a hard fact.

"There's I doot no one amang ye but has some one— friend or blood—wham he can turn to when things are sair wi' him. I've no one.

"I bear alane my lade o' care'—

alane wi' Wullie, who stands to me, blaw or snaw, rain or shine. And whiles I'm feared he'll be took from me." He spoke this last half to himself, a grieved, puzzled expression on his face, as though lately he had dreamed some ill dream.

"Forbye, Wullie, I've no friend on God's earth. And, mind ye, a bad man aften mak's a good friend—but ye've never given me the chance. It's a sair thing that, gentlemen, to ha' to fight the battle o' life alane: no one to pat ye on th' back, no one to say 'Weel done.' It hardly gies a man a chance. For gin he does try and yet fails, men never mind the tryin', they only mark the failin'.

"I dinna blame ye. There's somethin' bred in me, it seems, as sets ivery one agin me. It's the same wi' Wullie and the tykes—they're doon on him same as men are on me. I suppose we was made so. Sin' I was a lad it's aye bin the same. From school days I've had ivery one agin me.

"In ma life I've had three friends. Ma mither—and she went; then ma wife"—he gave a great swallow—"and she's awa'; and I may say they're the only two human bein's as ha' lived on God's earth in ma time that iver tied to bear wi' me;—and Wullie. A man's mither—a man's wife—a man's dog! it's aften a' he has in this warld; and the more he prizes them the more like they are to be took from him." The little earnest voice shook, and the dim eyes puckered and filled.

"Sin I've bin amang ye—twenty-odd years—can any man here mind speakin' any word that wasna ill to me?" He paused; there was no reply.

"I'll tell ye. All the time I've lived here I've had one kindly word spoke to me, and that a fortnight gone, and

not by a man then—by her ladyship. God bless her!"
He glanced up into the gallery. There was no one visible
there; but a curtain at one end shook as though it were
sobbing.

"Weel, I'm thinkin' we'll be gaein' in a wee while noo,
Wullie and me, alane and thegither, as we've aye done.
And it's time we went. Ye've had enough o' us, and it's
no for me to blame ye. And when I'm gone what'll ye
say o' me? 'He was a drunkard.' I am. 'He was a
sinner.' I am. 'He was ilka thing he shouldna be.'
I am. 'We're glad he's gone.' That's what ye'll say o'
me. And it's but ma deserts."

The gentle, condemning voice ceased, and began again.

"That's what I am. Gin things had been differ', aiblins
I'd ha' bin differ'. D'ye ken Robbie Burns? That's a
man I've read, and read, and read. D'ye ken why I
love him as some o' you do yer Bibles? Because there's a
humanity about him. A weak man hissel', aye slippin',
slippin', slippin', and tryin' to haud up; sorrowin' ae
minute, sinnin' the next; doin' ill deeds and wishin' 'em
undone—just a plain human man, a sinner. And that's
why I'm thinkin' he's tender for us as is like him. *He
understood*. It's what he wrote—after ain o' his tumbles,
I'm thinkin'—that I was goin' to tell ye:

> 'Then gently scan yer brother man,
>   Still gentler sister woman,
>   Though they may gang a kennin' wrang,
> To step aside is human'—

the doctrine o' Charity. Gie him his chance, says
Robbie, though he be a sinner. Mony a mon'd be differ',
mony bad'd be gude, gin they had but their chance

Gie 'em their chance, says he; and I'm wi' him. As 'tis, ye see me here—a bad man wi' a streak o' good in him. Gin I'd had ma chance, aiblins 'twad be—a good man wi' just a spice o' the devil in him. A' the differ' betune what is and what might ha' bin."

CHAPTER XXVIII

THE DEVIL'S BOWL

HE sat down. In the great hall there was silence, save for a tiny sound from the gallery like a sob suppressed.

The squire rose hurriedly and left the room.

After him, one by one, trailed the tenants.

At length, two only remained—M'Adam, sitting solitary with a long array of empty chairs on either hand; and, at the far end of the table, Parson Leggy, stern, upright, motionless.

When the last man had left the room the parson rose and with lips tight-set strode across the silent hall.

"M'Adam," he said rapidly and almost roughly, "I've listened to what you've said, as I think we all have, with a sore heart. You hit hard—but I think you were right. And if I've not done my duty by you as I ought—and I fear I've not—it's now my duty as God's minister to be the first to say I'm sorry." And it was evident from his face what an effort the words cost him.

The little man tilted back his chair, and raised his head. It was the old M'Adam who looked up. The thin lips were curled; a grin was crawling across the mocking face; and he wagged his head gently, as he looked at the speaker through the slits of his half-closed eyes.

"Mr. Hornbut, I believe ye thocht me in earnest, 'deed and I do!" He leaned back in his chair and laughed softly. "Ye swallered it all down like best butter. Dear, dear! to think o' that!" Then, stretching forward: "Mr. Hornbut, I was playin' wi' ye."

The parson's face, as he listened, was ugly to watch. He shot out a hand and grabbed the scoffer by his coat; then dropped it again and turned abruptly away.

As he passed through the door a little sneering voice called after him:

"Mr. Hornbut, I ask ye hoo you, a minister o' the Church of England, can reconcile it to yer conscience to think—though it be but for a minute—that there can be ony good in a man and him no churchgoer? Sir, ye're a heretic—not to say a heathen!" He sniggered to himself, and his hand crept to a half-emptied wine decanter.

.   .   .   .   .

An hour later, James Moore, his business with the squire completed, passed through the hall on his way out. Its only occupant was now M'Adam, and the Master walked straight up to his enemy.

"M'Adam," he said gruffly, holding out a sinewy hand, "I'd like to say——"

The little man knocked aside the token of friendship.

"Na, na. No cant, if ye please, James Moore. That'll aiblins go doon wi' the parsons, but not wi' me. I ken

you and you ken me, and all the whitewash i' th' warld 'll
no deceive us."

The Master turned away, and his face was hard as the
nether millstone.   But the little man pursued him.

"I was nigh forgettin'," he said.   "I've a surprise for
ye, James Moore.   But I hear it's yer birthday on Sunday,
and I'll keep it till then—he! he!"

"Ye'll see me before Sunday, M'Adam," the other
answered.   "On Saturday, as I told yo', I'm comin' to
see if yo've done yer duty."

"Whether ye come, James Moore, is your business.
Whether ye'll iver go, once there, I'll mak' mine.   I've
warned ye twice noo"—and the little man laughed that
harsh, cackling laugh of his.

At the door of the hall the Master met David.

"Noo lad, yo're comin' along wi' Andrew and me,"
he said; "Maggie'll niver forgie us if we dinna bring yo'
home wi' us."

"Thank you kindly, Mr. Moore," the boy replied.
"I've to see squire first; and then yo' may be sure I'll
be after you.'

The Master faltered a moment.

"David, ha'n yo' spoke to yer father yet?" he asked in
low voice.   "Yo' should, lad."

The boy made a gesture of dissent.

"I canna," he said petulantly.

"I would, lad," the other advised.   "An yo' don't yo'
may be sorry after."

As he turned away he heard the boy's steps, dull and
sodden, as he crossed the hall; and then a thin, would-be
cordial voice in the emptiness:

"I declar' if 'tisna David!   The return o' the Prodeegal

—he! he! So ye've seen yer auld dad at last, and the last; the proper place, say ye, for yer father—he! he! Eh, lad, but I'm blithe to see ye. D'ye mind when we was last thegither? Ye was kneelin' on ma chest: 'Your time's come, dad,' says you, and wangs me o'er the face— he! he! I mind it as if 'twas yesterday. Weel, weel, we'll say nae mair about it. Boys will be boys. Sons will be sons. Accidents will happen. And if at first ye don't succeed, why, try, try again—he! he!''

.   .   .   .   .

Dusk was merging into darkness when the Master and Andrew reached the Dalesman's Daughter. It had been long dark when they emerged from the cosy parlour of the inn and plunged out into the night.

As they crossed the Silver Lea and trudged over that familiar ground, where a fortnight since had been fought out the battle of the Cup, the wind fluttered past them in spasmodic gasps.

"There's trouble in the wind," said the Master.

"Ay," answered his laconic son.

All day there had been no breath of air, and the sky dangerously blue. But now a world of black was surging up from the horizon, smothering the star-lit night; and small dark clouds, like puffs of smoke, detaching themselves from the main body, were driving tempestuously forward —the vanguard of the storm.

In the distance was a low rumbling like heavy tumbrils on the floor of heaven. All about, the wind sounded hollow like a mighty scythe on corn. The air was oppressed with a leaden blackness—no glimmer of light on any hand; and as they began the ascent of the Pass they reached out blind hands to feel along the rock-face.

A sea-fret, cool and wetting, fell. A few big rain-drops splashed heavily down. The wind rose with a leap and roared past them up the rocky track. And the water-gates of heaven were flung wide.

Wet and weary, they battled on; thinking sometimes of the cosy parlour behind; sometimes of the home in front; wondering whether Maggie, in flat contradiction of her father's orders, would be up to welcome them; or whether Owd Bob would come out to meet them.

The wind volleyed past them like salvoes of artillery. The rain stormed at them from above; spat at them from the rock-face; and leapt up at them from their feet.

Once they halted for a moment, finding a miserable shelter in a crevice of the rock.

"It's a Black Killer's night," panted the Master. "I reck'n he's oot."

"Ay," the boy gasped, "reck'n he is."

Up and up they climbed through the blackness, blind and buffeted. The eternal thunder of the rain was all about them; the clamour of the gale above; and far beneath, the roar of angry waters.

Once, in a lull in the storm, the Master turned and looked back into the blackness along the path they had come.

"Did ye hear onythin'?" he roared above the muffled soughing of the wind.

"Nay!" Andrew shouted back.

"I thowt I heard a step!" the Master cried, peering down. But nothing could he see.

Then the wind leaped to life again like a giant from his sleep, drowning all sound with its hurricane voice; and they turned and bent to their task again.

Nearing the summit, the Master turned once more. "There it was again!" he called; but his words were swept away on the storm; and they buckled to the struggle afresh.

Ever and anon the moon gleamed down through the riot of tossing sky. Then they could see the wet wall above them, with the water tumbling down its sheer face; and far below, in the roaring gutter of the Pass a brown-stained torrent. Hardly, however, had they time to glance around when a mass of cloud would hurry jealously up, and all again was blackness and noise.

At length, nigh spent, they topped the last and steepest pitch of the Pass, and emerged into the Devil's Bowl. There, overcome with their exertions, they flung themselves on to the soaking ground to draw breath.

Behind them, the wind rushed with a sullen roar up the funnel of the Pass. It screamed above them as though ten million devils were a-horse; and blurted out on to the wild Marches beyond.

As they lay there, still panting, the moon gleamed down in momentary graciousness. In front, through the lashing rain, they could discern the hillocks that squat, hag-like, round the Devil's Bowl; and lying in its bosom, its white waters, usually so still, ploughed now into a thousand furrows, the Lone Tarn.

The Master raised his head and craned forward at the ghostly scene. Of a sudden he reared himself on to his arms, and stayed motionless awhile. Then he dropped as though dead, forcing down Andrew with an iron hand.

"Lad, did'st see?" he whispered.

"Nay: what was't?" the boy replied, roused by his father's tone.

"There!"

But as the Master pointed forward, a blur of cloud intervened and all was dark. Quickly it passed; and again the lantern of the night shone down. And Andrew, looking with all his eyes, saw indeed.

There, in front, by the fretting waters of the Tarn, packed in a solid phalanx, with every head turned in the same direction, was a flock of sheep. They were motionless, all-intent, staring with horror-bulging eyes. A column of steam rose from their bodies into the rain-pierced air. Panting and palpitating, yet they stood with their backs to the water, as though determined to sell their lives dearly. Beyond them, not fifty yards away, crouched a hump-backed boulder, casting a long, mis-shapen shadow in the moonlight. And beneath it were two black objects, one struggling feebly.

"The Killer!" gasped the boy, and, all ablaze with excitement, began forging forward.

"Steady, lad, steady!" urged his father, dropping a restraining hand on the boy's shoulder.

Above them a huddle of clouds flung in furious rout across the night, and the moon was veiled.

"Follow, lad!" ordered the Master, and began to crawl silently forward. As stealthily Andrew pursued. And over the sodden ground they crept, one behind the other, like two night-hawks on some foul errand.

On they crawled, lying prone during the blinks of moon, stealing forward in the dark; till, at length, the swish of the rain on the waters of the Tarn, and the sobbing of the flock in front, warned them they were near.

They skirted the trembling pack, passing so close as to brush against the flanking sheep; and yet unnoticed, for the sheep were soul-absorbed in the tragedy in front. Only, when the moon was in, Andrew could hear them huddling and stamping in the darkness. And again, as it shone out, fearfully they edged closer to watch the bloody play.

Along the Tarn edge the two crept. And still the gracious moon hid their approach, and the drunken wind drowned with its revelry the sound of their coming.

So they stole on, on hands and knees, with hearts aghast and fluttering breath; until, of a sudden, in a lull of wind, they could hear, right before them, the smack and slobber of bloody lips, chewing their bloody meal.

"Say thy prayers, Red Wull. Thy last minute's come!" muttered the Master, rising to his knees. Then, in Andrew's ear: "When I rush, lad, follow!" For he thought when the moon rose, to jump in on the great dog, and, surprising him as he lay gorged and unsuspicious, to deal him one terrible swashing blow, and end forever the lawless doings of the Tailless Tyke.

The moon flung off its veil of cloud. White and cold, it stared down into the Devil's Bowl; on murderer and murdered.

Within a hand's cast of the avengers of blood humped the black boulder. On the border of its shadow lay a dead sheep; and standing beside the body, his coat all ruffled by the hand of the storm—Owd Bob—Owd Bob o' Kenmuir.

Then the light went in, and darkness covered the land.

CHAPTER XXIX

THE DEVIL'S BOWL

IT WAS Owd Bob. There could be no mistaking. In the wide world there was but one Owd Bob o' Kenmuir. The silver moon gleamed down on the dark head and rough gray coat, and lit the white escutcheon on his chest.

And in the darkness James Moore was lying with his face pressed downward that he might not see.

Once he raised himself on his arms; his eyes were shut and face uplifted, like a blind man praying. He passed a weary hand across his brow; his head dropped again; and he moaned and moaned like a man in everlasting pain.

Then the darkness lifted a moment, and he stole a furtive glance, like a murderer's at the gallows-tree, at the scene in front.

It was no dream; clear and cruel in the moonlight the humpbacked boulder; the dead sheep; and that gray figure, beautiful, motionless, damned for all eternity

The Master turned his face and looked at Andrew, a dumb, pitiful entreaty in his eyes; but in the boy's white, horror-stricken countenance was no comfort. Then his head lolled down again, and the strong man was whimpering.

"He! he! he! 'Scuse ma laffin', Mr. Moore—he! he! he!"

A little man, all wet and shrunk, sat hunching on a mound above them, rocking his shrivelled form to and fro in the agony of his merriment.

"Ye raskil—he! he! Ye rogue—he! he!" and he shook his fist waggishly at the unconscious gray dog. "I owe ye anither grudge for this—ye've anteecipated me"—and he leant back and shook this way and that in convulsive mirth.

The man below him rose heavily to his feet, and tumbled toward the mocker, his great figure swaying from side to side as though in blind delirium, moaning still as he went. And there was that on his face which no man can mistake. Boy that he was, Andrew knew it.

"Feyther! feyther! do'ee not!" he pleaded, running after his father and laying impotent hands on him.

But the strong man shook him off like a fly, and rolled on, swaying and groaning, with that awful expression plain to see in the moonlight.

In front the little man squatted in the rain, bowed double still; and took no thought to flee.

"Come on, James Moore! Come on!" he laughed, malignant joy in his voice, and something gleamed bright in his right hand, and was hid again. "I've bin waitin' this a weary while noo. Come on!"

Then had there been done something worse than sheep-murder in the dreadful lonesomeness of the Devil's Bowl upon that night; but of a sudden, there sounded the splash of a man's foot falling heavily behind; a hand like a falling tree smote the Master on the shoulder; and a voice roared above the noise of the storm:

"Mr. Moore! Look, man! Look!

The Master tried to shake off that detaining grasp; but it pinned him where he was, immovable.

"Look, I tell yo'!" cried that great voice again.

A hand pushed past him and pointed; and sullenly he turned, ignoring the figure at his side, and looked.

The wind had dropped suddenly as it had risen; the little man on the mound had ceased to chuckle; Andrew's sobs were hushed; and in the background the huddled flock edged closer. The world hung balanced on the pin-point of the moment. Every eye was in the one direction.

With dull, uncomprehending gaze James Moore stared as bidden. There was the gray dog naked in the moonlight, heedless still of any witnesses; there the murdered sheep, lying within and without that distorted shade and there the humpbacked boulder.

He stared into the shadow, and still stared. Then he started as though struck. The shadow of the boulder had moved!

Motionless, with head shot forward and bulging eyes, he gazed.

Ay, ay, ay; he was sure of it—a huge dim outline as of a lion *couchant*, in the very thickest of the blackness.

At that he was seized with such a palsy of trembling that he must have fallen but for the strong arm about his waist.

Clearer every moment grew that crouching figure; till at length they plainly could discern the line of arching loins, the crest, thick as a stallion's, the massive, wagging head.   No mistake this time.   There he lay in the deepest black, gigantic, revelling in his horrid debauch—the Black Killer!

And they watched him at his feast.   Now he burrowed into the spongy flesh; now turned to lap the dark pool which glittered in the moonlight at his side like claret in a silver cup.   Now lifting his head, he snapped irritably at the rain-drops, and the moon caught his wicked, rolling eye and the red shreds of flesh dripping from his jaw. And again, raising his great muzzle as if about to howl, he let the delicious nectar trickle down his throat and ravish his palate.

So he went on, all unsuspicious, wisely nodding in slow-mouthed gluttony.   And in the stillness, between the claps of wind, they could hear the smacking of his lips.

While all the time the gray dog stood before him, motionless, as though carved in stone.

At last, as the murderer rolled his great head from side to side, he saw that still figure.   At the sight he leaped back, dismayed.   Then with a deep-mouthed roar that shook the waters of the Tarn he was up and across his victim with fangs bared, his coat standing erect in wet, rigid furrows from topknot to tail.

So the two stood, face to face, with perhaps a yard of rain-pierced air between them.

The wind hushed its sighing to listen.   The moon stared down, white and dumb.   Away at the back the sheep edged closer.   While save for the everlasting thunder of the rain, there was utter stillness.

An age, it seemed, they waited so. Then a voice, clear yet low and far away, like a bugle in a distant city, broke the silence.

"Eh, Wullie!" it said.

There was no anger in the tones, only an incomparable reproach; the sound of the cracking of a man's heart.

At the call the great dog leapt round, snarling in hideous passion. He saw the small, familiar figure, clear-cut against the tumbling sky; and for the only time in his life Red Wull was afraid.

His blood-foe was forgotten; the dead sheep was forgotten; everything was sunk in the agony of that moment. He cowered upon the ground, and a cry like that of a lost soul was wrung from him; it rose on the still night air and floated, wailing, away; and the white waters of the Tarn thrilled in cold pity; out of the lonely hollow; over the desolate Marches; into the night.

On the mound above stood his master. The little man's white hair was bared to the night wind; the rain trickled down his face; and his hands were folded behind his back. He stood there, looking down into the dell below him, as a man may stand at the tomb of his lately buried wife. And there was such an expression on his face as I cannot describe.

"Wullie, Wullie, to me!" he cried at length; and his voice sounded weak and far, like a distant memory.

At that the huge brute came crawling toward him on his belly, whimpering as he came, very pitiful in his distress. He knew his fate as every sheep-dog knows it. That troubled him not. His pain, insufferable, was that this, his friend and father, who had trusted him, should have found him in his sin.

So he crept up to his master's feet; and the little man never moved.

"Wullie—ma Wullie!" he said very gently. "They've aye bin agin me—and noo you! A man's mither—a man's wife—a man's dog! they're all I've iver had; and noo ain o' they three has turned agin me! Indeed I am alone!"

At that the great dog raised himself, and placing his forepaws on his master's chest tenderly, lest he should hurt him who was already hurt past healing, stood towering above him; while the little man laid his two cold hands on the dog's shoulders.

So they stood, looking at one another, like a man and his love.

.   .   .   .   .

At M'Adam's word, Owd Bob looked up, and for the first time saw his master.

He seemed in nowise startled, but trotted over to him. There was nothing fearful in his carriage, no haunting blood-guiltiness in the true gray eyes which never told a lie, which never, dog-like, failed to look you in the face. Yet his tail was low, and, as he stopped at his master's feet, he was quivering. For he, too, knew, and was not unmoved.

For weeks he had tracked the Killer; for weeks he had followed him as he crossed Kenmuir, bound on his bloody errands; yet always had lost him on the Marches. Now, at last, he had run him to ground. Yet his heart went out to his enemy in his distress.

"I thowt 't had been yo', lad," the Master whispered, his hand on the dark head at his knee—"I thowt 't had bin yo'!"

.   .   .   .   .

Rooted to the ground, the three watched the scene between M'Adam and his Wull.

In the end the Master was whimpering; Andrew crying; and David turned his back.

At length, silent, they moved away.

"Had I—should I go to him?" asked David hoarsely, nodding toward his father.

"Nay, nay, lad," the Master replied. "Yon's not a matter for a mon's friends."

So they marched out of the Devil's Bowl, and left those two alone together.

.   .   .   .   .

A little later, as they trampled along, James Moore heard little pattering, staggering footsteps behind.

He stopped, and the other two went on.

"Man," a voice whispered, and a face, white and pitiful, like a mother's pleading for her child, looked into his—"Man, ye'll no tell them a'? I'd no like 'em to ken 'twas ma Wullie. Think an 't had bin yer ain dog."

"You may trust me!" the other answered thickly.

The little man stretched out a palsied hand.

"Gie us yer hand on't. And G-God bless ye, James Moore!"

So these two shook hands in the moonlight, with none to witness it but the God who made them.

And that is why the mystery of the Black Killer is yet unsolved in the Daleland. Many have surmised; besides those three only one other knows—knows now which of those two he saw upon a summer night was the guilty, which the innocent. And Postie Jim tells no man.

CHAPTER XXX

THE TAILLESS TYKE AT BAY

ON THE following morning there was a sheep-auction at the Dalesman's Daughter.

Early as many of the farmers arrived, there was one earlier. Tupper, the first man to enter the sand-floored parlour, found M'Adam before him.

He was sitting a little forward in his chair; his thin hands rested on his knees; and on his face was a gentle, dreamy expression such as no man had ever seen there before. All the harsh wrinkles seemed to have fled in the night; and the sour face, stamped deep with the bitterness of life, was softened now, as if at length at peace.

"When I coom doon this mornin'," said Teddy Bolstock in a whisper. "I found 'im just sittin' so. And he's nor moved nor spoke since."

"Where's th' Terror, then?" asked Tupper, awed somehow into like hushed tones.

"In t' paddock at back," Teddy answered, "marchin'

hoop and doon, hoop and doon, for a' the world like a
sentry-soger. And so he was when I looked oot o'
window when I wake."

Then Londesley entered, and after him, Ned Hoppin,
Rob Saunderson, Jim Mason, and others, each with his
dog. And each man, as he came in and saw the little lone
figure for once without its huge attendant genius, put the
same question; while the dogs sniffed about the little man,
as though suspecting treachery. And all the time M'
Adam sat as though he neither heard nor saw, lost in some
sweet, sad dream; so quiet, so silent, that more than one
thought he slept.

After the first glance, however, the farmers paid him
little heed, clustering round the publican at the farther
end of the room to hear the latest story of Owd Bob.

It appeared that a week previously, James Moore with
a pack of sheep had met the new Grammoch-town butcher
at the Dalesman's Daughter. A bargain concluded, the
butcher started with the flock for home. As he had no
dog, the Master offered him Th' Owd Un. "And he'll
pick me i' th' town to-morrow," said he.

Now the butcher was a stranger in the land. Of course
he had heard of Owd Bob o' Kenmuir, yet it never struck
him that this handsome gentleman with the quiet, resolute
manner, who handled sheep as he had never seen them
handled, was that hero—"the best sheep-dog in the North."

Certain it is that by the time the flock was penned in the
enclosure behind the shop, he coveted the dog—ay, would
even offer ten pounds for him!

Forthwith the butcher locked him up in an outhouse—
summit of indignity; resolving to make his offer on the
morrow.

When the morrow came he found no dog in the outhouse, and, worse, no sheep in the enclosure. A sprung board showed the way of escape of the one, and a displaced hurdle that of the other. And as he was making the discovery, a gray dog and a flock of sheep, travelling along the road toward the Dalesman's Daughter, met the Master.

From the first, Owd Bob had mistrusted the man. The attempt to confine him set the seal on his suspicions. His master's sheep were not for such a rogue; and he worked his own way out and took the sheep along with him.

The story was told to a running chorus of—"Ma word! Good, Owd Un!—Ho! ho! did he thot?"

Of them all, only M'Adam sat strangely silent.

Rob Saunderson, always glad to draw the little man, remarked it.

"And what d'yo' think o' that, Mr. M'Adam, for a wunnerfu' story of a wunnerfu' tyke?" he asked.

"It's a gude tale, a vera gude tale," the little man answered dreamily. "And James Moore didna invent it; he had it from the Christmas number o' the *Flock-keeper* in saxty." (On the fol owing Sunday, old Rob, from sheer curiosity reached down from his shelf the specified number of the paper. To his amazement he found the little man was right. There was the story almost identically. None the less is it also true of Owd Bob o' Kenmuir.)

"Ay, ay," the little man continued, "and in a day or two James Moore'll ha' anither tale to tell ye—a better tale, ye'll think it—mair laffable. And yet—ay—no— I'll no believe it! I niver loved James Moore, but I think,

as Mr. Hornbut aince said, he'd rather die than lie. Owd
Bob o' Kenmuir!" he continued in a whisper. "Up till
the end I canna shake him aff. Hafflins I think that
where I'm gaein' to there'll be gray dogs sneakin' around
me in the twilight. And they're aye behind and behind,
and I canna, canna——"

Teddy Bolstock interrupted, lifting his hand for
silence.

"D'yo' hear thot?—Thunder!"

They listened; and from without came a gurgling,
jarring roar, horrible to hear.

"It's comin' nearer!"

"Nay, it's goin' away!"

"No thunder thot!"

"More like the Lea in flood. And yet—Eh, Mr.
M'Adam, what is it?"

The little man had moved at last. He was on his feet,
staring about him, wild-eyed.

"Where's yer dogs?" he almost screamed.

"Here's ma—— Nay, by thunder! but he's not!" was
the astonished cry.

In the interest of the story no man had noticed that his
dog had risen from his side; no one had noticed a file of
shaggy figures creeping out of the room.

"I tell ye it's the tykes! I tell ye it's the tykes!
They're on ma Wullie—fifty to one they're on him!
My God! My God! And me not there! Wullie, Wullie!"
—in a scream—"I'm wi' ye!"

At the same moment Bessie Bolstock rushed in, white-
faced.

"Hi! Feyther! Mr. Saunderson! all o' you! T' tykes
fightin' mad! Hark!"

There was no time for that. Each man seized his stick and rushed for the door; and M'Adam led them all.

.   .   .   .   .

A rare thing it was for M'Adam and Red Wull to be apart. So rare, that others besides the men in that little tap-room noticed it.

Saunderson's old Shep walked quietly to the back door of the house and looked out.

There on the slope below him he saw what he sought, stalking up and down, gaunt and grim, like a lion at feeding-time. And as the old dog watched, his tail was gently swaying as though he were well pleased.

He walked back into the tap-room just as Teddy began his tale. Twice he made the round of the room, silent-footed. From dog to dog he went, stopping at each as though urging him on to some great enterprise. Then he made for the door again, looking back to see if any followed.

One by one the others rose and trailed out after him: big blue Rasper, Londesley's Lassie, Ned Hoppin's young dog; Grip and Grapple, the publican's bull-terriers; Jim Mason's Gyp, foolish and flirting even now; others there were; and last of all, waddling heavily in the rear, that scarred Amazon, the Venus.

Out of the house they pattered, silent and unseen, with murder in their hearts. At last they had found their enemy alone. And slowly, in a black cloud, like the shadow of death, they dropped down the slope upon him.

And he saw them coming, knew their errand—as who should better than the Terror of the Border?—and was glad. Death it might be, and such an one as he would wish to die—at least distraction from that long-drawn,

ñaunting pain.   And he smiled grimly as he looked at the
approaching crowd, and saw there was not one there but
he had humbled in his time.

He ceased his restless pacing, and awaited them.   His
great head was high as he scanned them contemptuously,
daring them to come on.

And on they came, marching slow and silent like
soldiers at a funeral: young and old; bob-tailed and bull;
terrier and collie; flocking like vultures to the dead.
And the Venus, heavy with years, rolled after them on her
bandy legs panting in her hurry lest she should be late.
For had she not the blood of her blood to avenge?

So they came about him, slow, certain, murderous,
opening out to cut him off on every side.   There was no
need.   He never thought to move.   Long odds 'twould
be—crushingly heavy; yet he loved them for it, and was
trembling already with the glory of the coming fight.

They were up to him now; the sheep-dogs walking
round him on their toes, stiff and short like cats on coals;
their backs a little humped; heads averted; yet eying
him askance.

And he remained stock-still nor looked at them.   His
great chin was cocked, and his muzzle wrinkled in a
dreadful grin.   As he stood there, shivering a little, his
eyes rolling back, his breath grating in his throat to set
every bristle on end, he looked a devil indeed.

The Venus ranged alongside him.   No preliminary
stage for her; she never walked where she could stand, or
stood where she could lie.   But stand she must now,
breathing hard through her nose, never taking her eyes
off that pad she had marked for her own.   Close beside
her were crop-eared Grip and Grapple, looking up at the

line above them where hairy neck and shoulder joined. Behind was big Rasper, and close to him Lassie. Of the others, each had marked his place, each taken up his post.

Last of all, old Shep took his stand full in front of his enemy, their shoulders almost rubbing, head past head.

So the two stood a moment, as though they were whispering; each diabolical, each rolling back his eyes to watch the other. While from the little mob there rose a snarling, bubbling snore, like some giant wheezing in his sleep.

Then like lightning each struck. Rearing high, they wrestled with striving paws and the expression of fiends incarnate. Down they went, Shep underneath, and the great dog with a dozen of these wolves of hell upon him. Rasper, devilish, was riding on his back; the Venus— well for him!—had struck and missed; but Grip and Grapple had their hold; and the others, like leaping demoniacs, were plunging into the whirlpool vortex of the fight.

And there, where a fortnight before he had fought and lost the battle of the Cup, Red Wull now battled for his life.

Long odds! But what cared he? The long-drawn agony of the night was drowned in that glorious delirium. The hate of years came bubbling forth. In that supreme moment he would avenge his wrongs. And he went in to fight, revelling like a giant in the red lust of killing.

Long odds! Never before had he faced such a galaxy of foes. His one chance lay in quickness: to prevent the swarming crew getting their hold till at least he had diminished their numbers.

Then it was a sight to see the great brute, huge as a

bull-calf, strong as a bull, rolling over and over and up
again, quick as a kitten; leaping here, striking there;
shaking himself free; swinging his quarters; fighting with
feet and body and teeth—every inch of him at war.
More than once he broke right through the mob; only to
turn again and face it.   No flight for him; nor thought of
it.

Up and down the slope the dark mass tossed, like some
hulk the sport of the waves.   Black and white, sable and
gray, worrying at that great centrepiece.   Up and down,
roaming wide, leaving everywhere a trail of red.

Gyp he had pinned and hurled over his shoulder.   Grip
followed; he shook her till she rattled, then flung her afar;
and she fell with a horrid thud, not to rise.   While
Grapple, the death to avenge, hung tighter.   In a scarlet,
soaking patch of the ground lay Big Bell's lurcher,
doubled up in a dreadful ball.   And Hoppin's young dog,
who three hours before had been the children's tender
playmate, now fiendish to look on, dragged after the
huddle up the hill.   Back the mob rolled on her.   When it
was passed, she lay quite still, grinning; a handful of
tawny hair and flesh in her dead mouth.

So they fought on.   And ever and anon a great figure
rose up from the heaving inferno all around; rearing to
his full height, his head ragged and bleeding, the red foam
dripping from his jaws.   Thus he would appear momen-
tarily, like some dark rock amid a raging sea; and down
he would go again.

Silent now they fought, dumb and determined.   Only
you might have heard the rend and rip of tearing flesh;
a hoarse gurgle as some dog went down; the panting of
dry throats; and now and then a sob from that central

figure. For he was fighting for his life. The Terror of the Border was at bay.

All who meant it were on him now. The Venus, blinded with blood, had her hold at last; and never but once in a long life of battles had she let go; Rasper, his breath coming in rattles, had him horribly by the loins; while a dozen other devils with red eyes and wrinkled nostrils clung still.

Long odds! And down he went, smothered beneath the weight of numbers, yet struggled up again. His great head was torn and dripping; his eyes a gleam of rolling red and white; the little tail stern and stiff like the gallant stump of a flagstaff shot away. He was desperate, but indomitable; and he sobbed as he fought doggedly on.

Long odds! It could not last. And down he went at length, silent still—never a cry should they wring from him in his agony; the Venus glued to that mangled pad; Rasper beneath him now; three at his throat; two at his ears; a crowd on flanks and body.

The Terror of the Border was down at last!

.   .   .   .   .

"Wullie, ma Wullie!" screamed M'Adam, bounding down the slope a crook's length in front of the rest. "Wullie! Wullie! to me!"

At the shrill cry the huddle below was convulsed. It heaved and swelled and dragged to and fro, like the sea lashed into life by some dying leviathan.

A gigantic figure, tawny and red, fought its way to the surface. A great tossing head, bloody past recognition, flung out from the ruck. One quick glance he shot from his ragged eyes at the little flying form in front; then with a roar like a waterfall plunged toward it, shaking off the bloody leeches as he went.

"Wullie! Wullie! I'm wi' ye!" cried that little voice, now so near.

Through—through—through!—an incomparable effort and his last. They hung to his throat, they clung to his muzzle, they were round and about him. And down he went again with a sob and a little suffocating cry, shooting up at his master one quick, beseeching glance as the sea of blood closed over him—worrying, smothering, tearing, like fox-hounds at the kill.

They left the dead and pulled away the living. And it was no light task, for the pack were mad for blood.

At the bottom of the wet mess of hair and red and flesh was old Shep, stone-dead. And as Saunderson pulled the body out, his face was working; for no man can lose in a crack the friend of a dozen years, and remain unmoved.

The Venus lay there, her teeth clenched still in death; smiling that her vengeance was achieved. Big Rasper, blue no longer, was gasping out his life. Two more came crawling out to find a quiet spot where they might lay them down to die. Before the night had fallen another had gone to his account. While not a dog who fought upon that day but carried the scars of it with him to his grave.

The Terror o' th' Border, terrible in his life, like Samson, was yet more terrible in his dying.

.   .   .   .   .

Down at the bottom lay that which once had been Adam M'Adam's Red Wull.

At the sight the little man neither raved nor swore: it was past that for him. He sat down, heedless of the soaking ground, and took the mangled head in his lap very tenderly.

"They've done ye at last, Wullie—they've done ye at last," he said quietly; unalterably convinced that the attack had been organized while he was detained in the tap-room.

On hearing the loved little voice, the dog gave one weary wag of his stump-tail. And with that the Tailless Tyke, Adam M'Adam's Red Wull, the Black Killer, went to his long home.

.   .   .   .   .

One by one the Dalesmen took away their dead, and the little man was left alone with the body of his last friend.

Dry-eyed he sat there, nursing the dead dog's head; hour after hour—alone—crooning to himself:

> "'Monie a sair daurk we twa hae wrought,
>   An' wi' the weary warl' fought!
>   An' mony an anxious day I thought
>   We wad be beat.'

An' noo we are, Wullie—noo we are!"

So he went on, repeating the lines over and over again, always with the same sad termination.

"A man's mither—a man's wife—a man's dog! They three are a' little M'Adam iver had to back him! D'ye mind the auld mither, Wullie? And her, 'Niver be downhearted, Adam; ye've aye got yer mither.' And ae day I had not. And Flora, Wullie (ye remember Flora, Wullie? Na, na; ye'd not) wi' her laffin' daffin' manner, cryin' to one: 'Adam, ye say ye're alane. But ye've me—is that no enough for ony man?' And God kens it was—while it lasted!" He broke down and sobbed a while. "And you, Wullie—and you! the only man friend iver I had!" He sought the dog's bloody paw with his right hand.

> "'An' here's a hand, my trusty fier,
> An gie's a hand o' thine;
> An' we'll tak' a right guid willie-waught,
> For auld lang syne.'"

He sat there, muttering, and stroking the poor head upon his lap, bending over it, like a mother over a sick child.

"They've done ye at last, lad—done ye sair. And noo I'm thinkin' they'll no rest content till I'm gone. And oh, Wullie!"—he bent down and whispered—"I dreamed sic an awfu' thing—that ma Wullie—but there! 'twas but a dream."

So he sat on, crooning to the dead dog; and no man approached him. Only Bessie of the inn watched the little lone figure from afar.

It was long past noon when at length he rose, laying the dog's head reverently down, and tottered away toward that bridge which once the dead thing on the slope had held against a thousand.

He crossed it and turned; there was a look upon his face, half hopeful, half fearful, very piteous to see.

"Wullie, Wullie, to me!" he cried; only the accents, formerly so fiery, were now weak as a dying man's.

A while he waited in vain.

"Are ye no comin', Wullie?" he asked at length in quavering tones. "Ye've not used to leave me."

He walked away a pace, then turned again and whistled that shrill, sharp call, only now it sounded like a broken echo of itself.

"Come to me, Wullie!" he implored, very pitifully.

" 'Tis the first time iver I kent ye not come and me whistlin'. What ails ye, lad?"

He recrossed the bridge, walking blindly like a sobbing child; and yet dry-eyed.

Over the dead body he stooped.

"What ails ye, Wullie?" he asked again. "Will you, too, leave me?"

Then Bessie, watching fearfully, saw him bend, sling the great body on his back, and stagger away.

Limp and hideous, the carcase hung down from the little man's shoulders. The huge head, with grim, wide eyes and lolling tongue, jolted and swagged with the motion, seeming to grin a ghastly defiance at the world it had left. And the last Bessie saw of them was that bloody, rolling head with the puny legs staggering beneath their load, as the two passed out of the world's ken.

.   .   .   .   .

In the Devil's Bowl, next day, they found the pair: Adam M'Adam and his Red Wull, face to face; dead, not divided; each, save for the other, alone. The dog, his saturnine expression glazed and ghastly in the fixedness of death, propped up against that humpbacked boulder beneath which, a while before, the Black Killer had dreed his weird; and, close by, his master lying on his back, his dim dead eyes staring up at the heaven, one hand still clasping a crumpled photograph; the weary body at rest at last, the mocking face—mocking no longer—alight with a whole-souled, transfiguring happiness.

POSTSCRIPT

Adam M'Adam and his Red Wull lie buried together one just within, the other just without, the consecrated pale.

The only mourners at the funeral were David, James Moore, Maggie, and a gray dog peering through the lych-gate.

During the service a carriage stopped at the churchyard, and a lady with a stately figure and a gentle face stepped out and came across the grass to pay a last tribute to the dead. And Lady Eleanour, as she joined the little group about the grave, seemed to notice a more than usual solemnity in the parson's voice as he intoned: "Earth to earth—ashes to ashes—dust to dust; in sure and certain hope of the Resurrection to eternal life."

.   .   .   .   .

When you wander in the gray hill-country of the North, in the loneliest corner of that lonely land you may chance upon a low farm-house, lying in the shadow of the Muir Pike.

Entering, a tall old man comes out to greet you—the Master of Kenmuir. His shoulders are bent now; the hair that was so dark is frosted; but the gray-blue eyes look you as proudly in the face as of yore.

And while the girl with the glory of yellow hair is preparing food for you—they are hospitable to a fault, these Northerners—you will notice on the mantelpiece, standing solitary, a massive silver cup, dented.

That is the world-known Shepherds' Trophy, won out-right, as the old man will tell you, by Owd Bob, last and best of the Gray Dogs of Kenmuir. The last because he is the best; because once, for a long-drawn unit of time, James Moore had thought him to be the worst.

When at length you take your leave, the old man accompanies you to the top of the slope to point you your way.

"Yo' cross the stream; over Langholm How, yonder; past the Bottom; and oop th' hill on far side. Yo'll come on th' house o' top. And happen yo'll meet Th' Owd Un on the road. Good-day to you, sir, good-day."

So you go as he has bidden you; across the stream, skirting the How, over the gulf and up the hill again.

On the way, as the Master has foretold, you come upon an old gray dog, trotting soberly along. Th' Owd Un, indeed, seems to spend the evening of his life going thus between Kenmuir and the Grange. The black muzzle is almost white now; the gait, formerly so smooth and strong, is stiff and slow; venerable, indeed, is he of whom men still talk as the best sheep-dog in the North.

As he passes, he pauses to scan you. The noble head is high, and one foot raised; and you look into two big gray eyes such as you have never seen before—soft, a little dim, and infinitely sad.

That is Owd Bob o' Kenmuir, of whom the tales are many as the flowers on the May. With him dies the last of the immortal line of the Gray Dogs of Kenmuir.

. . . . .

You travel on up the hill, something pensive, and knock at the door of the house on the top.

A woman, comely with the inevitable comeliness of motherhood, opens to you. And nestling in her arms is a little boy with golden hair and happy face, like one of Correggio's cherubs.

You ask the child his name. He kicks and crows, and looks up at his mother; and in the end lisps roguishly, as if it was the merriest joke in all this merry world, "Adum Mataddum."

THE END